Also by Lance C Wilson

Other published books

The Laird of Braidwood

www.lancecwilson.com

Tears over the Kimberleys

by

Lance C. Wilson

Printed and published by Kimberley Cottage Press in
Chinese
German
English

National library of Australia
    Cataloguing-in-publication data:

    Wilson, Lance C., 1945- .
    Tears over the Kimberleys.

    ISBN 9780977550524 (pbk.)

    I. Title.

    A823.4

Edited by
Book and cover design   'Made in Ink' Hobart Tasmania
Typeset in 12 TimesNew Roman by

Acknowledgements

To Jo Grant my graphic designer who worked tirelessly assisting in the publishing of my novels. Jo's inspiration and encouragement has driven me on to finish my first two adult fiction attempts. Without her encouragement and hard work putting both together I honestly believe neither would have reached the printers.

The greatest thank you goes to my wife Cynthia who, through good and bad times, has put up with my eccentricities and dark periods. Cynthia has survived being chased by irate cows, stranded in crocodile infested rivers and a myriad of other adventures following her mad husband on his many escapades around Australia.

To my family who I am so proud of, thank you also. It has always been my opinion that not much else matters in life apart from your health and family, without either, nothing else really is of any significance.

Lastly to the many characters we have met in our travels around Australia who inspired me with their stories. Although my works are fictitious, many incidents actually happened.

I hope you enjoy my books; I have had a lot of satisfaction writing both to date and have three more in various stages which I intend to publish.

Introduction

Set amongst the magnificent red outback of New South Wales, the awesome Kimberleys of Western Australia and the green fertile hills of Tasmania, Tears over the Kimberleys tells of the heart wrenching love affair between three distinctly different people joined together by an act of fate at a very young age by the loneliness and vulnerability in the harsh world of the shearing sheds.

An erotic encounter on the return home of another, forming a three way bond between two women from opposite ends of social fabric and the man they both loved. A passionate and lifelong love affair begins, torn apart by family loyalty, war and human indifference. A story of unwavering lifelong love, human decency and commitment in an ever changing world over many decades and spanning the entire continent of Australia to the jungles of South East Asia.

Tears over the Kimberleys follows the lives of Anthony James Wilson, known simply as AJ to all those who knew him, and Sky Brown, a tall, strikingly beautiful girl of mixed Aboriginal, Spanish, Scottish and American Indian blood, and then there's Prudence Forsyth - grazing aristocracy also from Tasmania, born into money, spoilt, vibrant yet loveable. The three form a relationship that will last decades, an unbreakable bond of love and lust in a very unconventional relationship.

AJ was born into a Tasmanian family who farmed a small sheep and cattle property and his both parents were of Scottish ancestry whose ancestors migrated in the middle eighteen hundreds to the island. The Wilsons were not wealthy but lived a comfortable and stable life; AJ was the only son and child of the union and was taught at a very young age about family loyalty and the decency expected of both himself and his decisions in life. His father was a strict disciplinarian who expected his son to perform a fair share of the work and learn as much as possible while at the local school. Upon leaving school, with the blessing of his parents, he and two companions set out in a 1956 Holden packed with sleeping bags to travel on an adventure of a lifetime before settling down to a life of farming in the community into which they were born, as had previous generations.

Many young people at the time traveled to England but lack of money demanded that the three friends travel to the mainland on a working holiday to finance the trip. AJ waved a fond farewell to his parents as he drove out the driveway onto the highway to pick up his two companions in Campbell Town. His heart was beating with excitement, since his birth on the 12th of November 1945 he had never been far from the safety and love of his quiet and unassuming parents. He already missed them.

Pulling up outside the post office two smiling faces started piling cases into the car, a gift from his grandfather, the Holden had done a large mileage but was in sound condition and was his pride and joy. Michael Webb and Lyndon Fish had been lifelong friends attending school, social events and playing sport together since grade one. With a stern warning from the boy's fathers on the evils of drink and fast women, the three friends drove north for an adventure planned over many months; all were only seventeen and the year was 1962.

Sky was from a far different and more complicated background, one that instilled in her an immense mistrust of men, especially white men, at a very young age. Her mother was the result of a brief affair between her full blood grandmother when she was only sixteen and a Scottish seaman at the far flung Western Australian port of Wyndham. During the war her mother was only sixteen when she traveled to

Darwin with relatives from the Kimberleys; the war in the Pacific was at its height and Darwin was full of sailors and soldiers from Australia and America. Caught up in the atmosphere and excitement of the time, Rose Brown began a tumultuous affair with an American soldier of Spanish and Sioux Indian descent and on the 15th of December 1944, in the heat and humidity of Darwin, Sky Brown was born. The American lover soon transferred out of Darwin and Rose never heard from him again, as happened to many women in this time of passion and conflict. Rose, a pretty girl, soon became the attention of many men and spun into a life of abuse and heavy drinking. Sky was dragged along while she followed lovers, many who abused and beat her, from town to lonely town.

At a young age, Sky learnt to cover her growing beauty and appear disheveled and unattractive, so as not to place herself in danger when drunken parties were held in the hovels her mother often lived in. She became shy and withdrawn but fiercely independent. She had limited opportunity for an education but when she did, her inquiring mind allowed her to often surpass those in more stable conditions. At a very young age she made the decision that she was going to make something of her life. At sixteen her mother moved with a new lover to Bourke in outback New South Wales and with little opportunity for work, she began working for 'Smiley Foster', a shearing contractor of some repute who had a large run stretching over a huge area of New South Wales. Sky soon became his pet project as she became his best and most efficient rouseabout.

The word was soon out, 'Do not bugger around with Sky, or you will answer to Smiley bloody Foster and your next shearing job will be in the Falklands'. The shearing gangs soon got used to this disheveled, tall, gangly girl who ghosted around the board with an agility even the old hands had to admire. A loner, she kept to herself, never joining in the drinking sessions the other girls working in the sheds succumbed to. Quiet and unassuming, the other workers soon left Sky alone.

Chapter

——————

1

AJ, Michael and Lyndon traveled for a few weeks along the Murray River picking fruit in many small towns such as Mildura until they headed north to Condoblin in New South Wales. Camping out they all thrived on the freedom and adventure their lifestyle now allowed. During this period they met many other young people and had great times exploring, swimming and skylarking about, all displaying a great exuberance for life, but all knew a time would soon come when the adventure would have to end. The fruit picking had not been that lucrative and as all had shearing and shed hand experience they decided to seek a shearing contractor to spend their last few weeks in outback New South Wales working in the sheds, make a bit of extra money and learn about wool production in the outback.

Reaching Condoblin, the three friends decided to drop into the local bar and have a cold beer. The day was extremely hot and while enjoying their beer they asked the barman about the chances of finding work shearing on one of the stations. The barman, a gruff pudgy individual with cabbage ears who had seen better days, pointed to a couple of men sitting at a table and said, "Go ask old Smiley over there, he's always after men and I think he has a few sheds starting this week."

Michael Webb approached the table, introduced himself, and pointed to the other two and said, "Us Tassy boys are after some shearing work, do you have anything on the go?"

Looking up from his beer old Smiley soon summed up the

three lads. *Bloody Tasmanian hicks,* he thought, *wont stay longer than a month, but I am in a hell of a jam and need at least five before Monday and pickings are pretty thin on the ground.*

"Had any experience boys?" old Smiley drawled.

Michael, the extrovert of the three replied full of enthusiasm. "Bloody hell yeah, we can all shear a bit and rouseabout no worries."

"A bit? Can you or can't you bloody shear?" asked Smiley.

Somewhat deflated Michael said, "Well, AJ can do a hundred and me and Lyndon can shear eighty or so... or rousy."

With a low groan Smiley replied, "Well boys I will give youse a go as I am sorta short of a few hands. Go out to Tara Station, we start Monday. I need two shearers and a rousy, youse can work out that yourselves, who wants what, and see ya Monday. I'll draws youse a map."

There was much backslapping and bravado as the three friends left the pub, a roughly drawn map in hand they headed west out of town for Tara Station. An hours drive out of town the enthusiasm soon turned to alarm when they stopped at a sign which read 'Tara Station one hundred and twenty miles'. Swinging the old Holden onto the dirt track, a long and agonising trip over corrugated roads made of fine red dust that seeped into every item and crevice in the vehicle, ended at midnight. The tired and sleepy threesome eventually found the dilapidated shearer's quarters and all covered in dust they collapsed onto old dusty mattresses, drifting into an exhaustion fueled sleep.

AJ woke to the sound of a lone crow's rawkus cry and shot upright wiping the dust from his lips and quickly remembered how they came to be in this position. Looking around the room he saw the absurdity of the situation as his two companions were sprawled out on the floor covered from head to toe in red dust, the heat had already started to make the room uncomfortable.

He threw a pillow at Lyndon which caused the dust to explode and he rasped in panic, "What the hell have we got ourselves in for?"

Michael was sitting upright trying to wet his lips and squeaked. "Let's get the hell out of here, we must be in hell."

AJ immediately broke into a dry laugh and said, "Listen fellas, we gave our word to that old Smiley bloke and we will stick to it. Let's go clean up, find our rooms and we'll help each other make them livable. The shed lasts three weeks so better make the most of it."

Michael squeaked again, "Bloody okay, but can you two shear? I only have a few combs and cutters and this sand will soon bugger 'em. You can share mine and I'll do the rousing. God this heat will kill us."

Grudgingly the two friends agreed and all three went looking for the showers trudging across a large expanse of red dust made worse by large mobs of sheep. The three soon found the shower block and a refreshing shower made the deflated spirits rise.

Starving hungry, the three adventurers went in search of food and soon found the cook, Mrs Mancey, baking bread. Even though it was a Sunday the men still had to be fed. Looking up she saw the three boys enter and summing up the situation, her motherly instinct took over, and soon the three friends were indulging in fresh baked bread with bacon and eggs. So hungry was the trio they hardly noticed a tall olive skinned person enter and sit at the other end of the table. Mrs Mancey quietly dished up two eggs on fresh bread and placed it in front of the new entrant, who quietly began eating without a glance at the three boys. Mrs Mancey informed the boys that the others were in town boozing and that most would return in the afternoon ready for work in the morning. The shed had twelve stands so a workforce of twenty or so was needed to run it.

Finishing the welcome and excellent meal they thanked Mrs. Mancey profusely. Things had been a bit lean in the food department since leaving home and it was a good feeling to have a hearty, home cooked meal. As they left the room AJ glanced at the other diner, with a hat firmly over the head he was unable to say whether this lightly built person was male or female.

During the next few hours the trio busied themselves with cleaning up their rooms and moving their gear into them. They noticed several larger rooms had names already on them and guessed returning shearers had laid claim to these better facilities. Unperturbed and with enthusiasm the three soon had the accommodation clean and in some sort of order. With their gear safely stowed they went for a walk to inspect the woolshed and surrounding areas. It did not take long for all the fears of the previous night to abate and a sense of adventure to return. The homestead and surrounds had an eerie sense of beauty in many ways.

With the help of the shepherd they discovered yabbies and yellowbelly in the nearby river. Like excited children the three spent a relaxing afternoon catching a feed from the yellow waters of the river.

By mid afternoon and towards the evening, several cars began to arrive with men and women flopping out of them in various forms of health. Hard drinking and living seemed to be the cornerstone of the life of shearing gangs. The boys greeted each load with a cheerful g'day only to be met with a grunt or several of the girls giving a cheeky wave and bat of the much mascaraed eyelashes.

Quite surprisingly, very few, apart from the quiet one, turned up for the evening meal, a delicious stew of which the boys ate ravenously. As AJ got up to get a cuppa he met the lone figure at the urn and was shocked when he looked into the eyes of the most angelic face he had ever seen. His heart beat so hard he thought he was going to die.

His face flushed as he squeaked a weak, "Hello."

A slight smile entered the face of pure beauty as she turned away and left the room. Cup in hand, he turned, said nothing to his companions but gathered up his dirty plate and washed it in the sink and stacked it back on the shelf. Mrs. Mancey didn't miss the occasion and a wry smile crossed her motherly face. This was the first time she had seen a smile let alone the full face of Sky Brown.

Chapter

2

The next morning all three boys rose early and as they entered the kitchen dining room the place was mayhem. Unlike the previous day, the whole shearing gang was eating as a buzz of conversation bounced around the room. The entrance of the three hardly raised an eyebrow; a disappointed AJ did not see the absolute thing of beauty present he had seen the previous evening amongst the throng of hungry diners.

After a hearty breakfast, they made their way to the woolshed. One thing that was agreed on by all was that Mrs Mancey was one hell of a cook. It was no wonder old Smiley had her placed in the same category as Sky Brown and one whine about the culinary exploits of Mrs Mancey was akin to insulting old Smiley's expertise in the contracting game.

Michael was assigned to penning up and pressing by Smiley. Lyndon and AJ luckily drew pens four and five; it became apparent to AJ the non-appearance at breakfast of his angel was because she had been busy preparing wool bales for the bellies, and setting up the shed in preparation for the start of shearing. Old Smiley never had her in the elite class for nothing, like Mrs Mancey he knew he was on a good thing with Sky and god help the bastard who upset either of the women.

The two friends nervously set up their hand pieces the first morning. Apart from family sheds they had no experience interstate and it was a bit nerve-wracking. The other shearers did not seem too friendly but prepared in a very business-like manner for the day's work.

The temperature had already started to climb as the wool classer hit the bell for shearing to commence and both youngsters entered the pens and grabbed the first sheep for the day. AJ was surprised that his first sheep seemed smaller than he was used to, with bare legs, though he soon settled into the routine as did his friend opposite. Both were relaxed and the time soon passed to the first break. He was surprised to see he had shorn twenty eight sheep and Lyndon, who had less experience, twenty one. Even old Smiley nodded in approval as he also noted young Webb was strong and worked well.

AJ noted the easy loping stride of the angel faced nymph who glided along, easily scooping up a fleece and throwing it effortlessly onto the wool table. The board always seemed to be clean though he noticed that two other girls often held back having a smoke while the slender one did most of the work without hesitation or complaint.

The first week went by in a whirl of eating, sleeping and working long hours in the shed. All three boys settled in well and numbers for the two young shearers began to steadily rise much to the pleasure of old Smiley.

Bloody hell, he often said to himself, *during that first week even I can be wrong sometimes.*

AJ did not seem to come to the attention of two of the girls as much as his companions, maybe it was due to the fact he was shy and withdrawn. His experience with women was actually zero. During the breaks he usually went to a quiet spot and cleaned his combs and cutters ready for the expert to grind. He liked to contemplate on his own sometimes and seemed to settle into the shed life well with the other shearers having taken a liking to the quiet lad from Tasmania. His appearance and behavior gathered respect from all, especially from old Smiley who hated troublemakers, and this boy he was sure, was not one of those.

Of an evening AJ liked to walk in the cooler evening air. He often caught yabbies for Mrs Mancey to cook and everyone enjoyed the change of food. He often thought of his parents far away and missed them, but he realised this was his time to explore life and home would come soon enough. Besides, he quite liked the shed life and shearing came natural to him. The first week soon flew by and on the Friday night, as usual, he went for a walk down by the river checking his yabby traps.

AJ's companions flirted with the other girls making plans for a trip into town on the Saturday. He approached the bend in the river where his traps were tied to a log jutting out into the water. The breath flew from his lungs as he realised the angelic girl was sitting on the log his traps were anchored to. Approaching, he stammered hello which came out more like a squeak and he felt a real idiot until she spoke softly to him.

"Can I help you with the traps, I really love yabbying? My grandfather used to take me after Cherabaun prawns in the Kimberleys."

Sky felt safe and somehow trusted this quiet young man. She liked his work ethic and that he didn't flirt with the other girls but treated them with respect, and was not suggestive to them as the other shearers were. She was also lonely for conversation and companionship; everyone needs human contact and friendship. For years, she had met no-one she neither felt safe with nor trusted, yet for the short period this shed would last perhaps she would have a friend. It was amazing how soon after the ice was broken that both opened up and chatted for hours about their past and family. Sky spoke lovingly about her grandmother and grandfather, although he wasn't her biological grandfather, it seemed to mean nothing to the old aboriginal who treated her as his own granddaughter and an unbreakable bond existed between the two.

Loneliness had played a big part in Sky's life, though it seemed at last she had met someone with whom an instant bond of friendship evolved, two opposites sitting on the bank under the evening sky, completely oblivious to their surrounds, enjoying conversation as if they had known each other for years.

The pair arrived back at the shearers' quarters about midnight. AJ had forgotten to check the yabby traps much to the chiding of his mates and even the girls seemed surprised he and Sky had walked back to the quarters together, as if they were old friends.

On the Saturday, all hands attended to their washing in the morning and prepared to go into town that afternoon. AJ met Sky in the laundry, they helped each other with their washing then after lunch, they went to finish the job of emptying the yabby traps and resetting them. By now a platonic bond had settled in between the two friends. Though Sky still kept her head and shoulders completely covered and always wore jeans and sandals.

The couple returned to the quarters late in the afternoon after gathering the yabbies. They had walked the river looking for future spots and the time had flown past quickly. As they approached the huts the two Tassy boys and their companions ran up and to tell them the others had left for town and they had no way of getting there and that AJ would have to run them in.

Seeing the disappointment in their faces AJ agreed, he even offered to lend his car but the boys declined as they knew he worshipped his Holden and as they would be having a few drinks, better off not driving. Sky stood nearby and AJ asked her if she would like to go for a drive; at first she hesitated but he told her he was coming straight back and so she accepted. Piling into the car the six youngsters left for the arduous drive into town and a certain excitement pulsed through AJ as Sky, because of the lack of room, sat tightly next to him. A strange feeling came over him, one of contentment and happiness, something he had never felt before, a feeling he could not explain to himself.

The eager car load got into town around eight o'clock. Revelry was in full flight in the local pub as shearers and station hands had been steadily drinking all day. Parking the car behind the hotel the four passengers went straight into the pub. Sky and AJ decided to get a bottle of Coke to drink on the way home.

Crossing the road the two youngsters entered the shop, which was about to close, and purchased a couple of bottles of coke and a few packets of chips to eat on the return drive home.

Re-crossing the road, the pair now holding hands, made their way up the side street to the rear car park. In the shade of the hotel three very drunk station hands saw the couple coming and one lurched out of the shadows grabbing Sky and in doing so fell to the ground on top of the terrified girl ripping her top open. Without hesitation AJ grabbed the culprit and pulled him from Sky. He saw one of the other station hands rushing at him and in a flash his fathers words rang in his ears, *If you have to fight go for the snozzer, it will do wonders if you hit the right spot.* Drawing all his strength the fit young AJ slammed the attacker fair on the nose, he heard the sickening crunch of bone as the attacker slumped to the ground, yelping like a beaten dog. As he turned he saw Sky's attacker rushing at him. At the same time a bolt of fury shot through the air as Sky launched herself onto the back of the assailant, clawing like a cat at his face as the other hero ran screaming towards the pub for help. AJ slammed his fist into the gut full of beer with full force and a multitude of stubbies gushed out of the molesterer's mouth in a sickening stench of regurgitated beer. Hearing others yelling as they came out of the pub, AJ grabbed Sky by the hand and fleetingly the two ran to the car park and left town as the so called heroes told of a vicious attack by at least a dozen men.

It was the first time AJ had seen Sky without her hat; he was astounded by her beauty. Admiring her beautiful hawk like nose he caught a glimpse of her small, perked breasts between the tears of her shirt. A feeling of absolute satisfaction and love came over him as she slid close to him for comfort. They swigged on their coke and ate their chips on the way home in total silence. Sky had found her hero and AJ didn't know it but he was hopelessly and totally in love.

It was about two in the morning when the couple reached the shearer's quarters and both went straight to the washroom and tenderly helped to clean each other up. They were both swept up in feelings never felt before as they gently washed each other with warm water, bathing their bruises; it was a sensual encounter that completely bewildered both. Feelings ran through them, completely foreign to anything either had experienced before and they would have gladly died in protecting each other. An unbreakable union had been formed, never to be broken.

The two star struck youngsters walked back to the quarters and both had a fitful nights sleep as their feelings and passions had been aroused. Never before in her sad life had Sky felt so wanted and safe.

On the Sunday afternoon, the others returned with tales of a terrible assault on three of the revelers at the pub by a 'busload of thugs' and advised anyone going to town to keep a sharp lookout, it might be a rough gang of shearers passing through. The boys thought Sky's bruising and AJ's scratches were the results of energetic lovemaking, well everyone considered them an item now. Even old Smiley and Mrs. Mancey both accepted the union as a most satisfactory event and god help anyone who interfered with the new relationship.

The shed routine settled down now to a steady hum of activity. So happy was old Smiley he left to check on his other sheds. The gang got used to the two young lovers settling in a quiet corner facing each other, sharing lunch breaks together. They helped each other out, Sky would clean the combs and cutters and in turn AJ helped the clean up at the end of each run, much to the amusement of the older shearers and AJ's companions.

An uneventful week passed with AJ reaching a tally of one hundred and thirty sheep much to the respect of the older shearers who saw a challenge in the making for the top tallies held for years by the regulars.

On the second Saturday, AJ and Sky dropped the four passengers from the previous week in town and after picking up a drum of oil, decided to go for a drive and change the oil in the old Holden. On the return they stopped a few hundred metres off the road under a huge tree by the river where AJ scooped two channels of sand for the car to drive up on and let the oil out into a container. As this was taking place Sky undid the oil filter and in doing so covered AJ with oil. He came out from under the vehicle like a bolt of lightning much to the fits of laughter from Sky as he looked a ferocious sight covered in black oil.

Sky suggested that he dive into the river and try and wash it off. Stripping down to his jocks he dived into the water and as he surfaced he was surprised to see Sky too, stripped to her underpants, dive into the water with a big smile on her face. As he stood mesmerised, she broke surface and came straight out of the water close to him, the sight of her lithe body and small pear shape breasts took his breath away. He stood spellbound as she approached him with some soap and started to gently wash his body.

Overcome with feelings he had never had before he gently pulled her to him and kissed her on the lips, first gently, then with a passion that frightened them both. As they scrambled to the river bank he removed her panties while pulling his own down and then opened her legs and entered her in one brief explosion of passion.

During the afternoon they made love several more times , oil smeared over both of their naked bodies. All inhibitions were gone and both caught in the moment. Nothing mattered, an insatiable drive came over them both with neither able to saturate their passion.

With dreamy smiles from ear to ear they dressed then completed the old Holden's oil change. When they arrived back to their quarters they showered together finally removing the last traces off oil off their bodies. The hot water and the sight of each others nakedness saw them making love against the cold tiles of the shower wall, Sky's long slender legs wrapped around AJ's hips, thrusting into him until they collapsed into cries of ecstasy. Not wanting to spend a minute apart they swiftly retrieved her belongings to move into his room. A long night of lovemaking continued and an insatiable energy of almost frightening, uncontrolled passion, came over them.

Chapter

3

Monday morning arrived all too soon, the usual excited conversation about the weekend's events and the looming cutout at the end of the week made the kitchen abuzz during breakfast.

However, when Sky and AJ entered the room, a hush descended and even the breathing of all those present seemed loud. Sky had tied her unruly hair back with no hat hiding her features and instead of her usual oversized shirts, she wore a tight fitting feminine top. Instead of a shy girl, in walked a goddess that even AJ's two traveling companions coughed nervously over, the other rousy girls were speechless. Sky was now a confidant woman with a partner she both trusted and loved unconditionally and her life had changed for ever. No longer shy and frightened of life, her beaming smile said it all, no one approved more than Mrs. Mancey, her ugly duckling had come of age. Beaming with pride she personally served the young couple, smirking at the staring gob smacked females present who previously had hardly bothered to acknowledge Sky, only using her willingness to do others work to their advantage.

On the way to the shed there were envious looks and whispers from the girls, while the men still stared in utter disbelief, they could not believe this was the very plain waif who had worked amongst them unnoticed for months.

During the week the three friends discussed what they would do at the end of the shed. Both Michael and Lyndon decided to head for home, they would catch a bus to Canberra and fly back to Tasmania. AJ had decided to finish the season with old Smiley, much to his delight, he knew AJ would lose Sky if he left, and as only six weeks remained he did not wish to find more men at this stage. AJ also had no ideas of leaving Sky, he was totally infatuated with her, the sun shone from her, and she was his very reason for existing.

Friday came and everyone was paid. AJ and Sky dropped the two Tasmanian friends at the pub and bid them a fond farewell. AJ felt sad as his mates jumped on to the bus, but turning to Sky there was no second thoughts at all. Posting a letter to his parents advising them of his plans to stay and finish the run, he and Sky headed north to Longreach for the last shed which was to last five weeks.

The young lovers slept in swags on the trip North in absolute contentment in each others company until they reached Longreach where AJ stopped at the bank to cash his pay cheque. Sky then told AJ that she had no means of banking her cheque, as she had tried, but with having no identification and being aboriginal they had refused her.

Old Smiley had cashed her cheques in the past and gave the cash to her but she had longed to save for some land in the future and carrying cash made her nervous. AJ took her by the hand and strode her into the bank, walking up to the teller he passed his bank book over and deposited his cheque, he then said to the teller, "My fiancée wishes to open an account."

The teller looked at Sky and snorted, "Does your fiancée have identification?"

"No, we left it at home," AJ replied.

"Well, we can open a joint account as you are already a customer," said the teller getting anxious.

Looking at Sky and her look of bewilderment he passed his passbook back and said, "Ok put it in both names."

Sky passed her cheque over as well as a bundle of cash she

was saving and a joint account was opened.

A happy Sky tucked her book into her shoulder bag and the two young lovers left the bank with the incident closing the relationship more tightly than ever. An unbreakable bond, unspoken, was cemented further.

AJ turned eighteen at the next shed yet he showed a maturity beyond his age. Both he and Sky worked hard and the five weeks soon flew past. During this time, as they lay in each others arms, Sky told AJ of the Kimberleys, it almost sounded a magical place and he longed to visit and meet her grandparents. Sky had learned that her mother had taken ill and had returned home also, she longed to see her.

AJ again wrote to his parents, torn between returning home or going to the Kimberleys with Sky. He explained the situation to his worried family and set off via Mt Isa and Katherine with Sky on a quest to take her home to her ancestor's country.

Old Smiley and Mrs. Mancey had given the young couple a fond farewell and as a parting shot, old Smiley said to AJ, "If I'da known youse was gonna take me best rousy, I wouldna give ya a bloody job, ya young bugger."

AJ was fascinated by the changing scenery and the vastness of the country, entering the Kimberleys he was in awe of the landscape and Sky became so happy at the prospect of seeing her family which brought great happiness to AJ; she was the very oxygen of his life, every evening he melted into her arms in absolute bliss.

During the long journey Sky learnt to drive the car on the long straight stretches of road. She drove for hours turning out to be an astute student and a very capable driver.

Reaching the new township of Kununurra, AJ took Sky to the local police station and a helpful policeman gave Sky a driving test. Impressed he used her new bank book as identification.

On leaving the station, proudly examining her newly acquired license, she discovered he had inadvertently entered her name as Sky Brown-Wilson. Beaming with pride she placed the license in her pack safely with the couples small nest egg.

The closer Sky came to Wyndham, the more excited she became, chatting incessantly. She felt her life had indeed made a turn for the better and beaming with pride she looked lovingly into the face of the man responsible for it all. She now had two forms of identification, at last she was someone and she could not wait to surprise her grandparents and mother with her rock of strength and her reason for living, AJ.

Chapter

4

The faithful Holden fully laden pulled out of Kununurra on the last leg of a remarkable journey for AJ. Since leaving Tasmania his life had taken a direction that even in his wildest dreams he never would have imagined. The thoughts of his parents and friends in Tasmania was but a fond memory almost hidden in the mists of events over the last three months since Sky had came into his life. The pull of home was far outweighed by the holder of his heart and the beauty of the Kimberleys.

Two hours after leaving Kununurra and passing the junction of the Great Northern Highway heading south, Sky excitedly guided the car into a small track which seemed to head straight at the walls of a magnificent mountain range. A huge opening hidden from the road soon became apparent and on the side of this magnificent feature, AJ saw a series of small one room huts with an open structure in the middle from which poured thirty or so smiling aboriginal faces.

Oh the joy of this meeting. AJ had never experienced such open and unconditional love and happiness from a group of people towards a fellow human being.

Naked children and adults called out repeatedly, "Sky, Sky," with an enthusiasm beyond comprehension in white society.

In the middle of the group AJ noticed a tall distinguished aboriginal who looked in his early sixties, white beard and hair, tears streaming down his face and next to him, with moist eyes and staring in disbelief, a small, wrinkled female with a dress that had seen better days wrapped around her, exposing bare sagging breasts. AJ instinctively knew that he was looking at Sky's grandparents.

Sky was disappointed that her mother had already left with a man she had met in Wyndham, although unwell, her health had improved slightly. AJ noted Sky's disappointment but she never showed it or mentioned it again, a trait he observed amongst the aboriginals, life went on.

Huge hugs and total confusion seemed to reign with everyone talking at once, as AJ had came with Sky he too was swept up in the moment, never had he seen such a happy group of people in his entire life. He soon concluded these people were the poorest of the poor, disenfranchised and living on the edge of white society. It had never occurred to him until now why Sky had always kept to the fringe of the shearing sheds and why she felt inferior to the others. He had never thought of her as being any class of society but a living goddess. His life had began when he met her.

The first few days passed in a haze for AJ. Sky was busy catching up on all the news from her relatives and AJ went fishing with Sky's grandfather in the Ord River to the east catching Barramundi for the camp.

One day as he was standing on the bank of the Ord and feeling thirsty he scooped up a drink and Sky's grandfather looked at him and said, "Now you have had a drink from the Ord, you will always return."

Bemused, AJ knew that one day both he and Sky would leave but it never entered his mind when, at this time his life was one of pure happiness, his Sky was happy and with that being, so he was also.

AJ learned that this was only a wet season camp and during the dry the little group went south to a station on the banks of the Fitzroy River called The Big Sky. This was part of their ancestral hunting grounds where they would also work on the station there during the mustering season. He also woke up to the fact why his beloved was given the name Sky, named after the station that was so important to her people.

One evening while laying in each others arms and listening to the rumble of distant thunder, he was looking up at the sheer rock face watching the awesome display nature was putting on for them.

"Tomorrow I will take you to a very special place," Sky said quietly.

He thought no more about it and snuggled into her warm embrace and drifted into a blissful sleep.

To anyone else these two may have seemed an odd couple, she was at least three inches taller and slightly older than he. Standing side by side Sky almost appeared as a tall and lithe Amazon protecting her smaller partner. One can never understand the complicity of human nature when it comes to choosing partners. Perhaps there is a stronger chemistry that sometimes triggers an almost fatal attraction in human nature.

Early next morning as the sun came up in a red ball over the Kimberleys, some men appeared with two horses, both wiry station ponies that the group had used to transport their possessions between camps. Unshod and sure footed these small brumbies had some Timor horse blood flowing in their veins, from times past, when the first settlers landed years ago.

AJ used an old military coat his mother insisted he take, as a saddle blanket for Sky. He was amazed how she seemed to float from the ground onto the little horse and his eyes transfixed on her long slender legs as her dress rode up while she settled herself onto the pony.

It had never occurred to Sky what a natural beauty she possessed and AJ was constantly telling her that she had something women all over the world can only dream of. It was an absolute and natural feminine beauty, a beauty so great that men would turn their heads and gape. In a different time, Sky would have walked the world's stages as a super model, so natural and unassuming.

Mounting his horse the pair started the long climb upwards. The two ponies, surefooted and agile, picked their way slowly onwards and upwards, the heat of the approaching wet becoming worse and sweat trickled down AJ's back. Several times they stopped for a rest under the outline of a sheer wall, already AJ could see for miles across the stark and beautiful landscape. Sky spoke very little on her quest, she had been taken to this spot by her grandfather years ago as a child and she never forgotten it. She now wanted to share it with AJ.

They both took a long break in the middle of the day resting the ponies and eating some of the food they had packed.

The black clouds rolled in from the west giving the scenery a foreboding look and AJ wondered how they would find a way up the sheer wall to the top. He was soon to learn the answer late in the afternoon with the rumbling of thunder in the distance, a huge section of the wall had fallen away and a small path appeared which seemed to go straight to the heavens. Leading the horses on foot the pair picked their way carefully, it seemed like an eternity and both were exhausted by the time they broke out onto the top.

AJ felt as though he had entered another world. To the east he saw the five rivers and Wyndham Port, south, The Gibb River Road and in the distance, between the rays of sunshine, the whole scene appeared biblical. It felt as if he had entered a special place privy to only a few apart from the early inhabitants, perhaps few knew of its existence.

Sky kept up a steady pace, the plateau was only five hundred yards wide with sheer walls on both sides. Small scrub like trees littered the landscape and the only other feature was a huge rocky outcrop which ran parallel to the sheer precipice that dropped alarmingly away in what appeared to be eternity. Stopping near the outcrop, Sky tied up the ponies to some small trees and fed them the small ration they had carried with them, a pool of water had caught in the rock and both horses drank their fill.

A small cave lay on the western side into which Sky laid down the greatcoat and the provisions. Taking AJ by the hand they walked to the edge of the great range and looked west, eerie streaks of light pierced the landscape, cool blasts of air preceded the approaching storm and then warm rain began to splatter the pair.

Sky dropped her dress and stood completely naked before AJ and without thinking he stripped as well. Naked and unashamed they held hands as the rain wet their bodies to a glistening shine. Both raised their hands skyward without any reason and AJ felt he was in Nirvana, the experience out of this world, beyond explanation. So sensual was this he felt his life complete and he would have died happy at this time.

Sky led him to the cave and gently laying down, she pulled him to her body's moist and inviting embrace. They made love many times during the night, far more intense and passionate than ever before.

Thunder roared and sheets of lightening streaked over the landscape. AJ felt as though he was above the world and that this had to be like heaven. He would never again in his life have an experience that would come near to this one. A great sense of sadness, like the dark clouds, enveloped him.

The next morning the sky cleared and the couple started the long and arduous journey back to the camp. Neither spoke much, they did not have to. In Sky's mind she had given her heart to AJ and only death would part them.

They arrived back at the camp as evening approached and an afternoon storm again approached. Sky's grandfather came to meet them, taking them both by the hand, something he had never done before, and led them back to the meeting shelter out of the approaching rain.

The whole group was now quiet and reserved as they just sat and listened to the thunder, nature at its best, and seemingly they knew what the couple had experienced. After sitting silently for a while they all got up slowly and left, including Sky and AJ who went to their hut and fell in to an exhausted sleep, curled up in each others arms.

AJ noted that Sky had changed slightly on her return, she seemed sad and distant. This demeanor was one he noted from her aboriginal heritage as they had an uncanny ability to gauge the future or see a future happening. He thought nothing more of it at the time, and put it down to the arduous journey they had just taken.

On the following morning they went into Wyndham to collect mail and some supplies for the camp. Sky sat silently in the car as he collected the mail, one letter was from his mother. Opening it he frowned at its contents, his father had been admitted to hospital and his mother pleaded for her son to come home. He would have to make arrangements immediately as once the wet set in he may not be able to leave and time was of the essence.

Sky had known this moment would come. She also knew that she could not leave the Kimberleys; she had never felt comfortable in all the times she was away. In her heart she knew that they would only be happy in her country. Her mother was also on her mind and leaving for Tasmania was like going to another planet, she was fearful and terrified of leaving her family. Her love for AJ was unbreakable and although he begged and pleaded with her, she would not be moved. AJ knew he had to leave and fast as his loyalty to his parents was overwhelming though he promised to return to Sky as soon as possible and made her keep the money they had made together until his return. He promised he would write to her at every opportunity.

When AJ drove out the small drive towards the main road the image of Sky standing with her people was etched in his heart indelibly, a forlorn figure weeping. His heart was wrenched from his body, his very soul shattered.

AJ never stopped thinking about her for one moment on the trip to Katherine and down the Stuart Highway to Alice Springs, Adelaide and on to Melbourne for the voyage home. Her scent was in the car, he could feel her very presence and hear her sweet voice singing and many times he felt like turning back, but family loyalty and his mother's plea held him to his task. At every stop he wrote to Sky, as tears streamed down his cheeks at the very thought of her. He couldn't sleep, so he drove day and night until finally, fitfully sleeping at times through sheer exhaustion.

After nearly six months away AJ again drove up the familiar drive to his home, greeted by his mother crying with happiness at her son's return.

Chapter

5

For several weeks after the departure of AJ, Sky lay in a fetal position in the hut constantly looked after by her grandmother. She held her hand to her swelling stomach feeling the growing child within, weeping fitfully. She missed AJ as since meeting him this was the first time they had been apart. Her grandmother, on many trips to Wyndham, had called at the post office asking for her daughter's mail. Unfortunately although many letters for Sky sat in the post office, the postmistress looked in disdain at the quiet aboriginal woman before her and not understanding that daughter meant granddaughter to the old lady present, she never even looked.

"No and please stop annoying us," she just said.

At no time did the workers at the post office consider that an aboriginal would receive letters from down south in neat handwriting and did not even consider helping the old lady who meekly shuffled off after each inquiry.

Sky was confused and did not know why AJ had not written to her but in her culture she accepted that perhaps he did not want her. Many times she wished that she had gone with him to Tasmania, but many times while working in the woolshed, the other girls had tormented her about what Tasmanians do to aboriginals. Unfortunately she took this as fact and although she did not tell AJ, a great fear built up in her about the island that seemed so far away and of the awful things that may happen to her if she went there. Perhaps AJ could not protect her, maybe a great spiritual force existed as on the mountain she had taken AJ to, something unexplained, but one must be fearful of its power.

In March the mob packed to head south to the Fitzroy River. A heavily pregnant Sky accompanied them, she thought of AJ every day but turned her attention to the seed within, he was still with her.

Arriving a few weeks later they settled into the camp ready for the mustering season and the group went to the station store for supplies when Sky's life was to change forever because of one Mrs. Mary Jones.

Mary Scott had been a school teacher in Broome in her younger days and met her husband to be, at a function. A Sydney girl on an adventure after completing college, she had no idea of the life of loneliness she would endure after marrying the dashing Bradley Jones and moving to the Big Sky. The courtship had been brief and thrilling for a young girl. They had even traveled to Sydney for their wedding before returning to Fitzroy Crossing and the life of station owners. Mary Jones' first sight of her new home filled her with excitement, but loneliness and isolation soon took its toll and unfortunately the union produced no children.

With her husband now wheelchair bound, she needed help in the homestead. Mary was struck by the beauty of Sky and promptly offered her a job. Her interest in Sky's condition was also a factor as Mary had always longed for children and loved to watch the aboriginal children playing by the river.

Sky was found a room in the homestead and turned out to be a diligent worker and Mary soon warmed to the lovely youngster who perhaps was looked after more by Mary than Sky looked after her. Bradley Jones also took a shine to Sky, he was curious as to her background because of her striking looks, he guessed Afghan as this blood was quite common in the region.

Sky gave birth to a daughter after two months in the care of the Jones' and her health had improved. She glowed with motherhood as she held the tiny infant, Mary noticed the baby was white and her curiosity deepened.

Mary and Bradley Jones seemed to be more interested in the little waif who Sky named Mary much to the delight of Mary Jones, than running the station. She became their passion of love and interest. Sky never spoke of little Mary's father and the Jones' never made a point of asking her, they treated her as a daughter and an heir to their property. It was discussed many times as Bradley Jones' health deteriorated. Mary's wish had always been to return to Sydney after the death of her husband. Both sensible people they had discussed the move several times, but Bradley wished to die and be buried on his beloved station, leaving Mary free to return home to a house purchased years before to pacify her in her bouts of loneliness.

Great joy was had by Bradley Jones as he tenderly held the infant. His lifelong wish had been answered, the Big Sky would continue. Spinal cancer had forced him into a wheelchair and he knew his time was limited. He planned to form a trust with Sky as the manager, she was sharp and honest, he being a good judge of character was quite sure of that.

Time meant decisions had to be made and he arranged for the four to go to Darwin to set matters legally.

Bradley also felt Sky's people had the right to live on the station and that a legally binding document would ensure that in the future. He positively glowed with pride at his plans. Mary was financially set up for life and he felt no need for monetary gain anymore from the station, he wanted his legacy to live on and this seemed the best possible solution for all involved. Perhaps, to many, this scheme of Bradley Jones seemed preposterous, but in his cancer racked body with limited time on earth he did not wish to see his beloved Big Sky - over 1.7 million acres of the finest cattle country in

Australia - fall into the hands of strangers. Three generations of his family had carved a magnificent property out of the wilderness though he knew his wife, a great companion for over fifty decades, had endured all the isolation, loneliness and heat she could stand and longed for the comforts of civilisation.

Mary had been well catered for in case of his death, the family having invested well, she would only spend a fraction of what he had provided for her after his death, so immense was it

In his troubled mind, young Mary and Sky had been his salvation, he now slept at night in the knowledge he had set in plan a scheme to manage Big Sky even after his death. For weeks he tutored Sky in all facets of running the station and he was thrilled at her ability to learn and store knowledge.

He also planned for the education of young Mary Brown Wilson too, for his scheme to work she had to be well educated by her twenty first birthday in order to assist her mother in a changing world and for the continuance of his life's work at the Big Sky. Bradley Jones and his ancestors would now sleep on the hill overlooking the homestead in the knowledge his hand still ran the Big Sky and the station would endure for many more generations under people who knew and loved the Kimberleys.

The family line of Sky Brown Wilson, the tall and strikingly beautiful woman who had given him the option, would ensure the continuation and survival of the Big Sky; he was no longer depressed at the thought of the possibility of strangers taking over. In his pain racked mind he would always be in control, even in death and smiling he glowed at the little girl crawling across the floor; the little waif may well have been his own flesh and blood for how much he cared for her.

And what did Mary Jones think of her husband's grand plan? She didn't really care. The station had consumed her life and she could not wait to see the back of it. Sick of the loneliness, isolation, the lack of female companionship and the years she had endured of discomfort and deprivation. The town house in the exclusive suburb of Valcluse awaited her where she would willingly live out her remaining days.

One great gesture of Bradley's generosity, apart from the house in Sydney, was to give his wife at great expense a service that few other stations at this time had the privilege of, a phone service. He had installed from the line snaking north to the new Town of Kununurra, a branch line to the station, subject in the wet to breakdown and other problems though he spared no expense in maintaining the line and perhaps Mary's sanity.

Watching the little child playing on the floor she had long since decided her namesake would not endure the harshness of this country and although she liked Sky she was merely the vessel who delivered her long awaited child to her. Young Mary would be educated in the finest schools in Sydney, attend the best university, and yes, little Mary would live the life she gave up and always dreamed of.

Many times she had thought of leaving in the early days, but time slipped by and she always remembered her marriage vows. Bradley had been a good husband but she knew only in death would he abandon the Big Sky, at least now he would die happy. Mary only had one spinster sister still alive in her family and she intended to live to see little Mary fulfill the ambitions she once had.

Her thoughts were jolted by the phone ringing. A drawling voice asked to speak to Sky Brown, said it was Smiley Foster the shearing contractor from Bourke calling. Mary informed him that a Sky Brown-Wilson was on the station and that she was down by the river with some of her people.

"Ah well,' old Smiley drawled, "can you tell her and young AJ to get their bloody arses back here. I had to sack two girls who were friggin useless."

Mary was taken aback at the bad language. Bradley had never sworn in her presence and the aboriginal stockmen treated her with respect. However she was unprepared for the response when she informed him that indeed Sky and her baby were here, but no person by the name of AJ was present.

In the next few minutes she endured a barrage of expletives she had never heard before, among them castration, knocking up the best rousy ever and a two-headed Tasmanian arsehole before the phone was slammed down. She was left perplexed and astounded, however, she did note the name AJ and putting two and two together came up with AJ Wilson.

On her return from Darwin she would inquire more into the matter, she was aware Sky had worked in New South Wales in the woolsheds. The puzzle was beginning to become clearer.

During the rest of his illustrious career Smiley Foster never hired a Tasmanian. Many a baffled shearer wondered why Smiley went red and told them to piss off for no apparent reason. No bugger crossed Smiley Foster and got away with it.

.

Chapter

6

Perhaps in the human makeup there are many forms of love. The love of new partnerships formed for reasons that unfortunately, for many, do not last but fade and sometimes turn into hatred.

There's the love of a couple whose marriage has lasted the test of time through the many trials and tribulations that life can deliver. A love not passionate or perhaps sexual but one of mutual trust and dependence on each others strengths and the forgiveness of our weaknesses. This love is perhaps the best of all as it does not consume or destroy like the burning passion of the soul sapping total love experienced by a very small minority of humanity during their lives.

It was the overwhelming maternal love of a mother at its highest that embraced her son as he returned to her bosom. She was shocked at his unkempt and emancipated condition, so unlike the son she had raised and who left on an exciting adventure nearly a year ago.

Agnes Wilson was a short matronly woman who had worked in a local shop and had met her husband David and married at a later age. She had never traveled and with limited education she had thrown herself into being a homemaker and mother to her only child. She felt her life was complete. As for love, perhaps her older husband, like many of his generation, was unable to express any emotional feelings though the two had settled into a happy bond more of mutual respect and admiration than passion.

AJ's father had been discharged from hospital two days previously and with the aid of a walking stick came slowly down from the porch; even he was disturbed at the appearance of his son. Shaking his son's hand he began to inquire about the cause of his shocking appearance, when the stern intervention of Agnes put an abrupt end to the conversation. A hot bath, clean clothes and food was going to happen first, all other matters would come later.

David knew better than to carry on any further and retreated to the porch. He heard the bath running and Agnes singing in a low voice, he smiled in the knowledge that his wife was as happy as he was to see the return of their prodigal son.

He had been informed by the returning boys about the beautiful dark beauty AJ had met up with and hoped it was only puppy love and that the episode had ended and life would return to the usual cycle of seasons and farm life.

To the embarrassment of AJ his mother assisted with taking off his clothes and scrubbing him with vigor on the painful side with a large brush to remove the grime, his dull blonde hair soon began to show its lustre under the constant assault of copious quantities of shampoo and the twirling hands of Agnes.

It was during this event that Agnes noticed her son had indeed changed. Gone was the happy child and in his place, a quiet troubled young man had returned. As she went to collect some clean clothes, a frown passed over her face and she was troubled as to what had happened to her son since his departure all those months ago.

Returning with clean clothes and more embarrassment to AJ as she helped dress him, he inquired as to any mail waiting for him and as he seemed anxious, Agnes found and gave him a few letters she had collected for him. She was alarmed as he frantically sifted through them and gave a sigh of defeat that whatever he was expecting had not arrived.

For Agnes, enough was enough, she had to find out what had happened to her son since his departure. She was aware of Sky's existence but the returning boys had informed her AJ was fine when they left him and she had assumed it to be, like her husband, a case of puppy love and to her knowledge, AJ had never previously had a girlfriend.

She sat her son at the table and while the jug boiled and in the presence of his father, AJ told the full story of events since he had left home. Always honest to his parents he told every detail, every emotion and record of events since he had left.

Transfixed, both parents listened intently. Agnes unable to control her emotion sat quietly with tears streaming down her face listening to the unbelievable story that was given with such feeling and passion by her son. It is true to say that different people accept various events that happen in their lives in a totally different manner though Agnes felt a great sadness for her son and perhaps had the better understanding of the story that unfolded before her.

As a young girl she often dreamed of a dashing young man sweeping her off her feet into a passionate romance like the ones she had read in cheap romance novels sold at her place of work. Instead, she dated for over ten years and it was she who eventually raised the idea of marriage and David had agreed with little enthusiasm but at thirty four she had decided it was perhaps her only chance of marital bliss.

David listened intently in his usual no nonsense view of life and happenings and classed the episode as being similar to the many hot romances young men in his battalion had with the girls in the Middle East during the war. He believed that the situation would now resolve itself, with his son being home and working on the farm.

Evening came and the family settled down to sleep. AJ still never had a moment in his fitful sleep that he did not see the vision of Sky with her piercing brown eyes, a reminder of her

Sioux heritage mixed with the beauty of Spanish blood. Those eyes gently showing the patience and ability to accept whatever life threw at her from the aboriginal heritage.

In the morning he rose early to the smell of bacon and eggs cooking. Anxious to attend to the neglected duties of the farm, since his father's illness, he flew into work like a madman possessed.

Mustering the five hundred sheep the farm ran he crutched, drenched and changed paddocks in the first week home. Repairing fences and general maintenance filled the week in and on the Saturday night he wrote a long letter to Sky and in it he actually told her for the first time how he really loved her.

Working during the week he had thought back on all the times together and never once had either truly expressed loving each other. He recalled Sky saying at their time on the mountain that she had given him her heart, but he had naturally thought and assumed she had realised the depth of his feelings.

Attending church in town on the Sunday with his mother, he posted the letter, an event not missed by Agnes who also saw the address, *'Care of Wyndham Post Office.'*

On the return journey she had suggested that after his father rested and regained his health perhaps it feasible that AJ return to the Kimberleys to search for Sky. She realised his life would never have any normality whilst his heart was thousands of miles away.

For the first time she saw a smile on her sons face as he nodded in approval. Agnes suggested not breaking the news to his father at this time as she was of the opinion he may think such a move ridiculous.

Monday came and AJ went mustering the small mob of Hereford cattle to mark the calves, which because of the situation that had occurred, were well past the age of marking.

Agnes in her curiosity and with her wish to end her son's

agony phoned the local switchboard, manned by Linda, a friend she used to work with and requested she be connected to the Wyndham post office in Western Australia. Linda suggested she wait two hours, due to the time difference and she would try to ring the post office in Wyndham and connect the receiver of the call, if successful, to Agnes.

Excitedly Agnes paced the floor for the next two hours ready to pounce on the phone should it ring. On two occasions she received calls from friends keen for a chat and she quickly ended both conversations with the fact she was expecting a very urgent overseas call; to Agnes, Wyndham was overseas.

Finally after two and a half hours of absolute agony the phone rang and it was the Wyndham post office. Excitedly she explained the situation to an ever so helpful woman on the other end who checked to see if any mail was there for a Sky Brown-Wilson. Yes, in fact a large bundle of letters had been received and because all had no return address and had been posted from various parts of Australia she had just bundled them together and kept them.

"Please hold them," Agnes requested and told of another on the way.

Agnes then asked if anyone had visited the post office asking for mail for Sky but the woman said no and a very disappointed Agnes thanked her for her assistance and hung up.

Because Agnes never mentioned Sky being olive-skinned and part aboriginal the post office employee never connected her with the elderly aboriginal woman who had frequently come in asking for her daughter's mail. Sky's grandmother had never even mentioned the name Sky Brown-Wilson, the name Sky had proudly started using after obtaining her driver's license. Uneducated and not skilled in the business of post offices, Sky's grandmother had not realised she had to give a name and as in many cases with aboriginal people at the time, little or no help, nor compassion was given, to even try and find out any facts to assist.

An unperturbed Agnes was on a quest and soon ringing the switchboard again. She requested to be connected to the Wyndham police station. After a period of waiting, she was finally connected and a very cooperative sergeant answered the phone and briefly Agnes told him the situation. No, he did not know of a Sky, a mixed blood aboriginal woman, although many existed in the area and yes he did know the group who often camped where she had described but he had not seen them for months, apparently they had left the area. Trying to be helpful he advised Agnes that aboriginals were often unreliable and the girl he was seeking may be anywhere at this time, perhaps her son may be better off forgetting the whole matter. Again disappointed, Agnes thanked him for his assistance and replaced the receiver.

Instead of the delivery of good news when her son came home she disappointedly advised him of her phone calls. She saw the sadness in his eyes at the news and they both discussed the idea she may have gone to the station for the muster season with the others, but both agreed it being so isolated it was unlikely to have a phone. AJ mentioned she may have gone North looking for her mother, to Agnes it all seemed hopeless.

On the following weekend Michael and Lyndon, his childhood friends and traveling companions who were aware of the situation, called early on the Saturday. They wanted AJ to play football for the local team Campbell Town. They were a bit short and AJ had been a handy player in the past, the team had a chance of making the finals and the boys thought the game might cheer him up, as well as a few drinks after with old friends. Reluctantly, with the help of his parents, the lads persuaded AJ to go with them and much to the delight of the coach AJ assisted the team with a win that afternoon.

Life began to settle down for AJ but he always had the burning desire to head north to find Sky. He would never forget her. ever, and he made plans to set off after the end of the wet season. Even after all this time back home, at night he still sensed her body next to his and often woke thinking her long legs were entwined around his, only to lay there awake for hours thinking of her.

The shearing season had started and to earn some money AJ started back with the local shearing team. He also continued to play football even though he was unable to become enthused with either, but at the insistence of his friends he played football and to finance his return to the Kimberleys he worked hard in the shearing sheds saving every penny.

In early September his team had made the semi-finals and was to play Tunnack at Ross for a place in the finals. Although AJ never felt the excitement in the game as the other boys, he went along with the intention of playing as well as possible so as to not let his mates down. The day was chilly but fine as both teams entered the field. Tunnack was a tough team. known as the *'spud diggers,'* they were hard men, yet fair and capable of dishing out as much as any opposition team cared to foist onto them.

The game was a tough but a fair encounter watched by hundreds of screaming fans as well as Ross locals who in the main barracked for Campbell Town in the black and red.

In the crowd sitting on the bonnet of her Holden ute was Prudence Smythe, granddaughter of Col Charles Smythe, a well known grazier who owned Forth, a twelve thousand acre fine wool property in the district.

Forth was rumored to have been purchased by the Smythe family in order to banish the Colonel to the colonies for an indiscretion with the fourteen year old daughter of a politician in London in the early part of the century.

On the way to the colony he had met a flighty young woman

who he had married almost immediately on arrival, built a huge imposing home and settled into the marriage, producing a son Charles Smythe the second. Soon after the birth his wife absconded with a soldier leaving the Colonel to raise his son alone.

Resolved to make the best of the situation, Col Charles Smythe settled into the life of a grazier, building up the finest flock of ten thousand merinos and being the envy of the district. He employed a nanny to help raise Charles and on discovering that she was married to a local drunk who beat her and kept all the money she earned, he moved her into the huge homestead on a permanent basis and it was also rumored into his bed as well.

Charles Smythe junior was educated at the finest school and married a local girl of his own station in life. Her father also owned a huge sheep property nearby and the union produced Prudence. After the birth, Charles junior's wife Isabella, decided childbirth was a filthy business and retired to the spare room dedicating her life to social events and Prudence.

Prudence wanted for nothing in life. She was an outgoing girl, always the centre of attention and surrounded by friends. Even at private school Prudence was unable to behave herself and during an inter-school swimming carnival, she made an entrance with a bum busting splash that caused her to lose the bottom half of her bikini and an unperturbed Prudence then bounced out of the pool, swept back her hair and strode into the change rooms, much to the embarrassment of staff at the highly respected school she attended.

Now having left school and approaching nineteen, Prudence had no intention of leaving home again. She spent the days driving her prized ute into town and annoying her father and everyone else on the property. To Prudence life was one big blast.

The Colonel, along with the now aged Nanny Smith, had

long since moved into the manager's residence and Charles jnr and family moved themselves into the main homestead.

It was obvious the Colonel loved a whisky or two, the affection for the liquor evident by a rather large and red nose. Prudence assisted her grandfather in the pursuit of the malt by picking him up under the pretence of taking him to the football. In actual fact they would call at the pub for supplies to fill his portmanteau with spirits and he would sit under the pines with his mates on the pretext of watching the football and getting more inebriated as the afternoon went on.

As this particular game wore on Prudence became interested in a young blonde haired rover playing for Campbell Town who seemed to be getting cleaned up through lack of concentration by the opposition, either that or he had no fear of being severely injured.

Prudence had seen AJ about the town several times but she hadn't had the chance to meet him.

Taking it as a personal affront Prudence and her group verbally abused any opposition player who even came near AJ much to his embarrassment. Even so Campbell Town lost the game by just two points.

At the conclusion all the players, valiant in defeat and after hot showers, adjourned to the local pub for an evening of drinking and commiseration. AJ didn't really feel like it, but under pressure from his friends drove his old Holden to the hotel which was abuzz with drinkers from both teams.

Prudence collected her grandfather and safely delivered him home very drunk, muttering, "Bloody good show," so many times even Prudence was annoyed by the time she discharged him into the safe hands of Nanny Smith.

Immediately she drove back into town and parked her ute in the hotel car park and as usual Prudence made a grand entrance into the hotel and began drinking with her girl friends. As the drink flowed and voices became louder, things began to swing and Prudence intended to have one hell of a time as did her girlfriends.

As the evening wore on several drifted off and the hardliners, including AJ's mates and Prudence's friends, steadily drank on. Swept up in the moment AJ soon became very drunk and for the first time in months let himself go, singing along with his friends, far more seasoned in the consumption of alcohol than AJ. By midnight he was totally out of it when he bumped into Prudence who immediately grabbed hold of him to stop him crashing in a heap to the floor.

The barman was trying to empty the bar as it was past closing time by at least an hour and although he was sure the police on this night would not be to officious, he was not too keen to abuse their patience.

Prudence personally took it upon herself to escort the inebriated AJ home and with the help of his friends loaded him into her ute. Driving out of the hotel car park Prudence, as usual, put on a bit of a display of her driving skills, largely exaggerated because of the effects of the alcohol to which she was reasonably seasoned.

As the helpers poured back into the pub she realised she had no idea as to where exactly AJ lived. It was no problem for Prudence to unload him in the shearers' quarters at home as she had many times with her girlfriends after too much drinking, it was a safe place as even her parents would not be aware and she would deliver him back when he sobered up in the morning.

AJ groaned slightly all the way to Forth homestead and had very little recollection as to what was going on other than that his head was pounding and he felt terribly sick. Upon arrival, Prudence drove her ute as near as possible to one of the vacant huts, no expense spared here, all were clean and had good double beds. Dragging the hapless AJ out of the ute Prudence was not quick enough to escape being splashed with fowl smelling vomit as was AJ and it went all over the front of his shirt and trousers. Unperturbed Prudence pushed and dragged the very ill AJ onto a bed and immediately undressed him down to his underpants.

Taking off her own T-shirt and jeans she decided to doss down on the bed with him for the rest of the night. First she went to the wash room to clean the foul smelling clothes as well as getting a towel and some water to tidy herself up.

Back in the room she also cleaned up AJ and while performing this action she looked at the bulge in his underpants. Prudence, never a girl to be backward in coming forwards, could not contain herself and roughly pulled down AJ's underpants. A gasp came out of Prudence's mouth, hell she had never seen anything like it. In the future, she thought, if she had to produce an heir, here was a stud as good as any ram or bull she had ever seen serve a cow or ewe.She was transfixed in watching the rise of the most beautiful cock she had ever seen, Prudence felt wet between the legs and dropping her wet panties mounted AJ with a loud groan as her vagina was stretched to breaking point. A sensation came over her like she had never experienced before and gently rocking. her body arched and Prudence had her first mind blowing orgasm.

AJ groaned and in the midst of his mind was a picture of Sky, she had returned to him. As Prudence sat breathing heavily she felt hands grab her backside and AJ rose into her again with huge strokes bouncing her breasts up and down until no longer able to control herself, Prudence had another orgasm. She rolled off him, sated, the lust gone from her and she fell into a deep sleep.

The next morning it was rather late when AJ woke from an alcohol induced deep sleep, bursting to urinate and feeling sick he lurched out of bed and stumbled out the door grabbing hold of the bull bar of Prudence's ute, he was urinating and vomiting at the same time. As he straightened up he became aware of his surroundings as Prudence came bouncing out of the shed naked and squatted down in front of him to urinate also.

The sight of her was so erotic and as she stood up and bent over the bull bar his member rose and in a mad moment, head aching and feeling ill, he grabbed her and entered her from behind, riding her like a raging bull. Long strokes reaming in and out of her, her large breasts banging against the bonnet of the ute as she let out long muffled groans, making the occasion more exotic as he roughly banged into her buttocks for what seemed an eternity before he came in one giant explosion into her dripping vagina.

It was only after the event that the reality of what he had done began to sink in, he was ashamed. What would Sky think? He had betrayed her.

Prudence was in her full glee. What a story she would tell her girlfriends who always talked about their conquests, exaggerating no doubt in most cases. Hell, Prudence would make them green with envy, what a ride.

Both panting and dripping with sweat they decided to cool off in the showers, although there was no hot water it was a warm morning and the cool water was refreshing.

Returning to the hut Prudence suggested that they lie on the bed and eat some biscuits she found in the shearers' kitchen while their clothes dried.

Too ill to eat AJ watched as Prudence nibbled on the biscuits and then she faced AJ, still naked and positioned herself so he looked straight at her vagina. He returned her cheeky smile, her pink vagina still slightly apart from the long bout of lustful sex. Prudence slowly began to rub her foot on AJ's penis in small tickling strokes and unable to control the moment, he threw himself on her and in a rough and wild uncontrolled rush, plunged into her as she wrapped her legs around him. It seemed an eternity again before he came for the second time with such a powerful explosion, collapsing onto her heaving breasts, the pair had not even kissed. The encounter was one of pure lust and exhausted, both rolled apart and drifted into a sound sleep.

Late in the afternoon Prudence shook AJ awake and passed him his clothes, she had already dressed and was beaming. As he dressed he thought of what had happened. He was ashamed of what he had done to fulfill his need and angry at his weakness for lust. Prudence was short, big breasted and had a pleasant face but he had no feelings for her apart from the fact Prudence was erotic, likeable, confident and bold as brass. He could like her as a friend, she was exciting. Dropping him off at his car she gave him a quick peck on the cheek and with a happy wave made the usual stunning exit from the car park, spinning out her ute on the gravel edges.

While AJ slowly drove home, Prudence made a fast trip home, changed, scoffed down some breakfast, then bounced back in to her ute and drove into town to pick up her two girlfriends to tell them her story.

AJ had actually turned into a love machine with a cock so big Prudence had nearly passed out several times during the night of lovemaking. Wide-eyed the girls were more than green with envy and decided they would have to see this love machine in person.

On the Monday AJ returned to the shearing shed, much to the chiding of his friends as to how he got on with Prudence on the way home, or had he returned home at all. AJ never answered.

He continued to work hard as he had money to save, he could not continue his life until he found out what happened to Sky.

Prudence meanwhile in the first days after the encounter, felt sorry she had told her friends about the evening with AJ, although outwardly open she had indeed been putting on a front to impress her friends.

No softer hearted and kinder person existed than Prudence. Her mother had never discussed sex with Prudence and her only knowledge was watching the bulls and rams serve cows and ewes out in the paddocks. It all seemed in the natural scheme of things, and once while checking the cattle with her beloved grandfather, she had asked him what the bull was doing to the cow. Spitting and puffing, the Colonel had told her the cow was getting a good rogering.

Prudence said to herself, "I have just had a good rogering. No wonder the cows kept mounting the bulls after more."

As the week wore on Prudence thought more of AJ, not knowing if she was falling in love and even though she knew he was under her social status, it didn't matter as she was used to having her own way and would do as she pleased.

Even after the swimming episode, her discipline had been tempered by the generous donation of the old Colonel, who when told of the incident had roared laughing and exclaimed, "Bloody good show."

Prudence could do no wrong in the eyes of her grandfather but as for her mother, well that was a totally different story, absolutely embarrassed she refused to speak to Prudence for a month.

Chapter

7

The sun came up over the Big Sky homestead in a huge ball of life. The mustering gangs had gathered over thirty thousand cattle into the two holding paddocks of five hundred acres each. A rush was on to draft the steers for market and load them onto trucks to be sent to the abattoirs in Wyndham. They had to mark the calves, cull out the old cows and range bulls caught in the muster and return the breeder cows to the runs before the feed ran out.

Bradley had, through sheer will, held the angel of his impending death and trip to Darwin off. In the last three months, every day, he and Sky had overseen the muster and organising of trucks to ship cattle away. It had been a good season and the new Brahman cattle he had been replacing his herd of Shorthorns with were far better adapted to the Kimberleys.

Sky had became a crack shot at ridding the property of the last of the old scrubber bulls. She loved the majestic Braham bulls and fell into the organisation of running the property beyond all expectations of Bradley Jones. Firm and capable of demanding respect, purely by fairness and firmness, Bradley's education of leadership had been well taught.

Mary looked after the ever growing young Mary and life had changed for the better. No longer lonely, she now had purpose in life, she had even forgotten about longing for a social life in Sydney. Instead she turned Sky into a well dressed and respected figure with white akubra, long black plaited hair, sunglasses, Rossi boots, check shirt and blue jeans. The transformation had been amazing and a personal check every day by Mary assured this practice would continue.

Sky was now revered among her people and all those who came in contact with her. She had convinced Bradley to allow her grandparents into the guest cottage and her grandmother's shrill voice rang in the station gardens daily as she organised the women taking care of the extensive grounds and vegetable gardens.

Sky had obtained with the help of Mary a range of nice dresses and children's clothing and insisted, much to the wailing of the children, at least weekly baths and clean clothes. The event became a great source of amusement and fun, children running naked everywhere screaming with laughter.

Her grandparents had allowed as was the custom, several other members of the family into the cottage and all settled into a happy life. They would never leave the station again for their nomadic life was in the past. They now enjoyed the reliance and comfort of shelter and a stable diet of meat and flour, sugar and tea. Other staples they were given had made it impracticable to go wandering for food as their ancestors had. It was also the settling of Sky into the homestead and running of the station that assured her relatives would not move while this position remained.

The Big Sky was marooned by flood waters for months during the wet season and a good sized airfield had been installed for many years. Bradley had a small aircraft which he kept well maintained in the hangar; he decided weeks earlier to teach Sky the skills to fly the aircraft.

Early one morning he had wanted to go to Broome to pick up supplies and see the stock and station agent to deliver much needed fuel and veterinary products for the treatment of buffalo fly and other parasites. At first Sky was slightly alarmed at the coming event, also Bradley had to be helped into the plane in great pain but he was determined to see Sky fly the small plane.

Taking off, the little aircraft shot into the blue sky and looking out the window as they leveled off, tracked south west to Broome. Sky became hooked on the feeling of freedom and soaring with the eagles was infectious and thrilling. On the way Bradley started to explain the fundamentals of flying and again Sky showed her keen intelligence. She seemed to have an uncanny ability to maneuver the little aircraft and guide it within the first hour of flight.

Over the next several weeks, Bradley and Sky rose into the sky every morning as the sun's rays pierced the red mountain ranges and guided the ground crews to pockets of cattle hidden in the many valleys of the Big Sky.

Not only did Sky learn the exact boundaries of the Big Sky, but after only four weeks, took off into the clear sky soaring like a bird alone and with the exhilaration and feeling of total freedom.

Bradley sat on the homestead porch watching and a smile came over his face. He and his ancestors would not be forgotten on the station that had consumed three generations of his family. God, if there was one, had sent him an angel to protect the legacy that he and his ancestors had carved into the land.

The muster had been the best yet because of Sky's knack for finding cattle in pockets previously never detected. Her enthusiasm and ability for flying, along with her dedication, did not go unnoticed by both Bradley and Mary, just as others in the area regularly saw the little aircraft soaring about like a bird.

The tall striking beauty became a favorite and respected member of the community, many men admired her but she seemed to have an aura of untouchability, always respectful but distant. No-one had the inclination to even consider approaching Sky for any reason other than with respect.

Sky, because of her upbringing, did not drink alcohol or go near places where it was served as her memories of such places were distasteful.

A constant reminder of AJ was their offspring. She had given her heart to AJ and one day she seemed to know he would return and this she vehemently believed. Her mother had taught her a savage lesson about relationships with white men, though she had been lucky and often at night she felt his presence. All that had happened to her during their short time together had been life changing. He had given her a beautiful daughter and in fact, the position she now found herself in. Yes, her heart belonged forever, while the sun shone, to AJ. No other man interested her, nor did she even consider it. AJ was always with her in spirit, they had shared the sacred place and exchanged hearts, so while ever hers beat, she belonged to AJ. Her aboriginal ancestry still had a consideration in her makeup as a human, a quality she would maintain during her life.

As the muster came to an end, the cows, calves and new bulls were released in large mobs to wander back to the ranges and things started to quieten down.

Bradley knew he had to make his final trip to Darwin to enter hospital and spend his last days in a drug induced semi - consciousness. It would be with an agonizing heart that he looked back and watched his life long work and love disappear though it was a small comfort to know his body and spirit would return to be buried on the hilltop with his ancestors overlooking his beloved Big Sky.

He made many calls to his legal team in Darwin finalising the Bradley Jones trust and several times he made changes, much to the annoyance of his solicitors, he wanted it to be right so his legacy would continue. In essence the property would run as a trust with Sky as manager and one of the trustees until young Mary reached twenty one and then it would become her property. However, it must then pass to her offspring and never be sold. In the event of her death it would pass back to Sky, if she was still alive, or to her eldest offspring should she have anymore. Sky would have a wage and exclusive use of the homestead for the rest of her life. In the event that Sky and both Marys died and no other offspring were produced, the property was to be given to the relatives of Sky for their exclusive use and ran as a trust under management. A detailed and complicated document, but nevertheless, months of consideration had been given to the matter and it was the best result for Bradley Jones in his quest to take care of himself and that of his ancestor's remains, plus even after death, he would continue his life's work at the Big Sky.

It was in these last days before departure to Darwin that a lonely, light colored woman (with careful inspection still of some beauty) came up to the homestead surrounded by a group of aboriginal women all yelling loudly for Sky. It was Sky's mother. Rushing into her arms, Sky beamed, only one wish in her life now remained.

Cleaned up and moved into the homestead, over a wonderful meal, Sky and her mother caught up on the news since their last meeting nearly four years ago in Bourke. Sky made her mother agree to never leave her again. In ill health she agreed and Sky hoped this time she meant it. Apart from AJ, she was surrounded by all those whom she loved and she felt a bright and stable future lay ahead.

Chapter

8

AJ settled into the routine of the shearing sheds again. Several members of the shearing team were fellow footballers, including Michael Webb who found shearing a bit boring so he took to rousing. As well as being the comic of the team, much to AJ's embarrassment, he continually chided him about riding his way into a fortune.

On a Wednesday night after work he had returned home to shower and as usual, Agnes Wilson was preparing enough food to feed ten people for the evening meal. AJ decided that being a warm November evening, he'd wash and clean his old Holden, his late grandfather's prized possession. Dressed only in his shorts and while cleaning the interior of the vehicle, he thought of the special time and adventures traveling with Sky, it all seemed so long ago. It was nearly fifteen months since his last vision of her standing, watching him disappear... to him here and now, it felt like a lifetime ago. At almost the same time he thought of Prudence, the short auburn haired bundle of energy, the vigor and eroticism of her uninhibited lovemaking along with her large breasts somewhat excited him.

He had just emptied his shearing gear, greatcoat and other items onto the lawn and started to sweep out the interior of the car when he heard an approaching vehicle coming up the drive. To his surprise it was Prudence's ute making a grand entrance as she came to an abrupt stop before him. The vivacious, young woman bounced out of her car wearing tight little shorts, a shirt tied at the waist, unbuttoned to display her ample breasts and she wore a pair of Blundstones.

Running up to AJ she leapt into the air to straddle him around the waist in a bear hug and then set into giving him a hand to clean the Holden as if they had been an item for years.

Although he tried hard, AJ found no way of avoiding ogling at her perfect bottom that she seemed to be displaying just at the right angle for his gaze as she threw herself into the task of cleaning, as she did with every endeavor in her life. Picking up the gear on the ground she seemed to place her cleavage in full view of AJ, his shorts tightened no matter what other thoughts he tried to entertain in his mind while chatting away, in her glee, Prudence did not fail to notice the occurrence.

AJ found her good company and exciting. He had been, and was still in love with Sky, but now he was in lust with Prudence and even though he was annoyed with his own weakness, he really enjoyed her and having her in his life, she seemed to make it unpredictable and exciting.

Agnes had heard the car pull up and watching from the kitchen window informed her husband, whose thoughts quickly came to a happy conclusion that this may stop his son mooning over an aboriginal girl who was god only knows where. Life may settle down to some regularity. Agnes also seemed relieved that the young pair were chatting and laughing together and a great sense of happiness came over her for her son's sake.

Showing country hospitality as well as a mother's curiosity, Agnes made her way down the path towards the couple for the purpose of meeting the girl and asking her to join them for the evening meal. Upon seeing AJ's mother coming, Prudence rushed up and threw her arms around her, with a peck on the cheek, introducing herself to a surprised Agnes. Taken aback from such an enthusiastic introduction, Agnes was left to stammer an invitation for dinner which was accepted.

Prudence sprinted to her car and produced a beautiful bunch of roses that she presented to Agnes and the two women chatted away like old friends as they went into the house leaving AJ smiling as he finished the last of the polishing of his sparkling car.

Prudence had shown again her ability to organise, seize the moment, impress and delight. Agnes was sold, she immediately took a shine to Prudence as indeed very few people who met her failed to do so.

Over the evening meal, Prudence chatted away like a parrot and indeed impressed David Wilson with her knowledge of farming and animals. Even he became enthused by Prudence's vitality that won over everyone.

During the conversation the subject of marking the one hundred or so fat lambs they reared each year from the older ewes had Agnes bemoaning the fact she had to hold the struggling creatures while AJ attended to ringing the tails and testicles and earmarking. Again Prudence stole the moment by suggesting she come early on Saturday morning to help out.

Prudence offered to do the catching of the lambs, saving AJ from catching, then hold and restrain each one for AJ to perform the procedures on. Much time would be saved as Prudence was young and fit and it was her way of paying Agnes back for such a lovely meal.

AJ's parents at this moment gave a one hundred percent approval rating to Prudence. They had intended bringing the sheep in on the Friday ready for AJ to mark on the Saturday anyway and Agnes really did appreciate not having to carry out a task she didn't approach with much enthusiasm.

At the end of the meal a beaming Prudence informed everyone she would have to go early as her grandfather required a ride into Launceston early the next day, his health had been failing and he was making a visit to the doctor whom he had followed to Launceston when he ceased practice in

Campbell Town. Again Prudence received a tick of approval for the manner in which she apparently cared for her grandfather, the well known and respected Colonel Smythe.

Following her out to the car, AJ was in fact disappointed when she gave him a quick kiss against the car door, opened it and made a typical 'Prudence departure', leaving AJ more than a little excited. Prudence smiled with satisfaction as she drove home knowing her visit had been a success.

For two days AJ thought during the long monotonous shearing shed hours about the twists and turns his life had made since leaving school. All his mates dated girls, many had a number of relationships without any apparent problems though he seemed to become tied in a web of lust or love. Confused by the trials which had happened to him, he was unable to forget either women, who had impacted on his life.

Saturday came after what seemed to AJ an eternity. Sure enough while having breakfast at about seven, Prudence made her entrance and bounding up the front steps she plonked herself down at the breakfast table to join the Wilsons in a meal of bacon and eggs enthusiastically cooked up by Agnes. Agnes was very happy at having another female in the house; it made her feel young again. Prudence was the girl she longed to be in her younger days, she envied her to a certain extent.

After breakfast the young couple chatted away as they made their way to the sheep yards followed by the farm dogs, a pair of woolly looking Smithfields. Prudence was used to the sleek kelpies on her property and the sight of these unruly scruffy dogs amused her. Throwing herself into the task, they had all the lambs marked in under two hours. They turned the ewes out to match up with their offspring, many lying down on the ground in shock and pain at the rings around their tails and testicles.

Slowly they started to drift the ewes down the lane towards the river flats lined with willows and lush grass on the fertile soil. Of the entire nine hundred acres the property had perhaps only three hundred acres of good soil, the balance being wattle covered country of poor quality and situated higher than the rest with two large salt pans. The day was perfect as the sun rose to the centre of the sky and they finally herded the bleating and confused mob into the paddock and shut the gate.

As they made their way back up the river, AJ for once took the initiative and suggested a swim in the cool pond to wash of the blood from the earmarking and the dust from the yards. Does a duck swim, thought Prudence, who stripped and plunged in before AJ had his boots off. Splashing about in the crystal clear stream the pair refreshed themselves. AJ tried hard, as usual, not to look at Prudence's ample breasts and inviting mound of womanhood. He soon succumbed to lust and with Prudence feigning alarm, he dragged her onto the green inviting bank and plunged into her. Disappointed, he immediately exploded inside her, the moment so pent up he was unable to control himself. He had been having dreams of this moment since their first encounter.

Afterwards they lay on the fresh grass under the warm sun panting, gazing at the blue sky above. For the first time in many months, AJ felt somewhat at ease, life seemed to be returning to some form of familiarity.

Prudence lay against him, her pleasant, smiling face looking into his eyes showed the love she now felt for AJ. She began caressing his manhood as he again rose with excitement and they both became entwined in lovemaking, much slower and more controlled this time, ending with satisfaction for both in a mind blowing orgasm.

Holding hands they returned for a late afternoon meal prepared by Agnes and kept warm as the expected return had not eventuated in the time Agnes had worked out. However, she was not alarmed at the late return of the lovers and she had noticed the looks Prudence was giving her son, much to her approval.

Prudence took charge and gave AJ a birthday party for his nineteenth, as hers was two weeks earlier and Michael Webb's in the middle, so she threw a bash to combine all three. All the young ones in the district agreed it was the best show they had ever attended with a band in the Forth woolshed and Prudence's grandfather financing the food and alcohol to which he attended and consumed his share before heading home with Nanny Smith to guide him. Michael Webb had, for months, been in a relationship with one of Prudence's friends, Rachael Canning, a large likeable girl who had nearly finished her nursing training. The two couples often went out together.

One can never tell how, in the blink of an eye, the changes that can abruptly come into the tapestry of life we all face. Only two weeks after the party and before Christmas both Michael Webb and AJ received letters within two days of each other informing both they had been drafted into the army. On January the 10th they were to to attend a medical check in Launceston. Prudence was shattered as was Agnes. The awful war raging in Vietnam was something you saw on TV and it all seemed so far away from this little community that it did not seem real. Reality had hit two of their finest young men and they would be leaving the bosom of the community again.

Agnes did mention trying to get AJ out of the draft because of the condition of his father and the Colonel, seeing the anguish of his beloved granddaughter, also offered to help with such a course. But both AJ and his father did not entertain such a thought, they felt it was a man's duty to step forward if called upon.

All thoughts of going to find Sky now started to fade, the medical and interview soon came with the expected results and the two friends again bid farewell to family as well as two weeping girls at the Launceston airport later that month on route to Puckapunyal army camp for basic training.

Twice now AJ had seen the vision of a woman waving him a sad farewell, as the plane taxied down the runway and it seemed to him his life was out of control, that some dark force had diverted his life so fast and so quickly that it seemed fate was to intervene whenever life became ordered.

On the way home Prudence confided to her friend she felt rather ill and had been feeling sick the past few mornings. Alarmed, Rachael took her immediately to the surgery of the family doctor who gleefully informed Prudence that pregnancy was the main cause of the sickness and had been so for at least three months.

Not wanting to worry AJ, she did not confide the pregnancy to him for three weeks. In that time he had settled into the basic training of the yelling, marching and discipline of army life. When he heard of the pregnancy he did not consider anything but marriage, as always he accepted his responsibility and arranging a two week leave pass, both boys would return home after basic training for the wedding.

Prudence along with an embarrassed mother and a happy mother-in-law, planned a small family wedding on the lawns of the impressive Forth homestead, with a reception in the dining room to take place after.

During the next few weeks of training both boys, friends since childhood, helped each other and looked out for one another. Hit one and you hit both, one quiet and reserved the other outgoing and like Prudence, life was a blast. Twice weekly AJ wrote to Prudence and her to him daily. No girl was happier than Prudence, the matter of their wedding and impending childbirth had come much sooner than she had ever planned. Hell, she thought many times, life is short, strike while the iron is hot.

Though Prudence was no fool and she was aware AJ still carried a flame for the girl he met on his trip up north. On questioning his two friends she learnt sketchy details but in her own way she disregarded it, she would be a good wife and mother and keep him so satisfied he would eventually forget this wild northern nymph. For god's sake, the few dalliances she had never caused her a second thought, she was now totally in love.

Many times during the approach to his wedding, AJ laid in bed thinking of Sky, his heart somehow was still chained to hers forever. Had she met someone else? Now he would never know, marriage and a further twenty one months of national service would force him to block as much as he could from his mind. Life with Prudence wasn't that bad anyhow, he liked her in many ways, she made him feel good, not the heartache of true love. *True love can consume and destroy,* he thought.

On a visit to her doctor, accompanied by grandfather who also had a check up, the old Colonel sick of the lack of room in the ute and the infernal radio Prudence always had squawking away or the ten bloody fouring to everyone, he suggested he buy Prudence a new car. More room and suitable to a woman about to be married and produce the heir to Forth. With that thought Prudence drove home in a red Mercedes, more subdued and reserved in keeping with her status now. Why ever her driving, much to the acceptance of the Colonel, was more responsible.

As the two boys stepped off the plane in Launceston, AJ could see Prudence waving madly, beaming with a noticeable baby bump. He was glad to grab her in his arms and give her a passionate kiss, he had missed her greatly. Prudence was in her glee as she waited excitedly for baggage collection, holding AJ's hand while Michael grabbed the bags. She was glowing as those around her noticed the two dashing young servicemen who she seemed to command with unbridled happiness.

That night much to his disappointment, he was not allowed to stay with Prudence and he and his best man Michael stayed with his parents. Lyndon Fish was helping out on the farm while he was away and the three friends had a few drinks with AJs parents before turning in exhausted after the day's events.

AJ smiled as he thought of the new Mercedes they were picked up in. Prudence had matter of factly responded when they asked about the Mercedes, that it was a wedding pressy from grandfather. Nothing fazed Prudence he thought, what she wanted was what she got and now she had him.

Both boys resplendent in uniform were picked up by friends of Prudence an hour before the wedding, his parents and Lyndon having long since departed to help with final arrangements, which had been a waste of time as Prudence and her mother had everything finalised down to the last detail.

Pulling up outside the impressive homestead Rachael and Prudence stood on the front entrance steps with the minister. A tear came to Prudence's eyes as AJ and Michael walked up the steps and stood beside the two elegantly dressed girls.

Prudence had managed a wedding dress to hide the growing pregnancy and all present agreed she looked stunning.

The marriage ceremony was soon over as their vows were exchanged and AJ looked at Prudence and gave her a long kiss much to the oohs and aahs of the audience and the raising of the malt by the old Colonel with a, "Bloody good show."

It was great to be home and amongst friends after three hard months of army life. The boys intended to relax and enjoy their two weeks leave before heading to the jungles of Vietnam.

Michael read the wedding telegrams, many he had made up and he also gave a great speech about how glad he was to see his friend marrying such a nice girl. He was correct on all points, Prudence was indeed a catch many young men in the district would have aspired to. At the end of it he announced that he and Rachael had become engaged and would marry on his return from duty in the army.

Prudence was thrilled, as was AJ, it made the night a momentous occasion for the four friends.

After a wonderful evening they snuggled in the huge, soft bed at Prudence's and AJ never felt happier. Prudence did not wish for a honeymoon. Instead her parents left next morning for a holiday leaving the young newlyweds the use of the huge mansion undisturbed. Pregnancy did not diminish the sexual drive of Prudence and she threw herself into the sexual part of marriage with such vigor, AJ worried as to the wellbeing of his growing child. He enjoyed the two weeks which he thought perhaps the best two weeks of his life, he and Prudence ate, walked, visited his parents and made love.

Again it was a sad farewell at the airport as both boys looked out the plane window to the two girls. Seeing Prudence waving a tearful farewell as they faded from view, AJ made a commitment to return safely, he wanted to watch his child grow.

Prudence returned home to the care of her mother and visits of her doting mother-in-law Agnes, who awaited the birth of her grandchild with enthusiasm. Gone was the wild Prudence and she busied herself helping on the farm and with the gardening as well as preparing the nursery for the coming birth.

Chapter

9

The little aircraft bucked angrily as Sky nervously opened up the throttle. She anxiously looked down the runway, the wet had started early and Bradley Jones had stalled his departure as long as possible, the runway was sluggish, although well drained the tires of the overloaded plane would sink slightly into the runway as the plane gathered speed.

Sitting in the rear seats were Mary Jones and the younger Mary strapped in beside her, Bradley was seated in the front, a tear trickled down his face as he had been assisted into the seat, he was aware he had just stepped off his beloved Big Sky for the last time.

Born and educated on the station, very few times in his life had he left the safety and sanctity of his beloved country, it became his life's work, his passion. As the little plane lurched forward he waved to the aboriginal stockmen and their families lining the runway, he had empathy for them and their skill as stockmen and knowledge of the land.

Sky had never taken off with such a load, with passengers and luggage she was unaware of how the little plane would respond, used to only two passengers and mostly on her own she was alarmed at how the plane would perform under such duress.

As the little machine approached the end of the runway Sky pulled back on the controls and slowly the small plane lifted, struggling into the clear Kimberley sky; the departure was early in the morning as storms had been forecast later in the day. Banking slightly left, she followed the magnificent Fitzroy River now over-running its banks; the river ran wild and untamed through the magnificent gorges and flood planes of the best cattle country in the world.

No one spoke. Mary was still holding the hand of her namesake as Bradley gazed lovingly for the last time at his property, the grass was now lush and he could see the magnificent dark red cattle, sleek and contently grazing below.

He had requested Sky fly east over the station and following his request she kept the little plane as low as she dared, her forehead was covered in sweat from the exertion and stress of the takeoff. Reaching the boundary Sky banked north and flew over the hilltop where Bradley would return to be buried with his ancestors and continuing over the airstrip and homestead so he was capable of one last vision of the homes he had lived his entire life.

As the plane rose steadily into the clear blue sky the harsh Kimberley landscape opened up before them and taking in his last look as if breathing his last approaching breath, Bradley looked straight ahead and drifted off into a sleep helped by a shot of morphine he had received prior to departure.

Now isolated by the Fitzroy River, the residents still at the Big Sky would be unable to leave for several months. With the departure of the plane they were stranded. Sky had told her mother, who was living at the homestead as caretaker, to ring the hotel they would be staying at in Darwin in case of emergency and she would fly home as quickly as possible. The station store had been well stocked and a large supply of diesel stored for the generator with a back up generator in case of breakdown.

Sky's relatives who had all worked seasonally on the station for decades looked with sadness into the sky as the plane circled once overhead before climbing to a higher altitude. Bradley Jones had treated them with fairness and respect and they in turn had treated him the same; it was rare for a white man to treat the aboriginals with such consideration and kindness.

Sky had been the daughter Bradley had never had and in turn she had regarded him as the father she never had. As she glanced at him now sleeping next to her she tried hard to control her emotions remembering she had a valuable cargo on board. Sky wondered why everyone she truly loved seemed to come into her life, take her heart and leave. Both AJ and Bradley had treated her with respect and love no matter what, She would never forget them both, for as long as she lived.

Now at three thousand feet the little plane had leveled off as Sky settled into the task of guiding the aircraft to Darwin airport. As Kununurra passed under her she kept the highway on the right, following this she would strike the Stuart highway at Katherine then follow it north to the Darwin airport. Sky had never been to Darwin since her childhood and was more than troubled by the task ahead. However, Bradley had soothed her fears by telling her he had absolute faith in her skills as a pilot to guide the little family safely to Darwin. Several times she checked the fuel gauge, although Bradley had assured her he expected a reserve of fuel left on arrival, making it a safe trip. She worried about the amount of fuel used before departure and after flying over the Big Sky and taking off with such a load.

Looking at her passengers in the rear she saw both asleep, lulled by the drone of the engine. For Mary Jones the stress of the last few weeks had taken toll of her health and she was sleeping more than usual.

Fuelled with adrenaline Sky watched the road intently to her left, the Timber Creek store and settlement passed by and she settled into a routine of marking her flight east by checking the controls.

Sky was aware of the responsibility and new status in her

life given to her by the Jones family and she knew she would never let them down.

After what seemed an eternity Sky picked up the township of Katherine, again checking her fuel with satisfaction, she banked left and headed north for the last stretch into Darwin airport. This leg of the trip started to become more interesting as she observed landmarks vaguely remembered in her childhood and the thought of landing the plane in Darwin again raised her adrenalin levels as her hands became wet and clammy.

The radio started picking up chatter from the airport and checking in, she was told to approach from the north, on the main runway. She made sure an ambulance would be on standby upon arrival and her 'estimated time of arrival' was given as twenty minutes.

Sky anxiously peered north for signs of Darwin so she could bank south and approach over the harbor from the north. With all passengers asleep she felt frightened, her heart beat faster and she thought about waking Bradley for advice but then in doing so would wake and alarm her other passengers. Before she had time to think anymore Darwin appeared on the horizon and stealing herself, she banked south before circling right and coming in low over the harbor where the airport appeared before her. It was late afternoon and as she lowered the plane to approach the runway, she was surprised to see all the huge military aircraft lined up. Sky made a perfect landing. With the passengers now awake, Mary Jones started crying with emotion, congratulating Sky. Taxiing to the hangar allocated to her she saw the ambulance waiting and guiding the little plane to the hanger, Sky cut the engine. Opening the door she fell out of the aircraft and vomited, then fainted.

Sky came to as an ambulance officer waved smelling salts over her face and a worried Mary, holding her child, looked down at her. The first thing she saw was Bradley being loaded into the ambulance.

For the second time in her life Sky broke down with emotion and she sobbed uncontrollably. In such a short period of time in her troubled life, she'd had so much change and responsibility foisted onto her. She just let go, her head was splitting with a violent headache and she felt old, exhausted and worn out.

The taxi driver loaded luggage from the plane into the boot as the ambulance headed out of the airport towards Darwin Hospital where informed staff would be waiting. Mary and Sky felt relieved, over the past few weeks Bradley's condition had deteriorated and the task of caring for him had drained both women, while they had also prepare the station for the wet season.

The taxi pulled up outside one of Darwin's most exclusive hotels. On the few times that Mary did have the opportunity to leave the station, she did so in style. Though this time, under the circumstances, she was well aware of the traumatic time ahead and wished herself, Sky and little Mary to have the best of care. Porters removed the bags and placed them in the rooms, both rooms having been booked for several weeks as Mary did not want any problems of changing accommodation, she knew trying times lay ahead.

Mary suggested to Sky they wash and change, have a small meal in Mary's room and retire early. Sky feeling absolutely drained agreed and when the door of the room closed at the departure of the manager, she collapsed on the bed hugging her daughter sobbing uncontrollably.

Sky lay for the next two hours clinging to her little daughter before a knock came on the door and she had to drag herself off the bed to answer. It was Mary, she had rang the hospital and they had reported Bradley was comfortable and sleeping. She suggested, as had the doctor, that they not visit him until the morning and although worried about Bradley, Sky agreed.

She did not think herself capable anyway of leaving the room without a night's rest.

Mary played with little Mary while Sky showered and changed, a meal was delivered and although inviting, neither ate much. Mary helped Sky bath little Mary, who in her excitement at staying in the hotel, laughed happily. Little Mary ate a hearty meal, after which mother and daughter pulled back the sheets and snuggled into bed.

Mary hung up clothes, placed the food trolley outside the door and placing a 'do not disturb' sign on the door handle, turned to say goodnight, only to find both mother and daughter sound asleep. She stood quietly contemplating the pair and an overwhelming feeling of motherly love and emotion came over her. What would she have done all these long months without her adopted family? When they arrived she was near breaking point after years of isolation, loneliness and the fear of the future that had stretched her emotions beyond her control. As she closed the door quietly, she thought life must persevere. Her task now is to comfort her dying husband and help raise her namesake whom she loved unconditionally as the family she was not able to conceive herself.

Both Mary and Sky slept until late morning not waking until little Mary playfully woke her mother. Sky sat up abruptly, rubbing her eyes and immediately phoned Mary's room, also waking her up. Mary showered then ordered breakfast for them all to be eaten in Sky's room and then hastily went to help dress and feed little Mary, it was an important day.

The three ate breakfast, now hungry they enjoyed the meal and coffee. Feeling better they took a taxi to the hospital and were surprised to see Bradley sitting up in bed also eating breakfast. Although he looked grey and ill, connected to many tubes, he greeted his three most favorite people in the world with a huge smile. He told Sky how proud he was of her on the remarkable feat she had accomplished; even the doctor present congratulated her.

At eleven that morning, the firm of solicitors who the owners of the Big Sky had used over the decades arrived. All present listened as the document, crafted over several months, was read. Since the first draft was considered and with legal advice, Bradley had settled on the following course: a trust would now take over the Big Sky; Mary and Sky along with a solicitor appointed by them would act as trustees; beneficiaries of income would be Mary and Sky with a trust set up for young Mary for her education. The trust would maintain a bank balance always sufficient to insure the onward financial considerations of running the Big Sky. Both Mary and Sky would be signatories to any cheques signed, however, as Sky would perhaps in many instances find herself in the position of having to access money for the day to day running of the station, she would be capable of signing cheques to the value alone up to the sum of forty thousand dollars in any financial year. All books and transactions would be subject to audit and inspection by all concerned here, at a meeting to be held in Darwin, in the office of the company solicitors once a year. The younger Mary would become a beneficiary to profits from the station on her twenty first birthday and indeed take up the position of a trustee at that time or before in the case of Mary Jones's death. The trustees may appoint other beneficiaries being any further offspring of Sky or husband she may acquire in the future. Any children of young Mary or future siblings would become beneficiaries to the trust. If the line ever expires, then the trust would be run by the family solicitors with the relatives of Sky becoming beneficiaries of any profits and right of occupation of their camps on the station run under management. Many other minor details were explained to those present including maintenance of the family grave site to which an annual sum would be allocated for its upkeep and preservation.

It had taken a full two hours to explain all details to those present, including at Bradley's request, reports from the station accountant and bank manager both in Darwin.

At the conclusion, all papers were signed by those required and at the scolding off the nursing staff, left an exhausted but relieved Bradley Jones, along with the three women he loved, alone. He beckoned them up close and with effort sat the infant Mary on the bed. In a soft, but wavering voice as he held their hands, he looked at Mary and thanked her for her years of companionship and loyalty. He apologised for her years of isolation and loneliness, but he had no other option as he had never considered life apart from his beloved station, he now unchained her heart and set her free. "Please enjoy your coming years in Sydney, but remember me in your thoughts sometimes, for I always loved you unconditionally.".

To Sky, as he looked into her beautiful face, he spoke softly, "You are the child I never had, no father would ever be prouder of a daughter than I am of you. Thank you for my granddaughter Mary, no man hath a greater love for any human than I have for this child, and thanks to you my obsession and life in the Big Sky may continue on. May you all live a happy and long life. Now please go and let me rest, enjoy this beautiful day as life is short."

Tears streaming down their faces the two women left with young Mary holding both of their hands between them. Bradley had never told Mary how much he loved her, like many men he found it hard to express his feelings. As he watched them go he felt a feeling of relief, he would now die happily in the knowledge that the Big Sky would continue on.

Mary and Sky did not feel like doing much and went back to the hotel rooms, showered and played with young Mary, a happy little girl unable to comprehend the drama occurring around her. As Sky looked at her child, she thought of the uncanny resemblance of her father's features. Sky's aboriginal instincts felt his presence in the midst of all this turmoil somehow, she saw his face in her restless sleep, the look of happiness on his face troubled her.

As the weeks passed, Bradley Jones' life slowly and agonizingly marched towards his death. Visiting daily, the three who meant so much to him, did not enjoy the town life as much as they may have under different circumstances. Mary made Sky buy some new clothes and she looked beautiful in her new suits and long boots which were the fashion at the time. She also had her hair styled at the hairdressers. Sky was transformed into a stylish looking business woman and a big change from the shy, shabbily dressed girl Mary had first noticed. It all seemed so long ago.

Mary had never had anything to do with the business side of her husband's station nor had she wanted to, but now with her and Sky as trustees, she found a visit to the accountant was necessary. Both women found it hard to comprehend what they were now privy to.

The Big Sky had, that past season, sold over one hundred and eighty thousand dollars of beef cattle, after costs and taxation a profit of one hundred and two thousand dollars now sat in the trust account. As to Mary's position she had, apart from the house in the prestigious suburb of Valcluse in Sydney, a share and investment portfolio that Bradley had already signed over to her, after fees and government duties, worth three million dollars. The accountant asked the pair if they had any further instructions. An absolutely flustered Mary informed two dour faced accountants that she and Sky would indeed discuss matters and let them know.

At this time, the average weekly wage was fifty dollars, a huge amount of money. Mary was to learn later that Bradley's family had money invested in England and like most at the time never spent much and lived frugally. Sky found it impossible to focus on such large sums, she had thought the three thousand dollars in the pass book she still carried in her shoulder bag was a fortune. Mary had in fact never asked Bradley about finances and like Sky, money never became an issue, but even she was amazed at the amount squirrelled away by the Jones dynasty from the Big Sky over the decades.

After four long weeks, Bradley Jones died peacefully, surrounded by the three whom he adored. It was almost a relief to Sky and Mary that he was now at peace with all the awful suffering over. They made arrangements to take his body home hiring a twin engine plane to transport him the following Wednesday. On the Thursday and Friday they both attended to the last of the business matters and on the Saturday decided to have a coffee in the Darwin Plaza and go for a walk along the palm lined foreshore to try and relax while taking in the beauty of Darwin Harbor.

Chapter

10

The huge Hercules transport lumbered off from Townsville, fully laden with men and equipment heading west to Darwin. On board with their platoon were Michael Webb and AJ after having spent the past two months doing jungle warfare training in Northern Queensland. Both tanned and fit, they looked out at the red earth below many times during the trip to Darwin and AJ wondered if the roads he picked up below were any he and Sky had traveled. It seemed such a long time ago now.

He read the letters that he had received from Prudence at the Townsville base, always happy and full of good news about family life in general back home.

Her impending childbirth had slowed Prudence down somewhat and she now spent most days visiting her grandfather and Nanny Smith who doted on her. Tapping his finger to his nose as always, Colonel Charles Smythe commending his grandaughter on the fine job she was doing in the pregnancy stakes, *Jolly fine show,* he would often say.

AJ dozed along with most of his comrades as he looked forward to landing in Darwin. There they would wait for the balance of his battalion until the following Tuesday when all would leave for Saigon and the war that was turning nastier by the week.

The news was of body counts and the successes of the coalition forces, but even so many suspected it was bogged down in a quagmire. A sense of trepidation and fear of the unknown came over the fresh faced cream of Australia. Joking amongst themselves while waiting for planes or at other gathering points, and putting on a show of bravado, they hid the fact that they all feared the unknown and missed family and home.

The plane came in over the Darwin Harbor, screaming to a slow halt on the runway, a convoy of army trucks waited as men alighted and loaded into them. Driving to Larakeah Barracks, AJ and Michael were surprised at how small Darwin appeared. Safely accommodated in the barracks both boys wrote long letters home.

At role call they were informed that leave passes would be issued from Saturday at eight am until Monday at ten am when all would be expected to be back at least twenty minutes before roll call. Departure for Vietnam would be at one o'clock on the Tuesday morning and any person late or returning intoxicated would be severely dealt with.

AJ and Michael signed out of the barracks at ten that morning; in fact they had nearly not gone into town but decided to have a look at the old gun battery from the Second World War and then check out the city centre.

Catching a bus, they had been dropped off at the bus stop opposite the shopping mall and after a coffee they shopped around for sometime before buying take away food to enjoy while they walked along the esplanade. The pair sat on a seat under the shade of a sweet smelling frangipani, relaxing and talking about how fast life can change, what lay ahead and promising again to take care of each other.

Finishing the meal Michael made his way across to a garbage can to dispose of the packaging and he noticed a woman in her sixties and a tall, well dressed woman, perhaps twenty, with dark sunglasses and black knee length boots, approaching as they walked up the path. In between the two, holding hands, was little girl dressed in a polka dot dress happily laughing and skipping, occasionally lifting her legs and being carried by both women. Transfixed by the site and the beauty of the younger woman, Michael looked over at AJ staring out to sea, both hands over the back of his head. As they came closer, within a few meters of each other, Michael noticed the younger woman stop, place her hand to her mouth and give a muffled cry. AJ looked at Michael, who in an instant recognised Sky and was staring at her with mouth open, he knew immediately by the age of the child that she was AJs offspring. AJ stood up alarmed and then swung around to stare straight at Sky and the child he knew also in an instant was his. A stunned Mary also realised by the reaction of both that she was about to meet AJ Wilson. She bristled with anger at what she assumed he had done to her beloved Sky. Pent up with emotion AJs legs collapsed and he fell to his knees. Sky ran to him and held his face to her, tears streaming from her eyes. Mary started yelling at AJ and Michael, springing to his friend's defense, began to yell at Mary and young Mary, so happy a moment ago, started crying. Mary scooped up young Mary and decided that this course of events would not help and grabbing the hapless Michael by the arm she dragged him along with her to leave the two stunned lovers in the peace and quiet of their own presence. Hoping Sky heard, Mary said to come back to the hotel after they had regained some sanity and she and Michael would be waiting in the foyer.

Sitting on a seat, AJ and Sky holding hands so tightly as to nearly stop blood circulation, looking at each other, did not speak for some time until AJ asked why she had not answered his letters. Sky replied her grandmother had gone many times asking for letters and there were none, that was why she hadn't written and that she had thought he didn't want her and had forgotten her when he went home. He asked Sky what had happened after he left and she explained after a few months the family had gone south to the station and there she had given birth to their daughter. Sky also, in her unassuming way, did not tell the full story of her changed situation but merely stated she now worked on the station and was happy. She also explained about the death of Bradley Jones and that she would be returning to the station early the next week.

AJ never had thoughts of not telling Sky the truth about his marriage and Prudence. He never at anytime blamed Prudence and to his credit, even though he assumed that Sky would be devastated when he told her the whole story, he told her that he still loved her and always would, enough to set her free if she so wished.

Sky answered in a manner totally unexpected by AJ. He thought she may be angry and hurt, but instead she held his hand and told him he would always be her love and that she had given her heart to him, she was grateful to him for him bringing her home, giving her a lovely daughter, a new life on the station and lastly she told him that her people often had more than one wife.

Bewildered even more, AJ was anxious to see his daughter and the two walked hand in hand slowly back to the hotel. On the way Sky gave AJ the bank book and he was surprised that she had not withdrawn any money, even with a child to raise and the child was his responsibility.

Darwin was full of soldiers, both Australian and American coming and going for R&R in Sydney and as such banks and shops had opened for the day. On the way back to the hotel AJ suggested he withdraw the money and give it to Sky.

Leaving the bank they passed by a jewelers shop and Sky, out of the blue, requested AJ buy her a ring as he did his other wife. A stunned AJ entered the shop with Sky and while an assistant showed her wedding rings, he noticed a matching pair of ruby pendants surrounded by diamonds on glistening gold chains. On the spur of the moment he purchased both and placed one around the beautiful neck of Sky. She nodded in agreement that one should also go to his other wife. With a gold ring on her finger and the beautiful piece of jewellery around her neck, Sky was beaming, she had found her man and he still loved her. Bradley had gone but just knowing AJ was still around boosted her confidence, her aboriginality taught her many things including patience and lack of jealousy. All seemed in order to Sky.

Meanwhile, over coffee, Michael explained to Mary about AJs return, his anguish over no contact from Sky, the letters and phone calls and the result. Michael knew his friend so he also told her about Prudence. Mary was heartbroken and worried about Sky, what an unmitigated bloody mess Mary thought. What will happen to Sky?

Entering the foyer little Mary was playing on Michael's knee happy and contented again as the two walked in. Mary was surprised that they were smiling and holding hands. AJ scooped up little Mary as he beamed with pride. She was a beautiful little girl, a lighter skin color than Sky but still beautiful and having the same lustrous image as her mother, he also saw himself in many her features.

Confused and embarrassed, Mary did not know what to say. Always quick on the uptake, Michael, on seeing the pendants, decided to buy something for his Rachel also and jumping up invited Mary whom he now called Mrs J, to accompany him to help with the selection. They left Sky, AJ and young Mary to catch up as they left the hotel arm in arm. Two passing American sailors looked and said, "By gord, those Aussies sure are desperate."

AJ and Sky sat for a short time but the hustle of the foyer became annoying so Sky suggested they go to her room. AJ was impressed with the opulence but gave the matter no more thought as he thought Mrs Mary Jones obviously had plenty of money and paid for the accommodation. Laying their child on the bed, Sky, exhausted from the emotional day, lay down bedside her. AJ lay on the opposite side looking into Sky's angelic face and then at his sleeping daughter, all three of them drifted off to sleep.

Mary and Michael became good friends that day. Mary liked the outgoing and likeable young man and after choosing a beautiful brooch, Mary insisted on shouting him tea at the hotel and even suggested, as she had two rooms, he stay the night in the hotel to which Michael agreed. Both never mentioned Sky or AJ as Mary didn't wish to know what was going on, it all seemed surreal. Though Michael knew the power of love Sky held over his confused friend.

At about ten that evening, Sky, AJ and young Mary awoke and ordered tea to be delivered to the room. AJ was impressed with Sky, she was now more assured and confident but still quietly shy in many ways.

After tea Sky bathed Mary and played with her while AJ showered, his mind was so confused he knew he would never hurt Prudence, yet he would never let Sky leave his life again.

Then AJ amused little Mary while Sky showered and changed into a beautiful short nightdress and lacy pants. When she returned AJ melted at the sight of her, dreams of long ago flooded back and placing the child in the spare singe bed, both lay on the double bed and melted into each others arms.

When both failed to appear for breakfast, Mary suggested she and Michael take a tour of Darwin for the day on one of the buses operating. Michael was glad and wishing to save money jumped at the opportunity. Both found each other excellent company and enjoyed a fantastic day. Mary was happy to have the companionship after the emotionally exhausting few weeks she had just spent, it was refreshing chatting to her new friend.

Sky and AJ with little Mary went for a walk about midday along the Esplanade that had united them. Sitting on the lawn chatting and playing with their daughter life seemed perfect.

Both knew the chance meeting would be brief and soaked up the moment.

A passing tourist with a Polaroid camera, at the request of AJ, took several photos gladly of the young soldier and his beautiful wife and daughter, sadly aware they would soon be parted, wishing them well he shook AJs hand and strolled on.

In the afternoon they enjoyed a nice meal at the restaurant opposite their accommodation, little Mary soon became tired so they returned to the hotel. They did not re-appear until breakfast the next morning knowing they would be parted again for at least a year.

Mary and Michael were already at the table when the three appeared. AJ carried his daughter and as he held hands with Sky, Mary's heart missed a beat, she was worried for Sky. A fond farewell took place between the four adults on the street. Mary gave Michael a parting hug as Sky and AJ kissed passionately. AJ cuddled his daughter, breathing in deep her scent, then stepped onto the bus.

Once again he watched as Sky waved farewell to her one true love. Instead of crying this time she was smiling, he had came back to her which was all that mattered, she knew he loved her.

AJ knew he would be unable to see Sky again before leaving.

Mary was amazed how well Sky had taken the departure, AJ's marriage and leaving for Vietnam. Unable to contain herself she spoke to Sky about the dilemma. Unfazed, Sky explained she had given AJ her heart it was his to do with as he wished. She was his first wife, he still loved her and she was sure he would return to her and the Kimberleys. Her grandfather had told her often he had drunk from the Ord River so he would always come back. Sky's simple aboriginal logic amazed Mary.

Early Monday morning Sky, Mary and little Mary caught a

cab drove to the hangar and loaded up the little aircraft, checking that Bradley's coffin would indeed be delivered to The Big Sky airstrip on Wednesday. They taxied out to the runway as they radioed for clearance, more confident now, Sky with Mary holding little Mary strapped in the front seat, spun the little plane around and pouring on the power, catapulted the little machine down the runway. A rush of freedom came over her as she banked north in order to fly over the army base. AJ and Michael had both looked up at the little aircraft, unaware as to its passengers.

Sky flew along the coast on the return course. Mary did not question her as she had every faith in her ability to get them home safely. Cutting inland, Sky picked up the Ord River and following it, soon placed the Wyndham airstrip on the horizon. Instantly Mary knew what Sky had in mind and landing at the airport Sky called a taxi for the three and ordered the driver to the post office.

The three strode into the post office and requested the mail held for Sky Brown-Wilson. The post mistress exclaimed that she was told to hold that mail, but had just about given up on anyone ever coming to pick it up. Sky gasped when she saw the pile of letters that were handed to her.

Returning to the airport, Sky placed the letters in her case, she would read them when she got home, the contents did not matter as it was already proved he had never stopped loving her. Once again the little plane rose into the Kimberley sky, tracking the Gibb River Road she headed east to find familiar country. Landing back on a familiar and welcoming airstrip with confidence, she had returned them all home safely.

All the residents of the Big Sky had heard the approaching aircraft. A huge homecoming feast was prepared, even Mary was glad to be home.

On Wednesday, the body of Bradley arrived home and a small procession followed the coffin on the back of the station

Land Cruiser to the burial ground. The station women wailed as is their tradition, a simple ceremony was conducted by the local minister who had flown in. At last Bradley Jones was laid to rest. To Mary and Sky who had watched his suffering over many months, it was a final moment, he was now at peace with his ancestors. The view from his burial site overlooking the homestead and the country was breathtaking and indeed Mary knew he would be happy.

The next week life settled back to some normality. Sky read AJs letters and a feeling of peace came over her as she read the contents, "Come home my love," she whispered as she placed them in a box on her bedside table.

The wet season still had three months to go before mustering was due to begin. Mary begged Sky to accompany her to Sydney to help her open up her home 'Kimberley Cottage'. Mary did not want to leave her namesake behind, the thought alarmed her and Mary was infatuated with the child.

Mary explained that Sky would have to fly her to Broome anyway for a commercial flight to Sydney, the plane had to be serviced which would take a few days and she would appreciate Sky's help in opening up the house. Sky agreed, now more confident in her ability to cope with city living, she decided to accompany Mary and spend the three months with her before the dry and mustering season started. Sky had no worries about leaving The Big Sky as her family had coped well in her absence the past few weeks.

On the following Monday, once again, the trio were winging their way to Broome to catch a commercial flight to Sydney. Mary for once had misgivings and felt perhaps life at the station would not be so bad now she had family. Her spinster sister had died and apart from those in the little plane, Mary was alone.

The two young soldiers she now had in her family, currently winging their way to Vietnam, caused her anxiety.

Chapter

11

Rising out of bed Prudence again read the letter from AJ and looked at the beautiful pendant he had sent her. His letter seemed happy as he told her he had met Sky in Darwin and truthful as always told Prudence he now had a daughter, which he included a photo of the three sitting on the lawn in Darwin. Prudence had the unusual ability of never being jealous or thinking the worst of any situation but calmly concluded that if AJ had considered leaving her and the soon to be offspring he would never have sent the photo or in fact even informed her of the meeting. *Sometimes you can be so annoyingly honest,* she thought to herself, *What sort of man would deny spending time with his own flesh and blood?* Prudence did however note the beauty of Sky and the smile she apparently seemed to be giving AJ, the pendant she wore on her neck also seemed to match hers.

AJ had written and posted the letter on his last day in Darwin. Prudence missed him, her life had changed since the first night they had made love and now had purpose. Since he left all she had been doing was helping her beloved grandfather with the station books and his investment portfolio every evening as his practice was to spend at least two hours after tea attending to business matters. Prudence decided to go and spend the day with Nanny Smith and her grandfather as they had more sympathy for her heavily pregnant condition than her socialising mother who considered the whole affair a nuisance.

She waddled down to the manager's residence to find Nanny Smith and the Colonel sitting on the porch reading as they always did on a Sunday morning, enjoying the peace and beautiful view that lay before them.

Many times as a young girl Prudence remembers sneaking down to the manager's residence and getting into bed with Nanny Smith and the Colonel, it made her feel safe and important. Her mother became more distant as her own family's fortunes changed because of infighting between family members and the eventual sale of the family property.

The Colonel had fallen into a passionate affair with a dancer on the boat journey to Australia; the First World War had ended a year previously and returning from duty he threw himself into the social life of London. His extremely rich family were involved in trading and shipping, well known in London and respected. The Colonel a handsome looking young man caught the eye of Margaret Archer, daughter of the local member for parliament, only fourteen but she looked much older and well developed.

Colonel Charles Smythe had received an invitation, one of many, to attend the birthday party of the Honourable Guy Archer and socialite wife Kathleen, mainly because of the insistence of Margaret. During the party the Colonel now thirty two had been maneuvered by the charming Margaret down the bottom end of the extensive gardens of the mansion into a pergola and fuelled by whisky, a major weakness of the Colonel, he soon succumbed to the passion of Margaret as she launched herself at him. Taking in the sites also were Kathleen and two of her socialite friends on hearing the moaning and groaning coming from the pergola they rushed to investigate. The sight that confronted them caused Kathleen to faint and the Colonel to pull up his trousers and leave via the rear entrance, feeling more than embarrassed. The outcome was that a substantial sum of money exchanged hands to temper the fury of the local member and his wife.

Colonel Charles Smythe then found himself on a ship to the antipodes. Stepping off the ship and married to ex-dancer Jenny Thompson, the Colonel made arrangements to sail to Tasmania the next day. A son Charles junior was born six months later and from the start Jenny Smythe found life on the station more than boring. When Master Charles Smythe was only four she decamped with a soldier on maneuvers in the district never to be heard from again.

The Colonel had two families living on the property at the time, both had several children and neither seemed too keen to help raise another child, so the Colonel advertised for a Nanny.

Eileen Scott had been born to parents who both drank excessively, the eldest of nine children she had to often miss school and help with her siblings while her parents went on drinking binges. With the little money her father made working casually in the district she went many a night, along with her brothers and sisters to bed hungry, sleeping in two beds the children lived a life of misery.

At the age of just sixteen the parents had married her off to one Bull Smith, a bully, drunkard and nasty individual. Eileen was forced to find casual work in the district and pass the money over to Bull who beat her constantly. He was impotent caused by the heavy drinking and blamed the condition on Eileen taking his fury out on her at every opportunity; there was no welfare or women's shelters in those days so she was forced to endure the brutality.

At the instruction of her husband she had cycled on a borrowed bicycle twelve miles out to Forth and applied for the position advertised. Colonel Charles Smythe was impressed with Eileen and gave her the job of being nanny to Master Charles and she immediately commenced work for the Colonel.

Now aged twenty, Eileen found the homestead a place of

sanctity, the food was plentiful and the Colonel was a kind gentleman. Every Sunday she was given the day off and reluctantly went home to an abusive husband waiting for her weekly pay. On one particular Sunday he demanded that she steal whisky from the Colonel and bring home on her next visit. Eileen was shocked so she refused as the Colonel was good to her. In a rage Bull made the big mistake of hitting Eileen in places that would be seen, eyes swollen and with a broken jaw she lay whimpering on the filthy bed all that night. When she didn't turn up for work on Monday the Colonel went to investigate as it was not like the nanny to fail to appear for work as she was always punctual.

Pulling up in his Humber Super Snipe, that he affectionately called the Snipe, he noticed the door to the two-roomed hut standing open and peering in, he saw in the gloom, Nanny Smith laying on the bed groaning and the hulking Bull Smith sitting on a chair sleeping. A great feeling of rage and injustice swept over the Colonel; he had always treated the female gender with respect, even though in the past, a weakness for their affection had caused him some grief. Removing his shirt he placed it neatly on the seat of the snipe and entering the front room he kicked the chair out from under the surprised Bull Smith who fell to the floor now fully awake. The Colonel instructed Bull that he was going to give him a jolly good thrashing and if he had any sense at all, at the conclusion, he should leave the district never to return, nor to contact Nanny Smith again or he would not be responsible for his actions.

Bull staggered to his feet and rushed at the Colonel who had struck a typical Marquis of Queensbury rules pose. The Colonel deftly stepped aside from the raging and fast approaching man who then crashed into the hut wall. The Colonel taught Bull Smith such a lesson that Bull took the offered advice and was never heard from again.

Nanny Smith had seen the confrontation and it was the first

time any person had ever done anything to help her, let alone fight on her behalf. Scooping her up the Colonel drove straight to the hospital where Nanny was attended to immediately under his watchful eye. He visited her every day, with Master Charles, until he transported her home a few days later.

Nanny Smith was surprised to see new clothing stacked neatly on the bed, the Colonel had enlisted the assistance of one of the women who lived on the station. Coughing and spluttering the Colonel had instructed them to buy some of those unmentionable women's things also and tapping his finger twice to his nose, the helper understood completely, as a matter of fact she had wished the benevolence had been showered on her also.

Nanny Smith was never happier in her life as she snuggled into the clean sheets but being a born worrier she did wonder what would happen to her when Master Charles went to boarding school, a cause of concern for her over the next few years.

Life went on at Forth and the seasons approached and disappeared. On the way home from the local sheep sale one day, the local sergeant had cause as usual to pull the Colonel over as he was driving a bit slow and weaving slightly. He liked the Colonel but enough was enough so he employed a bit of logic and informed the Colonel that a new traffic squad was being formed and would patrol the area. It would be embarrassing if he was to appear in court on drink driving charges, especially as he was a Justice of the Peace.

"By Jove you're right," boomed the Colonel, tapping the finger to the nose, "understood old boy and thank you very much."

On the way home the Colonel decided to teach Nanny Smith the finer arts of driving, by Joves yes. He mused at the thought of her driving young Charles to school and out and about shopping, saving him from the monotonous task. As well, he knew he'd be able to indulge to his heart's content on sale days and have a driver to take him home. A very satisfactory arrangement he concluded.

Nanny Smith was terrified at the prospect but felt that she owed the Colonel a great deal and being ever so faithful, Nanny started lessons immediately under the guidance of the Colonel to learn the finer points of driving. The Colonel's previous teaching experience had been on the parade ground, yelling at soldiers. And so it was that Nanny Smith, terrified with white knuckles clasped to the steering wheel and in absolute fear, with the Colonel shouting instructions, pig rooted, stalled, crashed the gears and then came to stop with brakes locked, finally attaining some sort of driving method. Perhaps, the sergeant thought, a little less dangerous on the road than the Colonel, as he reluctantly issued her drivers license. The front paddock, where the instruction took place, appeared for months as if it had been roughly ploughed. The Colonel had problems sourcing his drenches, earmarks, fence strainers and a host of other items from the rear of the Snipe for some time after, with all having been thrown about and landing hopelessly entangled in one huge heap.

On her first foray into driving to town, with the Colonel sitting straight laced beside her waving his arms about gesturing and shouting, the terrified Nanny Smith drove with eyes glued to the road to pick up groceries. Unfortunately the Colonel had forgotten to tell her to pull up at the bank as he had cheques to deposit.

As they drew level with the bank the Colonel bellowed, "Bank, Nanny old girl,"and responding to the instruction, Nanny Smith swerved left, straight into the rear of a new Holden car parked outside the bank with a resounding crash of metal.

A few moments before, the new bank manager had been sitting at the window looking out at his pride and joy. Having just been transferred, he thought buying a new car would give him the prestige he now deserved and had taken a loan out to purchase the vehicle. On his desk, he was familiarising himself with his client base and was impressed with a few, including one Colonel Charles Smythe of Forth Sheep station. Indeed, he thought it would be nice to be associated with such wealth and not the penny saving riff raff he had to contend with as a teller for much of his career. Rudely awakened, he watched in dismay as a heap of crap slammed into the back of his new car. Running out of the bank, he immediately set into a tirade through the window at some terrified looking, stupid woman, who had almost destroyed his new car.

He failed to notice her passenger alight from the vehicle until a tap came on his shoulder from the Colonel's walking stick.

"Steady old chap," he said. "Hardly cricket a what, Nanny is an excellent driver, bloody unfortunate accident. Send the repair bill to Colonel Charles Smythe at Forth Farm."

With that the Colonel strode back onto the footpath and settled into the car in one quick flourish.

"Reverse Nanny," instructed the Colonel.

Nanny, still wide eyed and terrified, crunched the gears into reverse and shooting backwards, pulled the bumper bar off the new Holden. In a loud crash it fell to the road. Nanny shot out onto the street with the Colonel unfazed, still roaring loudly and gesticulating, about the obvious lack of respect around these days.

Standing dazed on the road, the new bank manager said to himself, "Holy shit, that's bloody done it, I'll be back behind the counter in some isolated, god-forsaken place now."

Thinking fast, he shot into the bank and wrote a long letter apologising to the Colonel and explaining that it was even his own fault for parking the car in front of the bank. Those parking spaces were for customers, especially customers of the Colonel's status.

The next time in the bank, the Colonel bellowed for all to hear, "Apology accepted,' and tapped his nose twice to the terrified bank manager.

He had, in fact, just banked the cheques left in the Snipe from the previous visit. In the confusion, he had forgotten to do so.

Young Master Charles, the Colonel decided, had to go to boarding school, so at the age of twelve, Nanny Smith packed his clothes ready to take him to the college the following morning.

That evening the Colonel, as usual, felt like a snack at about midnight and passing Nanny Smith's room he heard her softly crying. Entering the bedroom, he sat on her bed in his nightshirt, upset at whatever had made Nanny Smith so distressed.

Nanny Smith sniveled, "Where will I go? After Master Charles goes to school? Please don't send me away also."

Bemused and glad it was such a small problem the Colonel assured Nanny that she would never have to leave Forth, she was an important member of the family.

Bolting upright with such glee and emotion, she grabbed the Colonel, pulling him down onto her while hugging him with such ferocity, that the Colonel, so long without female companionship took it as an invitation. Tearing back the bed clothes, he gave Nanny Smith a jolly good rogering. After the encounter, still with passion, the Colonel carried her into his bed chamber where she has stayed until the present day.

As time went by, Master Charles left high school and attended agricultural college, settling into farm life well. On graduating, he was only twenty one when Isabella seduced him and becoming pregnant, was in her glee. She never liked the Colonel and thought him below his status living with the nanny. She soon had them moved into the manager's residence and from that time, never had the two back in the main house, nor talked to the Colonel or Nanny Smith unless she had to.

Prudence sat between her grandfather and Nanny Smith chatting away as usual, as her parents drove past on their way to church as was the habit on Sundays. The Colonel had not attended church for years since the minister gave a fiery speech on fornication outside marriage, taking it as a personal affront, neither Nanny nor the Colonel had attended since.

An hour passed and Prudence starting getting twinges and pains. Mentioning it to her grandfather he immediately sprung into action, knowing his son and daughter-in-law would go visiting friends after church.

"The Snipe Nanny. At once" he bellowed.

Prudence suggested the Mercedes, but unfazed, the Colonel bellowed something about unreliable new cars as Nanny slid to a halt and assisted Prudence into the front seat. The Colonel ordered Nanny into the back as this was an emergency and he would personally take charge, bugger the traffic police.

Not wishing to be left behind on such a great occasion, as the car took off, Nanny Smith launched herself into the back sprawling over the farm equipment; she had just positioned herself over the seat as the Colonel swung out the front gate leaving the back door on the gate post. Unfazed the Colonel drove the old snipe like a man possessed, pulling up outside the hospital in twenty minutes, a drive that should have taken forty minutes.

Rachael Canning had been working night shift and was not present, but a wheelchair appeared for Prudence to be rushed straight to the delivery room. Three hours later Prudence delivered a bouncing baby boy. Both the Colonel and Nanny Smith beamed at the little mite, no prouder man existed than the Colonel.

"By jove," he exclaimed, pulling back the shawl.

Prudence noted all was perfect, including his little manhood in which he took after his father. Noting all was well the Colonel tapped the old nose twice and ordered Nanny Smith to drive him home to celebrate with a few whiskies.

Prudence called her son David Charles Wilson, the name she and AJ had previously discussed. All the family appeared that evening and a tired Prudence was glad when they all disappeared home. She was knackered, she thought, hard work this childbirth. Still she wouldn't not mind more; good fun making babies.

Chapter

12

The two boys were glad to see that they were to take a commercial flight with Qantas to Vietnam and not the uncomfortable military aircraft.

Over the preceding twenty four hours AJ had written letters to Sky and Prudence, he was confused as to what he was going to do on his return. He knew both Sky and Prudence would have to play a part in his life, imagining not involving either was unthinkable.

The average age of Australians serving in Vietnam was only twenty years old and once airborne, the troops amused themselves by chatting to each other and showing photos of family and friends. When it was AJs turn Michael made him show photos of Prudence and Sky. It didn't take long for a message to come over the speaker from the pilot to warn stewardesses not to go near Private Wilson in seat 54 as his strike rate was 100% and to please avoid him at all costs. Although embarrassed AJ had to have a laugh, it was true what they said, he would avoid any contact with females in the future, two was more than enough.

As the plane touched down in Saigon airport, all on board looked out the aircraft windows at the scene that unfolded before them. Huge concrete hangers held dozens of fighter aircraft, trucks, men and helicopters were everywhere. It seemed an apocalyptic scene, huge aircraft stood side by side like giant bats, ambulances were loading a plane with wounded next to where they taxied.

"Remember our oath. We have to get out of here alive," Michael said as both boys looked at each other.

Disembarking down the stairway the hot air hit them like an oven; the smell was something they would never forget.

"Welcome to hell,"a sergeant greeted as they lined up. "From now on you carry your rifle with your magazine loaded, it may save your life. The enemy are around you even now, stay alert at all times and one other thing, keep your dick in your trousers, venereal disease is rife. Serve your time and hopefully you will all see home, family and friends in twelve months. Good luck to all of you. Do your country proud."

Fighter jets screamed off as he was talking while huge aircraft waited to land, the place was mayhem. Hot and sticky as he gripped his rifle AJ, clambered onto the truck that would transport them to the Australian base over one hour away.

And so started a routine of patrols in the surrounding area doing uncomfortable and unsettling night bivouacs, peering into the night. Ears strained listening for any sound, sweat pouring from your brow, too frightened to move from your uncomfortable position in case the enemy may hear you.

It was in the sixth week, on the last patrol, before their first promised R&R in Saigon, that the platoon both boys were serving in, was patrolling an area east of the main army camp.

Passing through a village AJ noticed although the occupants smiled they seemed frightened of either the soldiers or something else. He felt tense. Both he and Michael had the job as forward scouts and he told his friend to be alert as he felt unsafe, something did not seem quite right. Leaving the village with the two scouts in front of the main group, they wound their way along a path surrounded by thick vegetation. Michael was on the right and AJ ghosted along inside the thick foliage.

About a kilometer from the village, Michael signaled to AJ that he thought he heard something, pointing towards a rise ahead. Both crouched down listening intently as the platoon went to ground behind. After what seemed an eternity Michael rose slowly and was about to step off when it happened, a mortar exploded to his right knocking him onto the path. For an instant AJ froze. He saw blood oozing from Michael's nose as well as trickling down his back. The look on Michael's face was one he would never forget, a look of shock and horror. Without hesitating, AJ sprung to his feet, letting shots off in the direction of the rise as he hurled himself at his friend, rolling them both off the track. Gathering the limp body up in his arms, he ran with legs pumping, sucking in huge gasps of breath as he set off carrying his friend back down the track. He heard the smack of bullets hitting leaves as he ran, his arms ached, his head was bursting and he saw visions of Prudence, Sky and little Mary. The warm blood was soaking his clothes. Passing the first of his platoon, he kept running, spurred on by his companions who now laid down a covering fire. He ran for another hundred metres and collapsed, chest heaving, covered in blood and sweat and for the first time looked at his friend. Michael had been hit in the back with shrapnel from the blast, but he was breathing, thank god.

The medic rushed to his aid and the radio operator called for a Medivac helicopter to lift his friend out. Luckily the assailants had melted back into the jungle. It appears they had run into the patrol working in the area.

Watching his friend, AJ prayed for him, prayed that he'd make it back home to Rachael to live a long life in the peaceful midlands of Tasmania.

Carrying Michael back to the village, they heard the sound of the approaching chopper. AJ loaded his friend into the carry basket on the side and double checked the strapping to make sure he was safe. The machine rose into the air for the trip to the military hospital in Saigon.

AJ felt devastated. Since being called up he and Michael

hadn't been parted and were able to draw strength from each other. On return to the base, he cleaned up and then wrote letters to Mary and Sky. It seemed Mary wrote most of all, Sky was not very good at writing but at least she tried. He also wrote to Prudence telling her what happened and asking her to please take care of Rachael. AJ knew the army would inform her as she was down as his next of kin. He also knew Michael would be taken to Sydney when he stabilized, so asked Mary and Sky, both in Sydney, to check and assist Michael if they possibly could.

AJ never went on R&R. He was still in shock. He felt lonely as both had been there for each other. Laying on his bunk, staring at the two women in his life, he made a vow to return to Australia and never leave again. Several times he inquired about Michael and was eventually informed that, in fact, he was on his way home and yes he was going to the spinal unit at the Sydney North Shore Hospital. The chaplain assured him his friend would receive excellent care.

Other members of AJ's platoon noticed the change in him from that day. He went through the motions, remained quiet, hardly spoke and seemed to be extra careful on patrols. He tensed at the slightest sound and if attacked, went to ground and returned fire with aggression and purpose. He was trying to stay alive in the time he had to serve, survival was utmost in his mind. He knew Michael had been badly hurt and swore to help his friend whenever possible on his return home.

Chapter

13

Mary had not found the Sydney move as exciting as she had dreamed of over the years. Many a night she lay bed in the huge home and wondered what she would do when Sky and little Mary left and the thought caused her worry.

During the last few weeks both Mary and Sky had busied themselves opening up and cleaning the huge home. Mary had never let the property, but paid a caretaker to maintain the house and gardens. Even so, there seemed a lot of work to do.

Time flew by and only three weeks remained before Sky had to return. Mary had decided to go back with her though she didn't let Sky know at this stage that she had made up her mind.

Mary wandered down to the mail box with little Mary to collect the mail, it was a daily excuse to be with the child. Seeing a letter from AJ, she excitedly opened it calling to Sky to tell her there was one addressed to her too. Reading the contents as she walked back up the path, Mary was crying when Sky approached her. Alarmed, Sky's heart missed a beat. Mary told her the awful news and running to the house, they phoned the hospital. Yes, Michael Webb was there, he had been brought in in two days earlier.

Without hesitation, all three were soon speeding in a taxi to the hospital. Mary was quiet, she liked Michael and his company in Darwin made it all seem somehow ok. He had given her a laugh when she needed it most. Well Mary Jones was coming, Michael, have no fear and if money can do anything, nothing will be spared.

Prudence had been home a few weeks. She settled into motherhood like all her endeavors, at full throttle, she was thriving on it. As she sat in the chair feeding her child on her ample milk supply, baby David gurgled in satisfaction.

The phone rang, it was Rachael in tears sobbing uncontrollably, "Michael has been wounded," she sobbed. "He's on his way home to hospital in Sydney."

"No problems Rachael, I'll pick you up in half an hour. Book ahead and I'll pay for the tickets at the airport, hopefully we'll be in Sydney tonight," Prudence replied without hesitation, always ready to take charge.

Two days later, Prudence would have heard the news from AJ.

Informing her mother of the situation, Prudence threw clothes into a case and then strapped the baby into the car seat. In typical fashion, she rushed out of the drive to pick up her friend to do whatever was possible to help, no matter how long it took or what it might cost, Prudence was on the way.

Stepping onto the tarmac that evening, Prudence collected the luggage while the distraught Rachael cuddled the baby. Hurrying out of the terminal, they hailed a taxi and instructed the driver to drive, post haste, to the hospital. Caught up in all the drama, the women did not seem to notice the driver screech to a halt in front of the hospital in record time, even he was pleased to have carried out the task without police intervention.

On finding out the room Michael was in, both rushed up the stairs to the second floor. The three burst into the room, so caught up in the moment, that Rachael hurled herself at the bed sobbing, grabbing Michael's hand. He looked absolutely awful, but as always, put on a cheerful face. Prudence looked right and saw two seated women, a child sitting on the knee of the elder. Instantly she knew and overcome with emotion, she rushed over and hugged them both, grateful they had taken care of her and AJs best friend. Sky held David while Prudence caught up with Michael.

Mary insisted that Rachael and Prudence stay with her and as they had not organised a booking ahead, both thankfully agreed. At midnight, all alighted from a crowded taxi outside Mary's palatial residence.

In the drama, Mary had not thought of the consequence of the event that had just occurred. She was amazed that both of AJ's lovers were chatting like old friends and fussing over the distraught Rachael. Sky carried the baby while Prudence had little Mary in hand, as well as carrying her suitcase into the house.

Over the next three weeks Sky warmed to Prudence. She began to think of her as the sister she never had, she made her feel good, her personality was infectious.

Michael found it hard to believe the attention he received from so many women fussing over him. Sky and Prudence did all the shopping and errands, while Mary cared for the two children, she was in her glee.

Prudence introduced Sky to lingerie. Sky warmed to the femininity of the undergarments that Prudence insisted she buy. Prudence also thought of Sky as the sister she never had, quiet and friendly. Both formed a friendship so close, even Mary was surprised and happy at the idea that she now had a growing family. The two women seemed drawn to the offspring they had both given birth to, drawn together by the bond AJ had formed.

Several times while Mary and Rachael went to see Michael, the two young women, in their twenties, sat together and chatted on the lawns of Kimberley Cottage watching their children, both fathered by the same man that each shared a strong love for.

Unable to contain herself Prudence extracted from Sky how

she met AJ and both laughed heartily at the oil incident and the three drunks. Sky loved the humor of Prudence. Life had always seemed so hard at times and the light hearted banter of Prudence made her, for the first time, roll on the lawn in fits of laughter. Prudence told Sky of how she helped herself in making love to AJ the first time and again, Sky laughed at the way Prudence told the story, it all seemed so natural. The bond in their relationship strengthened daily. Prudence suggested, in one of her mad schemes, that they get some photos done together of themselves with the children and also send AJ a photo or two to cheer him up and make him yearn to come home to them.

Calling a taxi Prudence told the driver to go to this Kings Cross place she had heard about. Pulling up outside an adults only shop, she told him to wait and asked Sky to watch the children. She waltzed in and came out a short time later with a small parcel. They had only driven a short distance when Prudence noticed a photographic studio that advertised portraits. Paying the driver both girls entered the studio and Prudence requested a family portrait of the four.

After many photos Prudence approached the photographer, a middle aged man. She whispered to him that she and her friend would like a few sexy photos taken for their husband and would he oblige? Without hesitation, the photographer agreed, finding it hard to believe his luck. While young Mary played with the baby on the studio floor, Sky and Prudence changed, each coming out in the briefest of crotchless panties, giggling and laughing. After several poses, and while laying facing each other, propped up on their elbows with one leg intertwined and the other up, Prudence shouted to Sky, "Point towards your vagina and look sexily at the camera."

"What vagina?" Sky yelled, unsure of the word vagina.

"Your bloody twat!" yelled Prudence as all three adults broke into hysterical laughter.

The studio informed the pair that the photos would be ready at ten the next morning and he would have a range of nice frames to choose from. At exactly ten the next day, both visited the studio anxious to see the results. Prudence insisted on the negatives much to the studio's disgust.

On the way back in the taxi, Sky asked Prudence why she insisted on the negatives; Prudence replied that if she hadn't, their tits and fannies would be all over Sydney the next day. Sky had not heard the term fanny and was perplexed.

"Your bloody twat!" shouted Prudence as the two burst into laughter, rolling about in the back of the cab, the driver fighting hard to concentrate on his driving as he was laughing also.

Sky had to head home as it was impossible to wait any longer. She didn't really want to go, since Prudence arrived it had been the best time she had ever had. Worried still about AJ so far away, she had found peace and laughter that she associated with Prudence. Mary and Rachael had planned to stay, at Mary's insistence. They were going to discharge Michael and bring him to Kimberley Cottage to recuperate. Mary had hired the best physiotherapist that money could buy in Sydney. She also hired a cook and made a room ready for the patient.

It was a sad event three days later when the four made farewells to each other at the airport. Sky and Prudence hugged each other, shedding a few tears, as both departed within thirty minutes of each other, one south to Tasmania and the other west to Broome. Mary was glad she had Rachael whom she got along with so well, it eased the pain of parting with little Mary which was heartbreaking. She was determined to take care of her new friends, Rachael and Michael, promising both Sky and little Mary she would phone constantly. She waved as both planes disappeared into the sky.

Chapter

14

Prudence was lucky enough to grab an Ansett flight directly to Tasmania, stopping off in Launceston and taking off again for the short hop to Hobart. With her son happily feeding at her breast, Prudence already missed Sky, Mary and little Mary. What a happy time it had been.

Some may have thought Prudence vulgar but the opposite was in fact true. Prudence drank in the nectar of life, vibrant, sensual and grabbing without reservation the very essence of living for the day in every hour and every minute. She ached for the companionship and intimacy of AJ; he had been her focus since the first meeting and with his child suckling at her breast, it only made the feeling worse.

Prudence had also raised the female sensuality stakes in Sky. Never before had Sky talked about sex. In the short time they had known each other, Prudence had somehow made the subject open and natural, something a woman should enjoy and be proud of.

As she winged her way west, Sky also thought about AJ. Strangely she missed both Mary and Bradley terribly, she felt alone. She was troubled by what awaited her, without Bradley as her mentor and tutor, she suddenly felt a little unsure of how she would cope.

"Why are we apart all the time? Why can't we keep our little family together? Something always interferes."

Sky had enjoyed sitting and watching the two children while talking to Prudence, or at least listening to Prudence. Holding her child to her, a tear trickled down her cheek as she settled in for the long flight home.

Prudence was jolted into reality by the announcement to buckle up as they would be landing shortly. A kindly gentleman in the next seat helped her to replace the food tray and prepare for landing and she was grateful for the assistance.

Prudence collected the luggage and made her way to the car park, unlocking the Mercedes she strapped baby David into his seat, paying the fee at the boom, she drove south towards home. She looked forward to seeing her beloved grand father, her rock in times of all crisis and Nanny Smith, quiet and reserved, exactly the opposite of herself and indeed the extrovert Colonel Smythe.

Prudence's mother was a panic merchant, always complaining and her father never said much as the Colonel had always been in charge. Because Isabella made life such a misery, he worked long hours on the station, coming home as late as possible in order to avoid her whining. Prudence was the exact opposite of her mother and her father found it hard to believe Isabella had produced such a happy, outgoing bundle of dynamite.

Driving in the front laneway with the Snipe door still leaning against the fence post, Prudence was alarmed to see an ambulance parked in front of the manager's residence. Several people, including her distraught father with his head in his hand, were sitting on the front porch. Two empty chairs stood where her grandfather usually sat with Nanny Smith.

A lump came into Prudence's throat as tears welled in her eyes, she instantly knew something terrible and unbelievable had happened. Prudence rushed up to her father as a covered stretcher was placed in the ambulance. She was gently told by her father that the Colonel had died the previous evening, peacefully in his sleep.

"Then who is being loaded into the ambulance?" Prudence

sobbed.

"Nanny Smith," her father informed her. He had come down to check on the distraught Nanny two hours ago and she was lying in the bed she shared with the Colonel with a look of peace on her face, quite dead.

Many in the district reckoned Nanny Smith had died in sympathy after the old Colonel's death, but Prudence knew she had died of a broken heart. Her white knight had died, the man who saved her from a life of misery, who treated her with respect. He never forgot her birthday, always buying her a beautiful antique jewel of some type. There was breakfast in bed and always a pat on the backside and peck on the cheek every morning and night. Nanny Smith had no further reason to live when her warrior prince died.

Prudence also knew she would be unable to bear life if anything happened to her man. She would do all in her power to keep the little family he had together.

Three days later Prudence, with Mary, Rachael and Agnes standing beside her, watched as the coffins of the Colonel and Nanny Smith were laid side by side in the huge family plot. The old Colonel had prepared it years before when he had ideas of establishing a family dynasty in those days. Sky had been given the bad news and was upset, the time being too short to attend the funeral, so she rang Prudence and they both had a good cry over the phone. Prudence picked up that Sky was struggling a bit even though she had the support of family. Running the station must have been a daunting task for a twenty one year old.

Mary and Rachael stayed for two nights after the funeral.

Michael had written Prudence a lovely letter and in it, he told her of how AJ had saved him. The army chaplain had informed him of the circumstances and he would be eternally grateful to his childhood friend for the risk he took in carrying him to safety, under enemy fire. Michael had been writing to

AJ and in AJ's replies, Michael also picked up he was struggling a bit. AJ was a good person and he found mankind's inhumanity to man very sad. The thousands of orphan's mutilated bodies, planes napalming civilians, planes spraying defoliants over thousands of acres. He began to doubt the legitimacy of the war.

Prudence was proud of AJ. Taking Rachael and Mary to the plane she was unable to stop sobbing all the way home.

"What a fucking mess," she shouted to vent her frustrations. "What a shit show of a bloody disaster."

Thankfully Prudence never wavered from the belief that AJ would come home. To suggest any other thought was incomprehensible.

Three weeks later Prudence and her father attended the family solicitors for the reading of the will. The solicitors informed them both that Isabella's presence would not be necessary. This infuriated Isabella making living in the same house even more distasteful.

On the prescribed day, Agnes was more than happy to pick up her husband's namesake, her grandchild, and take him to her place for the day to be absolutely spoilt rotten. Agnes had been told about the meeting with Sky and that she had another grandchild. Even Prudence was shocked that her mother-in-law was happy both women had become friends; at least she may now have the opportunity of spoiling two grandchildren.

Entering the office of the station solicitors, both were ushered into the opulent office of the senior partner to find two members of the firm and a secretary seated, looking very solemn and efficient looking. Prudence grinned, thinking of her grandfathers opinion of the profession. *Lice on the arse of society*, was just one opinion he'd openly expressed..

Clearing his throat, the senior partner took a nervous sip of water and started reading.

"Due to the demise of one Nanny Smith, I feel no need to

read the instructions of the Colonel and the remuneration, as well as life tenancy of the manager's residence, to one Nanny Smith. At the conclusion of the reading of our esteemed deceased clients final will and testimony, we shall in fact read the will of one Eileen Smith known to all as Nanny Smith."

For fucks sake get on with it you pompous old fart, thought Prudence. Taking a further sip of water, he commenced, now very nervously.

"To my daughter-in-law, the most miserable bitch I have ever had the misfortune to meet, I leave nothing. To my long suffering son, Charles junior, I leave life tenancy in the manager's residence upon the expiry of Nanny Smith, my beloved and faithful companion over the last fifty years. I also leave an annual income payable each year on the first of January, at the sum of sixty thousand dollars, which even allowing for inflation should keep both he and his miserable wife in the manner to which she is accustomed. These monies shall not come from income derived off Forth but from my investments."

The senior partner, now looking rather drained, looked up from the document and went into a long speech about how the Colonel's family had been wealthy traders and that the last of the line, a penny pinching old spinster, the Colonel's words he quickly added, gulping down further water and in fact now looking rather ill, left the entire estate to the Colonel twenty years previously, now worth over fifty million Australian dollars. The stipend for Charles junior would be drawn from interest and dividends from these investments.

He read on, becoming hard to hear, almost a whisper.

"To my beloved grand daughter Prudence, I leave the following: Forth station, all the livestock, plant and equipment. Lastly, the Snipe, in which care I hope she will keep it in good condition and repair. I also leave her all my investments subject to the payment to her father of the monies, this will has stipulated for the balance of his life. I suggest Prudence may wish to employ her father as a manager. I suggest he is possibly the most skilled wool and sheep man in Tasmania, but that is left to her discretion. Finally, I leave the sunshine of my life, Prudence, all my art collection and books to whose care I now pass."

Prudence was shocked. She was never aware her grandfather had so much money, although she helped him with bookwork and his share portfolio, never in her wildest dreams imagined it was so much money. The old Colonel was in fact very frugal and careful with money. Prudence looked at her father and she felt sadly sorry for him. He just sat there and smiled, holding his daughters hands and explained he was aware the old Colonel would have the last laugh on Isabella.

"He suffered her insolence in silence for my sake but I bet he is having a good laugh now. To be honest Prudence, I am glad. All I want to do is work on the station and live the rest of my life in peace."

As she felt her life was in such a mess, Prudence suggested that her father manage the farm and for the pair to split profits. AJ would also help on his return. All those present felt relieved at the benevolence of Prudence to her dad and of her father's acceptance of the will. They thought a battle may erupt and all breathed a sigh of relief, agreeing to draw up the agreement; the senior partner now seemed to relax.

"Let us move on to the last will and testament of Eileen Smith, known to all as Nanny Smith," he chirped, his confidence and decorum returned. "This will is very simple," he now nearly boomed. "It states: To Prudence, the light of my life, the daughter I never had, I leave all my jewels lovingly given to me by your beloved grandfather and if I should pass away after his death, please make sure I am buried beside him. Signed Eileen Smith and in brackets Nanny."

Leaving the office both father and daughter had a cup of

coffee. It was the first time she could remember spending quality time with her father. Her mother was always intervening, complaining about Prudence's dress or something her father had done. Prudence glancing at her father decided to give her mild father some valuable advice.

"Dad," she began, "why don't you put and end to the misery mum heaps on you, stand up for yourself for once. Why do you put up with her crap? Never once have I seen you argue or lay down the law to her miserable harping."

The two chatted on the way home, it was a beautiful afternoon and Prudence thought about the money. She thought she would rather give it all up for the return of AJ safely and strangely, she thought to include Sky also.

Agnes had to go into town late that afternoon had agreed to bring little David home to Forth that evening. She and David senior had planned with Prudence to have a small meal on the verandah at the Forth homestead.

On arriving home, Prudence went straight to the kitchen to prepare the evening meal. She heard her mother screaming at her father. Twenty years of tantrums and bitterness was enough for Charles junior and he thought of the advice from his daughter.

Drawing up to his full height, he roared, "Shut up you miserable bitch. Enough is enough. It was your bloody fault and I am glad you reaped what you've sown. Dad was too bloody smart for your scheming, he knew you would have sold the property. Here is the new state of events that will happen at Forth from this day, if you can't live by it with enthusiasm, you can go live with your miserable bloody family."

Isabella with her mouth agape started to whimper and slobber as Charles, now in full flight, informed her, "As of now, we will be moving into the manager's residence to give Prudence and her family some peace. If you complain, even one time more, you'll be thrown out the front gate. Further to that you can burn those long nightgowns and jump back into my bed and show some enthusiasm, in fact I expect you to be naked from now on, not covered in bloody yards of material."

Hell, that felt good, he thought. Still having feelings for Isabella, even after years of torture, he was surprised as she went roaring and sobbing out of the house towards the manager's cottage. Prudence smiled as she went to her father.

"Well done Dad. I think life has just taken a turn for the better at Forth for us all."

That evening, still sniveling, Isabella, to Charles's surprise, was waiting in bed in the raw and threw herself into the task of seducing her husband much the same way she had when they first met. It seems the idea of having no money and living like poor people was not such a good idea to Isabella, so overnight she became quite friendly to all, quite amicable and even tried to be helpful to husband Charles on the farm.

Prudence felt good that her father was happy, more so than he had been in years and her mother even made inquiries about the sexy lingerie Prudence flounced about in.

Prudence settled once again into life at the station, until she received a phone call from Mary. It seemed Bradley had taught Sky to fly well, muster and run the station, but all good plans are never perfect. He had forgotten the day-to-day bookwork that needed to be done to run a station. Mary felt unable to offer assistance and as Bradley had done all the work in that department, she was at a loss to know what to do. She asked Prudence for some advice. As Prudence had been a bit lonely since the death of her grandfather and Nanny Smith, the trumpet of battle sounded in her ears and without being invited, informed Mary that if Michael and Rachael would be okay to fend for themselves for a few weeks, to pack her bags. Prudence said she'd be coming to Sydney the next day to arrange transport for Mary to the Kimberleys.

Informing her father she would be absent for a few weeks, she phoned Sky that evening.

"Have no fear, Prudence is on the way. Pick us up at the airport. I'll advise arrival for Mary and myself on the way."

Prudence made several phone calls informing Agnes and others of her departure. She sang to herself as she packed her bags, the old Prudence had returned.

Sky was more than happy to hear from Prudence; she was more than relieved as she was in a bit of a mess. The muster was going well but arranging trucks, ordering supplies and doing wages, on top of everything else, was getting her down.

Chapter

15

AJ sat on the bed in the billet he was sharing with six other soldiers. The sweat was pouring down his back; the weather had been hot and humid for weeks which added to the misery of the position he found himself in.

He missed his friend Michael, who had shared the room and army life with him. They'd both supported each other and kept each others spirits up.

Again, he read the letters from Michael who was lapping up the attention of so many women. He was satisfied that all found themselves in Sydney together but still, under the circumstances, he would rather it not have happened. However the last letter had informed him that Mary had hired an ambulance and moved Michael into her house. He read the letters again from Prudence and Sky, not really surprised they had become good friends; he knew both were lacking in jealousy and anger. Hatred seemed unknown to both women.

His thoughts were interrupted when 'mail call' was called. He quickly sprang up from his bunk, pulling on a shirt and joined the queue of men, all anxiously waiting for news from home. For many like himself, mail played a big part in keeping some sort of normality in the crazy world they found themselves in. When it came his turn, he was happy to see several letters and a large parcel; he recognized Prudence's handwriting on the parcel. There were two letters as well; one from Sky and the same from Mary and Michael as well as his mother.

Hurrying back to his tent, he lay on the bed and read every letter several times. He was glad to read that Michael was improving and Mary wrote that the two women in his life were now firm friends and his two beautiful children were growing like mushrooms.

He turned his attention to the parcel and carefully started to unwrap it. It was packed in layers of bubble paper and he was curious as to its contents, but knowing Prudence, nothing would surprise him. Yet when he unwrapped the beautifully framed photo of Prudence and Sky with his two children, AJ was overcome with emotion. Clutching the photo, he covered his head so that any returning comrades did not see the tears running down his face. He really missed them both.

Another frame appeared to be wrapped even further and composing himself, he carefully unwrapped it. On the paper covering the glass with the photo under was the words *'Here is something to make sure you will come back to your family, signed Prudence and Sky'*. Peeling off the note, he was spellbound as he saw both dressed only in brief panties, with feathers around their womanhood, pointing to the dark hair visible between their beautiful legs; they both had the most seductive smiles on their faces. AJ knew this would be the cheeky work of Prudence. For the first time in weeks he had a grin from ear to ear, he felt so happy. From this day on, he thought, I will keep only good thoughts in my mind.

"Yes my beauties, I will return home." he said aloud.

As he continued to look spellbound at the photo, a soldier, Sam Stewart walked in and looking over AJ's shoulder shouted, "Bloody hell."

After that day he was the most popular soldier in the camp. Everyone heard about the photos and all made excuses to see AJ in the hope they might catch a glimpse of his women. They all knew he had children to two good looking women. AJ's elevation in the camp rose sharply.

Prudence was right; it lifted his spirits and he once again decided to make the most of his situation. The little idea that Prudence had thought up indeed made a bigger difference than even she imagined. AJ sat down and wrote all a long, cheerful letter with a special thanks to both girls for the lovely photos. He wondered how the situation would resolve on his return.

The following week, Prudence wrote and gave him the sad news of her grandfather's death and that of Nanny Smith. He replied with a long letter to Prudence, he knew she would be upset; beyond the bravado he knew there was a soft and kind heart beating.

The war raged on and was becoming unpopular at home as AJ was informed. Most of the finest of Australia's young men, were now far from home, in the middle of a worsening situation.

In the next few weeks, AJ thought about the dilemma he would face on his return home. He also worried about the financial situation both Sky and Prudence may be facing; both rearing children that were ultimately his and his responsibility. He had given Sky the contents of the joint savings and was having his army pay forwarded to Prudence. He wasn't aware that her grandfather had made sure Prudence wanted for nothing and with his death, was unsure as to how she would be coping.

He was also unaware of how much Sky would be collecting in pay for the work she was doing at the station. He learned from Prudence that she was going to the Kimberleys as Sky was having a few problems. Worried, he wondered what the problems might be, but knowing the abilities of Prudence, he was rather relieved to hear the news.

AJ need not have worried as three weeks later he received a ten page letter from Prudence. The letter put his mind at rest and he finally relaxed, with a grin from ear to ear.

With uplifted spirits, he started a fitness routine, the envy of all his comrades and gave up drinking his cups of tea served in the mess; instead he boiled his own jug and made coffee from powered milk, coffee and sugar he purchased in Saigon. He now went on R&R with his fellow soldiers, a complete change from his normal routine.

AJ now had only one major hurdle to contend with; to fly out of Vietnam alive and uninjured back to his family in Australia. Well perhaps not a traditional family, but a family he would do all in his limited power to return to, safely, regardless of all obstacles that may lay in his path. He hoped never to have to leave or break up that family again.

Chapter

16

Before departure to the Big Sky, Prudence had been working on several projects. She sat down with her father and explained the position and stage of work she had achieved to date, with all instructions written out carefully. She was assured by her grateful Dad that he would finish all and on her return, hopefully see the results. Prudence had arranged for the Snipe and AJs Holden to be picked up at the two locations the vehicles were garaged at, to be repainted, serviced and mechanically checked, then returned to Forth. There, they were to be garaged securely, covered to protect the new paintwork, and yes, of course, the rear door of the Snipe was to be repaired.

A new wing was being constructed on the Forth homestead, to display her grandfather's art collection as well as a library for the books he had left; all had been stored in two rooms of the manager's cottage and in a large container in one of the farm sheds.

Prudence had the collection valued and cleaned, then stacked in three bedrooms of the main homestead. Now insured, both collections were ready to be placed for display in the new wing when completed. She also installed a safe to safeguard the jewelry collection Nanny Smith had left her, along with a few items she treasured and were inherited from her beloved grandfather, such as medals, his war diary and a few other personal possessions.

Her father was happy to oversee the arrangement of the

collections. He regarded the advice his daughter had given him for his changed circumstances. Isabella had, after removing from the manager's residence all the 'Colonels crap' as she regarded it, turned the house into a comfortable and welcoming home. She gave up her social commitments, apart from the church committee, and devoted her time to her husband. In fact, Isabella seemed happier. On investigating why her father's Land Rover was parked outside the shearer's quarters at midday, Prudence was surprised to hear noisy lovemaking coming from the same room in which she and AJ had once also spent a lustful night.

Placing the valuation and insurance papers in the safe, Prudence locked it and thought about what her mother would have thought of her 'grandfather's crap' if she realized it was worth three million dollars.

Placing her ever growing child into the safety of his car seat, Prudence glanced around with a satisfied look at the builder's work in their final stages of the new wing.

She started up the Mercedes and cruised on out the front gate, determined to assist her fellow concubine, Sky. The idea of a new adventure perked her spirits up; she had been a bit down since the death of the Colonel and Nanny, as well as missing AJ.

Rachael had driven Mary to the airport to meet Prudence in the new car Mary had purchased for Michael. Taxis were inconvenient and the car was better suited for medical appointments, shopping and other duties. Mary was not confident enough after years of living in isolation, to drive in the mad traffic of Sydney; however Rachael was very competent.

Much to Mary's pleasure, she was informed that Rachael and Michael would stay at Kimberly Cottage until the return of both she and Prudence; the couple also told Mary that they would marry on the return of AJ as he was definitely going to be the best man, with Sky and Prudence as bridesmaids.

On arrival at the airport they both noticed a young woman, baby on hip, waving madly as she came towards them. It was Prudence. Mary and Rachael smiled as they watched her flouncing down the aircraft gangway and it seemed to them that anything was possible with Prudence around; no problem ever existed. It seemed that Prudence, in her uncanny ability to sum up a situation, always come out smelling like a rose, her effervescent personality was infectious to all around her.

Throwing her arms in the traditional Prudence manner around all three, they collected the luggage and left the airport.

Prudence was anxious to see Michael and during a slow drive though Sydney's heavy traffic, the trio chatted happily exchanging their news.

On their arrival at Kimberley Cottage, Michael was so happy to see Prudence he started to cry, causing Prudence also to have a bit of a sniffle, hugging Michael in a protective bear hug while Mary ordered afternoon tea. The two longtime friends, bonded together by AJ, chatted for the next few hours.

Michael was improving, even though doctors in the early days thought he may never walk again, he in fact was walking with the aid of a frame and was determined to walk unaided with a walking stick. Prudence told him she had no doubt that would be the case and in fact she would not participate in his wedding unless he did; typical Prudence logic.

Mary was already packed to leave and although glad to see Prudence and baby David, she really missed her little namesake. Sky had told her on the phone that little Mary was missing her Grandma Mary too.

At seven the following morning, Rachael waved the trio off as they left for Darwin to then link to a flight to Kununurra, where Sky would pick them up.

It was a long and tiring trip. When they finally arrived, Mary was exhausted; she had helped Prudence with the baby during the trip, giving her a spell many times during the journey. Mary was amused at how Prudence flopped out her huge breast and fed the infant whenever he showed any signs of hunger, something Mary would have been too embarrassed to do if she'd had a child of her own. She really admired Prudence for her natural ability to get on with it and bugger anyone else who might be offended.

Sky was waiting for them at Kununurra airport, ever so grateful to see Prudence. Throwing their arms around each other it was a happy reunion as all three had missed the company of one another more than they realized.

Mary looking tired, was sorry to see little Mary had stayed at home. Sky had come in earlier to complete her course for instrument flying and proudly informed them that she now was in a position to fly non visual. Prudence was a bit bemused by the conversation, having never been told Sky flew a plane. She smiled and not wishing to sound uniformed nodded at the conversation while harboring more than a small fear of what lay ahead.

Collecting the luggage and a typewriter Prudence had packed, ever on the ready, the three walked through the car park and then Prudence saw it, the smallest bloody aircraft she had ever remembered seeing parked on the tarmac adjacent to the car park.

Sky opened the door and began packing the luggage into the rear of the little aircraft. Mary suggested she sit in the rear seats with little David so that Prudence could enjoy the views from the front. Prudence gave a weak grin and nodded. Sky noticed Prudence had stopped chatting like a parrot as usual and put it down to the long trip. Squeezing into the back, Mary secured the infant in the seat next to her as Sky helped Prudence into the front passenger seat; she then sprang into the pilot's seat, started the little aircraft and taxied down to the end of the runway. Sky lined up and gunned the engine, hurtling down the runway to rise steadily into the air.

In exactly five minutes, as the magnificent Ord Scheme passed under them, Mary and the baby had fallen asleep. Prudence was hooked on the sheer exhilaration as the air rushed under the little plane and the landscape that opened up before them was intoxicating.

Sky banked left and told Prudence she would take her over the Bungle Bungles on the way home for a look. Prudence was impressed at the ease with which Sky controlled the little plane; she was obviously a natural pilot. At that exact moment, Prudence made a decision to learn the finer arts of flight and immediately she inquired as to how Sky had learnt to fly. Sky told Prudence that Bradley Jones had taught her and that she would willingly teach Prudence over the next few weeks if that's what she really wanted; however, she would have to go to Broome for tests to get her license. Prudence thought, does a bird fly? She started straight away, under the guidance of Sky, to get a feel for the control of the light aircraft.

Dusk was settling as the little aircraft glided on to the runway at the Big Sky. Prudence got a shock as about two dozen aboriginals rushed out to the little plane, clapping, laughing and waving their hands in the air, so pleased Missus Boss had returned.

The happy procession, seated in two station land cruiser utes, wound its way along the red dusty road to the homestead. It was dark when the group arrived and Sky's mother Rose and little Mary were waiting on the porch. Mary felt revived as she rushed, scooping the little girl into her arms.

Over the evening meal, Sky told them all the news since her return. It was a good season, mustering was well under way and though she felt she managed the field operations well, she admitted to sadly lacking in the bookkeeping tasks of the station office department; it had swamped her and basically things were a mess.

Prudence assured Sky she would soon set matters right.

"Don't worry. In the morning, can you show me over the station so I can get a handle on the logistics of the property, then I'll return to check the office out and start cleaning up the backlog."

Besides, Prudence wanted another plane ride in the station aircraft, the feeling of flight in a small plane was exhilarating.

The Big Sky station homestead was really only four bedrooms, a large open eating area and a kitchen with a store attached. Before any discussion on room allocation, Sky matter of factly said to everyone around the table that she and Prudence would share the master bedroom and Mary the next door room. She knew Mary did not want to go back to the room she had once shared with her husband. The children and Rose would have the other two smaller rooms on the other side of the hallway with a bathroom existing in the middle.

Glancing at the clock, Prudence realized it was near midnight. Rose and Mary, along with the children had retired earlier, yet having so much to talk about both Prudence and Sky had not been aware it was so late. As an early morning beckoned, they climbed the stairs, had a quick shower together, then climbed into the huge master bed. It was two in the morning before both exhaustedly drifted off to sleep.

Prudence was awakened by Rose banging on the door, shouting, "Breakfast ready."

Sky had rolled over next to her during the night and Prudence had snuggled into the arms of the woman who shared the love of her husband. It all seemed so natural thought Prudence and as she bounced out of bed, she understood why AJ loved Sky; the angelic face, lithe body and long legs was something no man would be able to resist falling in love with.

Prudence gently shook Sky awake and then dressed in her

shorts, shirt and boots bounded down the stairs for breakfast, ready to enter the trenches for the day ahead.

She fed her son and then left him in the capable hands of Rose and Mary, assisted by little Mary fussing over him.

Sky and Prudence drove to the airstrip and pushed the little plane out of the hangar to do a pre-takeoff check. Sky started the engine to allow the plane to run a few minutes before taxiing down the runway in a cloud of red dust to then rise like a bird into the blue Kimberley sky.

Prudence had never questioned anyone about the size of the Big Sky or numbers of stock it ran, or even the ownership. As they explored the station from the air, Sky told Prudence everything she wanted to know about the Big Sky; the acreage, that the property was now a trust with her and Mary the trustees along with a solicitor in Darwin; the beneficiaries were Sky and Mary. Sky informed her it ran forty thousand head of cattle and how the muster ran from May to September in the dry when all parts of the property were accessible and the trucks able to cross the Fitzroy to the station yards. At this time the station hands were busy drafting cattle, marking calves, culling aged cows and bringing in the last stragglers that Sky found from the aircraft and guided the ground crews to. Sweeping low over a large outcrop, Prudence, by now extremely impressed, spotted a herd of cattle on her left and Sky radioed ground crews to pick them up.

On the return path, Sky flew over the holding paddocks. Thousands of sleek red cattle with big humps grazed below. Prudence's property back in Tasmania ran three hundred Hereford cows and ten thousand sheep. The scene below was hard to comprehend. Yes, Prudence was bloody impressed and she fell in love with the place. This is big she thought, and I mean bloody big. It's no wonder Sky has difficulty running this juggernaut.

Returning to the airstrip, Prudence, under the guidance of

Sky, tried to land the aircraft but Sky had to take control as Prudence came in a little fast, but not bad for two short lessons she told Prudence.

Over coffee, the girls sat in the station office that even Prudence thought looked as if a cyclone had passed through it. Sky explained where ledgers should be, unpaid bills might be and the chalk board where truck movements and deliveries used to be.

Unperturbed, Prudence suggested Sky return to the yards, as usual, to overseer drafting and selection of cattle destined either for slaughter or to be returned to the runs. They both decided that Prudence would accompany Sky in the mornings on search missions in the plane, to learn the fundamentals of flying as well as being another spotter, and in the afternoons, Prudence would do the office work while Sky supervised the hectic drafting and loading of cattle.

First things first, thought Prudence, and with the assistance of Sky's grandmother, she pressed three of the women into cleaning the office. Setting her typewriter on the desk with other items she had brought from home, she began to sort files. A head popped around the door and then a vase of flowers appeared and was placed on the desk. Perfect, she thought. Prudence attacked the outstanding paper work.

By the end of that evening, Prudence had a grasp of proceedings by the time Sky and Mary came to get her for tea. They found she was waiting for a return phone call from the owner of the cartage company that the Big Sky had used for several years. As they sat Mary and Sky were congratulating Prudence on the pristine state of the office when the phone rang.

"Yes hello, Mr. Balsley? Thank you for returning my call," began Prudence.

"Yes, Mrs Prudence Forsyth-Wilson speaking. What can I do for you?"

"Mr. Balsley, can you please explain why cartage costs have increased one hundred percent this year?"

Prudence winked as she flicked a switch so that Mary and Sky could hear what was being said.

"Well Mrs. Forsyth-Wilson, costs have gone up and wages also you will note," came Mr Balsley's impatient voice over the speaker.

"Well Mr. Balsley, that is total crap, wages have not risen, not for your drivers anyhow, and diesel has risen only two cents per litre, so I cannot see how you justify the rise. Also, I have received a quote less than your last season's price."

"Mrs. Forsyth-Wilson, are you calling me a crook?"

"Exactly Mr. Balsley, I am calling you a fucking rip-off merchant, for taking advantage of a situation, caused through the death of a man whose business helped build your bloody company."

"Listen Mrs. bloody Forsyth-Wilson, pay the account or I'll take legal action."

"Well Mr. Balsley, I can assure you, that subject to hell freezing over and my fifty fucking million being gobbled up in court costs, you will not receive as much as a postal stamp ever."

There was a slight pause.

"Ok, steady down Mrs. Forsyth-Wilson. Now please tell me how we may settle the situation?"

"It will be settled this way Mr. Balsley; we will pay the same as last year and tenders will be called for next season. The free rent, food and rooms your drivers usually receive here will now cost two hundred dollars per week from here on, as a matter of fact, we will backdate it to the beginning of this season. Do you understand Mr. Balsley? If not, I can repeat myself."

"Please Mrs. Forsyth-Wilson, I have new trucks to pay for, be reasonable," he replied in a completely beaten down voice,

"Mr. Balsley, all I require is yes or no. Any other of your bullshit is immaterial."

After a long pause Mr Balsley sighed and said, "Ok Mrs. Forsyth-Wilson, yes I will have to accept."

"Thank you Mr. Balsley, please tell your drivers to keep to schedule, we have a business to run, thank you and good evening."

Banging down the phone Prudence smiled to the two women present and in a most demure voice told them, "Excellent day ladies, lets have dinner," and swept out of the office.

Holding hands, Mary and Sky burst into giggles. Yes it sure was good to have Prudence around again.

Chapter

17

Over the next two weeks, the routines of Sky and Prudence settled down to the schedule discussed, and the station started to run like a well oiled machine, much to Mary's delight . The word soon spread that some wealthy, arrogant bitch ran the office at the Big Sky and to not try and put anything over her, she has a tongue like a King Brown's deadly poison.

The station workers soon warmed to 'Auntie Pruey' as she became known, with the aboriginals being unable to grasp the name Prudence. She amused them also with her little legs swinging about and breasts flying up and down, always wearing a revealing shirt tied at the waist.

One day after the two girls returned they went for a walk down to the river that now had clear pools of water in different parts of the sandy bottom. Several aboriginal children frolicked naked in the water watched by Mary, Rose and about twelve aboriginal women, including Sky's grandmother, all chatting loudly while watching the children. Little Mary joined in the frolicking while baby David sat in front of Mary playing in the sand. Unable to contain herself, Prudence, thinking as all the others in the water were naked, this must be the acceptable way, so she dropped her gear and ran at a deeper section at the end of the pool and did a big bum buster.

As Prudence yelled out, "Bum buster," screams of delight came from the seated women the children squealed noisily. Caught up in the madness, Sky followed by over half the aboriginal women, all undressed laughing and yelling as they plunged in and a huge water fight started. The area veterinarian coming in to inspect cattle before live shipment was approaching the station airstrip and gazing at the scene below, nearly demolished the homestead, but managed to pull up at the last moment.

From that day, Auntie Pruey was a favorite with the children and their mothers. Many a time, when little faces appeared at her office waiting for her come out and play with them, Pruey obliged. She loved the life and the station children, but was worried that they didn't have a schoolteacher to teach them to read and write.

One day, she mused, if all goes as planned I will rectify the situation and then roared out of the office as a gang of little bodies scampered away towards the river squealing with delight.

The next afternoon, as she sat in the office after the morning flight, one of the station hands delivered the mail. There was a letter addressed to Prudence from AJ and one to Sky. Opening her letter Prudence read it several times. AJ mentioned two things that made Prudence realize the poor boy was in agony over money to keep his children. Without coming straight to the point he tentatively asked what they would all do on his return to the family fold. Setting up the typewriter Prudence wrote a full ten pages in the hope it would calm the obvious fears he held for the future.

In the letter, she informed AJ about the financial situation, explaining everything to him; her inheritance and the position Sky was in and how she was a beneficiary to the station. Prudence went on to state how she had liked Sky from the day they had met, the bond both had formed very quickly and the tie they had, both having children belonging to AJ. Prudence had been impressed with the honesty of Sky and her simple philosophy on the situation they both faced. Prudence wrote that she understood why it would be impossible for AJ not to have Sky and his child play a role in his life. She was prepared for this and wished for the three to in fact form a relationship upon his return, if he wished. She told him the truth that she loved him enough to share him with Sky and then asked, what is conventional love, anyway? What are the boundaries of love?

Watching the news from Vietnam, the suffering and death, Prudence wondered if perhaps the world would be a far better place if all believed in more love and had a better understanding. It was also the practical Mary's wish that this would happen; Bradley Jones had taught her forward planning and the reality of any situation.

Perhaps, she went on, they may join forces and run both stations together, spending summers in Tasmania, the peak season there for shearing and hay baling, helping her father, then returning to the Kimberleys to work the mustering season. As the dry only lasted five months, the two would fit together perfectly.

Sky was a very good at organising, mustering and sorting cattle, but the office work was something she was unable to handle along with the other duties. She had also revealed in one of their nightly talks in the sanctity of the bedroom that most of the finance was completely beyond her limited education. All the details would be discussed when he, the third member of the little family, safely returned to the arms of both who loved him.

Prudence then, as was her usual ending to any letter in the hope of cheering up AJ, wrote that she was aware the army added some sexual inhibiter to the tea and that if he was happy with the family plan, perhaps drinking it may not be such a good idea, as he had double duties in the bedroom on his return.

Prudence showed Sky the letter. Sky was delighted as she'd been worrying about a future without both Prudence and AJ.

Hugging Prudence she felt relieved.

Mary realized it was the only course that would be handled satisfactorily. Mary really loved both young women and their children. Her life again had purpose and although she would live in Sydney, the children would stay with her once they reached school age. As she aged, hiring a nanny would solve the problem if she found it hard to cope. Yes she mused, life has changed drastically since I saw Sky standing at the station store over two years ago.

The incoming letters from AJ now arrived addressed in the one envelope to both women. He seemed more relaxed, though anxious to finish his army service and begin the life planned out for him by fate. It seemed Prudence was the outgoing one, a born leader, with both AJ and Sky being somewhat reserved and glad to follow the 'she wolf' of the pack. The leadership of Prudence could be vicious if a member under her protection appeared in danger, yet motherly and kind to those she loved. Since the hangers on disappeared after her marriage to AJ, Prudence now looked to the little family, gathering around her, as her brood, and she became fiercely protective towards them.

In two short weeks, Prudence had all the book keeping in order and started helping Sky to count and record loading cattle. A fast learner, Prudence soon became an astute drafter of the cows and calves into the marking yards along with any yearling heifers chosen to remain for breeding. Culls and steers for sale went into the loading yards for transport to either Wyndham abattoirs or to Broome for live shipment; old scrubbers and cull breeders to Katherine slaughter house.

Auntie Pruey always seemed to have a load of excited aboriginal children on the back of the land cruiser. One day she decided to take the children back to their camp that was a kilometer from the main homestead on a rise overlooking the Fitzroy River. She found it hard to comprehend the sight that met her. The farm workers back in Tasmania had small but good cottages to stay in. What she saw now before her were nothing but shanties constructed out of tin. Prudence was appalled.

Standing surveying the scene, she was amazed at the happy women in the camp, so happy and carefree yet they lived in such poor conditions, with no toilets or laundry facilities.

That evening, Prudence raised the matter at dinner with Mary and Sky. Both replied that it was the way it had always been and Sky even told Prudence that she herself had lived most of her life in such camps with the mob. However, both agreed that this did not in fact make it right and on reflection now, perhaps something could be done to make things better for the workers and families. Prudence repeated to them what her grandfather had always believed, that the troops should be well looked after as workers perform better when consideration is given to their welfare and that of their families.

The following morning Prudence was in the office at nine, having come in early from her flying lesson and by ten she had a price on twelve new, portable, two bedroom dwellings constructed in Perth for the mining camps. They had a kitchen facility and also a laundry combined shower facility for a total cost of seven thousand dollars each. She then phoned Mr. Balsley, the trucking contractor and on answering the phone she heard a low groan when he heard her name.

"Hello Mrs. Prudence Forsyth-Wilson. What may I do for you? Perhaps give blood?"

"Certainly not Mr. Balsley, I need a quote to transport fourteen portable buildings, each twenty four feet long, from Midland near Perth to the Big Sky."

Now Mr. Balsley had purchased two new trucks and was financially overstretched so the mood of the conversation changed immediately.

"Thank you Mrs...."

Prudence cut him off at this point.

"Please call me Prudence Mr. Balsley, it is so much easier."

"Please call me Bill, Prudence," he shot back in an amicable way. "Well Prudence, I can do the job for ten thousand dollars."

"When would delivery be Bill?"

"Best I can do is over four weeks Prudence."

"I will give you a bonus of five thousand Bill, if you can do it in three weeks, from now."

"Geez Prudence, you're on, where do I pick them up?"

Prudence gave the address and placing the phone back in the cradle, gave a sigh of satisfaction. So did Mr. Balsley on the other end; perhaps this Prudence sheila was not so bad after all, he thought.

At lunch, Prudence asked Sky where the station bulldozer was situated, aware by office records one existed along with a grader. Prudence had never operated a dozer, or in fact even seen one up close, but the task ahead unfazed her. She proudly informed Mary and Sky that in her dealings for Big Sky, she'd been able to save the money required for the new buildings and freight from Perth, but if any more was required, she would make up the shortfall.

Mary and Sky would not hear anything of it. Mary had stated, on reflection, she felt ashamed at her indifference to the workers' housing situation but it had always been that way since her arrival and it seemed the natural order of things.

Sky drove Prudence down to the river crossing where the dozer sat on the bank, mostly used to pull trucks across the river and make a new crossing after each wet season. Prudence thought that a better method must be possible, but Sky reported that in the wet, the river levels ran twenty feet above the bank at its peak. Still unfazed, Prudence thought there must be some way and decided to look into that as her next project.

As no trucks were due until the next day, the dozer was available for use elsewhere for that short time. Sky jumped up on the tracks and helped Prudence up in order to show her the fundamentals of bulldozer operation.

"Where is the damn steering wheel?" Prudence said looking at Sky, who broke into laughter.

Sky showed Prudence how the machine steered by foot brakes as well as by pulling the long gear-like controls. Starting the engine, Prudence was impressed how Sky easily maneuvered the huge beast. She thought she could practice on the way back to the camp site and bravely asked Sky to take the ute back and hold the fort at the cattle yards. Prudence would clear a site for the new camp, chosen because of its height above the wet season flooding.

Sky was more than reluctant to leave Prudence to walk the D7 Caterpillar machine back to the new camp site, but Prudence told her, matter of factly, that all machinery was capable of being operated mainly by commonsense, as well as trial and error. How quickly had she learnt to fly the aircraft, she asked Sky, and then revealed she would be going to Broome soon to get her license.

Sky had to agree and watched apprehensibly as Prudence lurched off in the huge machine. Sky was amused how her legs were too short to operate the machine from the seat, so she stood up so as to stand on the turning brakes to steer the thing. Having faith in her ability, Sky went back to her drafting duties for the day.

As the huge, steel machine rattled along in the red dusty soil, Prudence raised and lowered the blade, finding it difficult to imagine how one was supposed to know what was going on in front of the blade, when commonsense dictated that the operator was unable to see in front. However, during the long and slow crawl back to the new site for the camp, through trial and error, Prudence worked out a satisfactory arrangement between her and the monster she fought to control.

Passing the station workshop she saw Billy, Sky's grandfather and another station worker repairing a damaged drafting gate. On seeing the predicament Prudence was in to operate the machine, because her bum slid off the driver's seat when trying to turn it, Billy Brown pulled her over and in true, ingenious aboriginal fashion, placed a wooden block on each pedal and twitching them on with wire, extended the pedals in order for Prudence to remain seated while operating the machine. Prudence was to learn that improvisation was a trait the aboriginal had stockmen become famous for, making do with available items in all circumstances.

Prudence now felt more in control and upon reaching the chosen site, she soon had a main track pushed in the centre of her new village. After removing the trees, she found it was easier to drag the blade in reverse to flatten a good road surface than try to fathom what was going on in front of the huge blade. She then made inroads into the bush in six opposite directions so as to place six buildings either side and have the shower block and washing and laundry facilities in the centre of the compound. By evening, Prudence proudly surveyed her creation and with a sigh of satisfaction, spun the big machine around, found a higher gear than she had previously and went clanking along back to deliver the machine from where she had picked it up. On the way she yelled to the workshop workers to come and pick her up in about an hour.

While waiting for the ride back to the homestead and a welcome shower, Prudence surveyed the crossing. After each crossing, the dozer had to be used to flatten the track across the sandy river bottom, as in most cases the trucks, when loaded, sank into the sand and had to be pulled out which was hard on the drivers and indeed the truck differentials and gearboxes.

That evening over a hearty meal both Mary and Sky were anxious to find out how Prudence had managed with her clearing of the proposed village site. Prudence promised to take them down, first thing at daylight, to show everyone what a magnificent site she had created.

As they lay in bed that night, Sky was glad when Prudence, so full of enthusiasm, stopped prattling on at midnight and finally dropped off to sleep. With a smile, Sky pulled the sheet up over her slumbering friend and wondered what she would have done had this little bundle of energy not entered her life. Somehow Prudence made everything seem to be in the right order, everything as it should be.

Chapter

18

The following day they received a letter from AJ. He wrote that he had decided to do another tour of duty in Vietnam, mainly because, in doing so, he would be allowed extended leave on his return and so would be home six months from the date he had posted the letter. That was in time to spend Christmas with them in Tasmania. He went on to say that he would still be in the army for two months before discharge, but it would be on leave and that way he would never have to say farewell again. He went on to explain that if he did return home anyway, he would still serve his full time at Townsville and would only be in the position to see them for a couple of short leave periods. He wished to get it over with as soon as possible.

The letter was received with much happiness at the prospect of a Christmas reunion. Prudence gaily announced to all that she would organize the best Christmas ever at Forth homestead. Everyone, including Mary was excited at the prospect, but still worried about the safety of AJ.

In the next three weeks, all buildings as promised by Bill Balsley were delivered. On the first trip he was more than amused at the site of Prudence on the phone. He imagined he was dealing with a six foot muscle bound female wrestler, not a petite good-looker. He noted the bouncing, energetic stride as the large breasted little girl came up to him to offer a firm handshake. That day, both became firm friends and Bill apologized for over charging and went on to explain that he was trying to grow his freight yet business finance was always very tight. He felt rather ashamed over the incident. Prudence waived her finger at him and made him promise to be a good boy in the future and with a blushing face, he promised her faithfully never to do such a thing again.

The Big Sky had been the first station to start transporting cattle by truck and most still drove huge herds overland to various destinations. The road from Canarvon's north was little more than rough corrugated tracks and throughout the Kimberleys, progress was slow and hazardous. Although Bill Balsley had a huge fleet of trucks, it was a monumental task to move the large numbers by road but he was, in fact, a pioneer in road transport. Had he not purchased three new trucks in Perth and contracted out moving the dongas to other truck operators, he would have never fulfilled the order for Prudence as it was a hazardous sixteen day journey from Perth.

Prudence constructed a large tank tower; it was filled by a pump drawing water from the Fitzroy. A large water hole sat below the new settlement that held water during the dry season, connecting water to the laundry, shower block and kitchen block ready for the inhabitants to move in. Sky, Mary and Prudence inspected the new village with pride. Mary wondered why no one had thought of it before. Both Sky and Mary gave Prudence a big hug, congratulating her on such a terrific job.

The following morning, now capable of flying alone, Prudence decided to go to Broome to order furniture and bedding for the new quarters, as well as service the plane and have a test so she could be issued with a restricted license. She asked the aboriginal woman to pick three people to accompany her to Broome to choose the required equipment for the village. As she approached the hangar, Prudence was amazed that all the women had turned up wanting to go, making it her hard task to decide which three would go. Choosing only three, Prudence promised the remaining ladies that she would take all, in turn, to Broome over time on shopping expeditions. All present were delighted and accepted the decision, waving madly as the little plane lifted off for Broome.

As it was the first time any of the passengers had been in a plane, it was an exciting trip for them. Prudence flew down Gieke Gorge and out over Derby following the coast to Broome. The pilot for once drowned out by the excited chatter of her passengers on the biggest adventure of their lives. Landing in Broome to the nervous giggles of the passengers, Prudence arranged later for her test as the engineers started immediately to service the aircraft.

Hailing a taxi, the four requested to be driven to Wing & Co emporium in China Town. It was the first visit for Prudence's three passengers to Broome and they were absolutely spellbound with all the cars and people. Like school children, they entered the store with Prudence at the head of the little group. Picking out double and single beds, plus mattresses, Prudence requested Mr. Fong to also order another twelve double beds, mattresses and pillows plus blankets. Included in that order was twenty more singles, again with mattresses, pillows and linen. Immediately she had his undying attention. Even the wife came out trying to be of assistance. Prudence gave Mr. Fong her name and said that she would be paying for the complete order, along with what her friends wished to purchase as well; a Mr Bill Balsley would pick up the order when ready and deliver it to the Big Sky.

And so it was that 'Missy Ploodence' became a favorite customer of Wing & Co. Mr. Fong and his wife ran to the door welcoming Missy Ploodence and her entourage whenever she came to Broome.

Prudence also decided that the women should have bras and

panties along with new dresses. Much giggling and humor occurred during fitting of the apple catchers and boulder holders, as Prudence described them to Mr. Fong. Prudence asked that perhaps they may stock some more feminine lines? Looking perplexed as to what Missy Ploodence was on about, Prudence solved the situation by opening up her shirt and dropping her shorts to display what she required, much to the bowing of Mr. Fong and clapping of Mrs. Fong in delight. The women squealed with laughter. Never surprised at the antics of Missy Ploodence, Mr. Fong soon had a special display, hidden of course, of ladies delights to which Missy Ploodence and her entourage were ushered on each subsequent visit.

After an enjoyable morning shopping, Prudence shouted lunch for the ladies and dropped them off at Cable Beach to fill in a couple of hours, while she went for her flying test. As expected Prudence excelled and flew home legal. She failed to inform the instructor she had actually flown the plane to Broome that morning.

On arriving home to much excitement from those who had missed the flight, Prudence became more of a celebrity and her shopping expeditions became a standard routine over the next few months. Indeed it was to continue for decades later, unbeknown to those who experienced the initial trip.

Bill Balsley delivered the goods as arranged two weeks later much to the pleasure of the station workers, anxious to move into the new village. With the help of Bill and a co-driver, plus all the station women, the buildings were soon fully furnished. Water was turned on to both service blocks, although only cold water as no power existed at the site. The weather was always warm and showers became a game to the children.
Prudence soon taught the women to shower daily and change undergarments along with dresses, wash their dirties and hang them on the line.

Mary arranged a huge feast that evening as all moved from

the old campsite to the new village with much enthusiasm and excitement. Billy Brown, the elder, chose who would have what and then all settled in, thrilled with the new surroundings. Prudence arranged drums to be placed outside each residence for rubbish and the cooking was all done in the communal kitchen on the new gas stoves. Life changed for the Big Sky station workers.

Bill Balsley had a talk to Prudence about the question of the river crossing,. He had come up with the solution of pouring a cement bridge over the river, although it would be covered with sand and debris during the wet each season. all that was needed was a grader to clean it off before the start of each dry as the river stopped flowing.

Prudence again used the station bulldozer to dig a huge pit to push all remains of the old campsite into it and then covered it up. She then pushed a new pit for rubbish from the new site and rostered two of the women to clean up and dump refuse in the new pit twice a week. A new sense of pride came over the camp and palm trees planted down the avenue between the dongas made the whole village look inviting and orderley, much to the delight of Sky and Prudence.

Prudence did not wish to make too many new ventures in her first season on the Big Sky. She continued on with the office and helped to finish the last of the shipments of cattle out of the yards before the onset of the wet season. It was during a dinner conversation that she raised the subject of a cement bridge over the river and claimed the benefits it would bring to the station. Mary was so enthused Prudence wondered why she had not raised the subject before. Such a construction would allow easy access to and from the station not only of the trucks, but station vehicles, that always seemed to be bogged in the soft sand. Mary even went on to say how they would not have managed without Prudence over the past weeks and it was enthusiastically seconded by Sky, and her mother, on behalf of the station workers. It was, of course, like fuelling a fire to praise Prudence; she immediately, with the eager help of Bill Balsley, planned the construction of the new access viaduct over the river, to begin as soon as possible, for the following season. Prudence even chose a new crossing place with the help of Bill Balsley, a much shorter span where the river narrowed, although the banks were steeper, she would cut a new road through them and cement the gradient so the vehicles would have a better grip. Shaking hands as he departed with the last of the season's cattle, Bill Balsley was indeed impressed with Prudence, his new business partner.

Station life slowed down with the release of the last of the breeding stock out to the wet season runs. The station workers attended to maintenance and helped stock provisions for the coming wet season. In general they relaxed, fishing and hunting, as had their ancestors; it was the best part of the year, a time to relax with the family.

Sky wanted her mother to accompany them to Darwin, Sydney then on to Tasmania, but she refused. Her life was now settled, happy amongst her people. Memories of a violent past instilled in her a wish to stay in the comfort and safety of the station and her soft bed in the main house.

October came with a sense of excitement at the homecoming of AJ. The three women, along with the two children both running around, loaded cases into the little plane for the trip to Kununurra and then onto Darwin, to a meeting with the station solicitors and accountants.

Sky found herself, fully loaded this time and with a co pilot, hurtling down the runway for the trip to Kununurra. She was much more relaxed now. Happy with her situation and looking forward to the return of AJ, her dreams looked like coming true sooner than she had anticipated.

Prudence thought of Forth homestead, wondering if all her renovations had been finished. Her father was sure she'd be surprised at the appearance of the wing stacked with books and paintings hanging on the walls. The two vehicles had been returned and covered after his close inspection. Prudence also thought of AJ and his long awaited return. The thought aroused her, so much, she had to snap herself out of it to concentrate on the flight. The passengers in the little plane agreed that they would never tire of the magnificent scenery and awesome beauty of the Kimberleys now before them and looked forward to returning with AJ next season.

Arriving in Kununurra, Sky arranged for storage of their aircraft while Prudence, Mary and the excited children booked in for the flight to Darwin. Having an hour to kill, the little group enjoyed a coffee. They all agreed it had been a very successful season at the Big Sky and Mary knew that Bradley would have been impressed with the job all three had done.

Mac Robinson Millar ran a Fokker turbo prop to Darwin from Wyndham and Kununurra twice weekly, apart from shipping into Wyndham, this was the lifeblood of the North. All roads were only passable for a few months in the dry season.

Landing in Darwin and collecting their luggage, they made their way to the hotel where Mary and Sky had stayed before. Booking in they decided to have a light meal in the rooms before having an early night; everyone was tired after the long day.

Mary put the two children to bed in her spare room while Sky and Prudence shared the room Sky had stayed in before. Prudence asked Sky if this was the bed Sky had shared with AJ and she nodded yes. Prudence felt aroused at the thought and had to forcefully control her emotions. The electricity charged relationship she shared with AJ turned her on and she missed the intimacy. Sinking into the bed, Sky also felt his presence and she too was aroused. Prudence had stirred the sexuality in her with her openness on the subject of intimacy and relationships.

The next few days were taken up with meetings and business. Mary didn't like these meetings as she had never been interested in the business side of the Big Sky and found them quite boring.

The accountants were obviously very impressed with Prudence's efficient bookwork. Mary requested that arrangements be made to include Prudence and her husband AJ as trustees and benefactors. She went on to explain that she did not wish to make the journey the following year as it was tiring and she wished to spend a few years of her life, stress free, at her Sydney residence.

Mary was instructed in the way the trust had been set up and according to her husbands wishes, the changes would be possible. Documents would be forwarded by post for her to sign.

Clearing his throat, the solicitor requested clarification, as he had heard that the children of both Sky and Prudence had been fathered by AJ and that his interest was purely, of course, for future reference as to benefactors of the trust that ran the big Sky. Before any one else answered Prudence stated, "Well sir, Sky owns his heart, I have his wedding ring and we both intend to share his bed. And yes, he is the father of both children; we hope and intend that there will be many more to come."

Coughing and spluttering the solicitor escorted them to the door. Mary had a wide grin on her face. Somehow Prudence always had the answers and good god they all seemed plausible, thought Mary.

Two days later the family boarded a flight to Sydney. Mary was not looking forward to the trip as she found travel very tiring at her age. She intended to go to Tasmania for Christmas with her family to attend Michael and Rachael's wedding. As the event was also planned at Forth by Prudence upon AJs return, it was not nearly as arduous a trip as the one she was undertaking.

The trio, with children, arrived in Sydney that evening and a happy reunion occurred at the airport. Rachael noted how tanned Prudence looked and saw that her hair had a gorgeous natural sheen from all the time in the sun. Sky was now beaming and looking more assured, unlike the time she had departed into the unknown of running a station solo.

Michael had stayed at home reluctantly because of a lack of room in the car, but sent his love to all. He was eagerly waiting with the barbecue fired up, a supply of cold beer and a nice bottle of red specially set aside for Mrs. J.

It was a happy and tear filled reunion that night. They had missed each other dreadfully. A decision was made to wait three weeks for AJ to return before heading to Tasmania for the wedding and Christmas celebrations. Expectations and excitement were already building for the two big occasions, even Mrs. J, Michael noticed, got a little carried away with the coming events, drinking two glasses more than he had ever seen her indulge. Giving Michael a big kiss she staggered off to bed waving to her large family and blowing kisses.

What a brood, she thought; years of absolute loneliness and now look, with more to come. She felt so happy for her two lovely girls; the future looked bright for the first time in Mary's life. Sky put the two exhausted children to bed and the four of them sat on the lawn watching the night sky and the lights of Sydney. Only one obstacle remained; AJ was to join them, then life would be perfect.

Chapter

19

Mary was glad to be back in civilization. The station life was harsh, that awful red dust seeped into everything, and she was tired of always feeling hot and gritty. It had only been the last few years that the homestead even had electricity but still the power was turned off overnight and the refrigerators ran on kerosene.

Mary was more than happy to pass her role over to the young and enthused members of her new family. She had noted with confidence how the two younger women operated as a team. She mused how Bradley would have been more than impressed with the first muster after his death.

Kimberley Cottage now seemed more civilized and clean, with many extras to make life comfortable. Mary had even found an Italian couple to live in the gardener's cottage. Maria was an excellent cook and housekeeper, her husband Giovanni was the best gardener, growing the best vegetables she had ever seen, always cheerful, they loved the children playing games with them in the lush gardens.

During the first week back in Sydney, everyone worked feverishly preparing for the homecoming of AJ. Mary hired a limo to bring AJ, Prudence, Sky and the children back from the airport, while the rest of the family would follow in Michael's car with the luggage. Every detail was discussed to make the homecoming a memorable one for AJ.

The three girls then visited boutiques in Sydney, finally purchasing dresses to wear to greet AJ at the airport. They also shopped for bridesmaid's dresses and Rachael's wedding dress for the nuptials at Forth on Christmas Eve; with all the families staying overnight and having Christmas dinner together the following day.

The time seemed to drag, the last week at Kimberley Cottage took on an air of excitement; the final member of the small family was coming home to the fold.

Arrangements for the trip to Tasmania were booked and confirmed. Prudence was busy sending constant messages to home, double checking final arrangements with Agnes and her mother, who both eagerly threw themselves into the excitement of the coming event. Prudence also phoned a real estate agent in Launceston and gave instructions that both she and Mary had agreed on.

AJ was glad to see Saigon airport with its frantic military activity disappear as the plane rose on the trip home to Australia. The last few weeks had dragged by, he had become miserable thinking this day would never come. The excitement of his homecoming was building, he felt dry in the mouth, and although he tried to visualize both Sky and Prudence, it seemed so long ago. He was angry that they both seemed distant in a cloud, he tried to remember the aroma of them both, distinctly different yet exciting. He longed for their touch, to see and hold them both, to sit and play with his children.

AJ tried to relax on the flight home but found he was unable to do so. Memories of the last few years, since the trip undertaken with his two Tasmanian friends, came flooding back and he relived them all. Events had changed so fast it almost seemed a dream. His one wish was to settle down to a normal and quiet existence to allow order back into his life; he knew this was perhaps difficult in the relationships he now found himself in. But AJ was happy he did not have to make a decision that he knew was impossible for him to make, he would be eternally grateful to both Sky and Prudence for making that for him.

AJ was jolted into reality as the plane landed in Darwin. Here he was to stay overnight, be de-mobbed and signed out on two months leave before final discharge. He slept fitfully that night.

With several of his comrades, he eagerly boarded an afternoon flight to Sydney, although extremely tired he was kept awake by adrenaline. When he landed in Sydney he was so excited he found himself shaking and in a cold sweat, fighting hard to control his emotions.

Passing through customs he walked briskly along to the exit, immediately he saw them, he fought to control his emotions. Sky and Prudence had chosen the same dresses, high above their knees, showing the full benefit of their beautiful legs; not sheer material but one that showed the outlines faintly of their undergarments: low cut displaying their beautiful breasts, both far more beautiful than he could remember. His two beautiful children both held by Mary were looking at the arriving throng. One he had never seen, apart from photos, and little Mary who seemed to have doubled in size since he last saw her out of the bus window in Darwin.

Michael and Rachael were waving madly as he rushed to both women, who clasped him to their bosoms sobbing madly and raining kisses on him. Overcome with emotion and exhaustion, he broke down and sobbed, drawing in the smells he had tried so hard to remember. He made an oath, at that time, that he would never leave them again. In an effort to control himself, he scooped up his two children. With everyone overcome by the moment and all talking at once, Michael collected the luggage as the group left the terminal.

Mary had the limo waiting and she ushered the family into the roomy interior and ordered the driver to head off. She and the others would follow with Michael, Rachael and the luggage, they would all reunite at home.

On the way to Kimberley Cottage very little was spoken, only lots of hugs, kissing and nervous giggles as the passengers rekindled old feelings and passions, as well as bonding as a family unit. Even the children became caught up in the electricity of love and suppressed lust as the limo made its way to Kimberley Cottage hugging their parents, especially their father, the man their mothers constantly reminded them of.

AJ was again mobbed, this time by Maria and Giovanni waiting at the footsteps of the mansion with huge hugs and kisses. Having never seen Mary's home he was impressed with the neatness of the gardens and inviting entrance.

Maria insisted on serving a meal at once for the arrivals in order for AJ to have a shower and retire early. He was glad of this as he was exhausted. The instructions had been given by Mary to Maria that this was to be the course of events; she knew both Prudence and Sky wished to be alone with AJ.

Mary, Michael and Rachael arrived shortly after, AJ relaxed a bit chatting to them all; it was a feeling he found hard to describe, being home amongst his family and friends. AJ ate sparingly, too emotional and pent up with feelings of expectations of things to come. Looking at both women, he remembered past memories, he was glad, when at Mary's insistence, she ushered them of to their room, promising to bath and put the children to bed later.

Holding hands with both he was led to the bedroom, especially prepared for his arrival. A huge bed sat at the end of the room; an ensuite and changing room adjacent. Closing the door, the sexual tension vibrated around the room.

Unsure what to do, AJ stood watching as both women slipped their dresses off the shoulders, letting them slide to the ground; both had white lacy underwear which they seductively dropped to the floor. The girls approached AJ, both slowly undressed him, pushing him back onto the bed; he felt their womanhood slide up his legs moist with anticipation. Still unsure, but bursting with unbridled lust, his decision was taken from him as Sky slid over onto him; he felt her inviting sex as he slid into her. Prudence placed his hand over her dripping vagina. Both women groaned in pent up ecstasy at that moment and with short, sharp gasps of energy came in throbbing orgasms so intense, all three were panting, totally covered in sweat.

The ice had been broken, all three showered together. As AJ lay on the bed, he watched Prudence come back into the bedroom, still drying herself and unable to contain himself, he dragged her onto the bed making slow and passionate love, drawing to a shattering climax that even Rachael heard as she went down the passage to her bedroom.

During the night, between snatches of sleep, AJ drank in the smell of both women; the musky aroma of sex filled the room. Even though exhausted he woke several times, as if driven by the loneliness and lack of female company he had endured over the past months. He even surprised himself with what seemed to be his inability to satisfy his sexual urgings. As daybreak came he found himself making love to Sky, with the sleeping Prudence spread-eagled next to them, her presence making it more erotic and fuelling his lust even more.

Over the next few days while waiting for their flight south to Tasmania, members of the household enjoyed lunches on the lawns of Kimberley Cottage; they played with the children while catching up with the news.

AJ was impressed with what his two loves had achieved. It seemed unreal as he looked at Sky that she was the same shy girl he had fallen in love with so long ago; if anything her beauty was far greater now than then. Prudence equally caught his attention: a bundle of energy; good looking and erotic, she knew how to turn him on. He now couldn't imagine life without either.

His attention was diverted by Prudence who announced she was going for a shower. Unable to restrain himself, AJ made an excuse to go to the room to change into shorts and catching Prudence getting undressed, he grabbed her, pulling her protesting onto the bed. Aroused she wrapped her legs tightly around him and they made love, ever so gently. He kissed her tenderly, telling her how he loved her, thanking her for what she had done for him. Prudence shed a little tear, it was what she had wished for; it made her a happy woman, contented and in love with a man whose love she shared, but who loved her.

The few days since his arrival seemed like an eternity ago. As the little group stood at the departure gates of Sydney airport, waiting for the call to board, Michael and AJ were chatting while the four women tried to control both children, who were excited about the plane ride. Michael and Rachael were coming back to Sydney after Christmas, to take a leisurely honeymoon back to Tasmania. Michael, to everyone's amazement, was walking with the aid of a walking stick; he was in continuous pain, but as always cheerful and looking forward to his marriage.

Boarding the aircraft, both boys sat together to let the excited women nurse the children and go over plans for the next few days, for perhaps the one hundredth time; even Mary was showing more than the usual signs of excitement.

Landing at Launceston airport, Lyndon Fish and Agnes Wilson greeted them. Agnes was thrilled to see her two beautiful grandchildren. She hugged Sky, now fully aware of the beauty AJ had described; he hadn't exaggerated, maybe he even understated her natural looks. Agnes was also glad to see Prudence who gave her an affectionate hug with a beautiful smile; all seemed to be so happy.

Mary and Agnes struck an immediate bond as the group gathered the luggage and headed to the car park. Prudence had a flat battery, but fortunately, Lyndon had jumper leads in his car which saved a call to the RACT. Prudence, Sky, AJ and the children went in the Mercedes, whilst Mary, Agnes, Michael and Rachael went with Lyndon in his car.

It didn't take Agnes long to inquire about how the two women in her son's life appeared to be so friendly and have such a good relationship; Mary came straight out with it. Although initially shocked, she listened as they all spoke about the great relationship experienced by the three; they made it seem so natural; a good ending to what may have been a sad story. Lyndon laughed and said several times 'lucky bastard'. He hadn't been very successful in finding a permanent relationship with his many girlfriends; he found it hard to believe that AJ, the quietest and shyest of the trio, ever found himself in the position he was in.

The arrival at Forth was bedlam; friends of Prudence, Rachael, Michael and Sky, along with relatives, parents, football club mates and general hangers on, had been waiting for some time for the arrival and the party was already in full swing.

Prudence's parents put on a barbecue with free beer for all, as it was such a momentous occasion. Tears, hugs and laughter intermingled as the two cars discharged their cargo. Prudence hurled herself into proceedings whilst Mary and Sky stood in shock ,until dragged into the crowd, drinks thrust in hands as well as food. They were hugged by just about everyone and given a big welcome home.

Isabella, never a drinker, flushed with her new found position in life. She had consumed more than was usual for her and was passionately kissing and hugging all the newcomers.

David and Mary joined in with the other dozen or so children running madly up and down the wide verandah of the Forth homestead, squealing and laughing madly. Mary and Sky looked at each other and burst into laughter; what else would you expect from Prudence? Mary laughed as Rachael invited them to come inside the homestead as Prudence was otherwise engaged. They were shown around what was to be their home for the next few weeks.

Mary and Sky were impressed; unlike the Big Sky homestead, it was furnished in beautiful old English furniture: leather chairs; the bedrooms with elegant beds had canopies of lace over them; fine art on the walls; three bathrooms with cast iron claw foot baths and Georgian fittings. This home even made Kimberley Cottage look down market. As they entered the new wing, Prudence, breathless, caught up with the little group, anxious to see the finished product. She was more than impressed, it blended into the homestead better than she had anticipated.

Rows of beautiful, leather bound books sat on Blackwood shelving; all the walls displayed large paintings of hunting and military scenes; in the centre a large mahogany table sat with beautiful leather armchairs placed around it. Mary and Sky stood speechless they found it hard to comprehend that Prudence, who bounced about in ripped shorts, shirt tied at the waist and wearing an old pair of blunnies, was actually the mistress of all they gazed upon.

Prudence, still breathless, gave them all a hug, she was so pleased with the results that she then told the three women she was going to give her dad the biggest hug ever for doing such a great job of finishing her project.

Prudence yelled to Rachael to take them to the kitchen for something to eat; the barbecued food was like eating raw meat as the cooks were rather inebriated. With that said, she made a typical Prudence exit, flouncing down the hallway.

If Mary and Sky were impressed with the homestead so far, the dining room proved to be more unbelievable. A massive table with twelve chairs either side, covered in red velvet, ran down the centre of the room. On either side stood magnificent serving tables, each with a silver candelabra and utensils. The walls were adorned with grand paintings and stags heads on the embossed wallpapered walls and a huge crystal chandelier hung from the ceiling. Off to the right, Rachael led them to the kitchen with beautiful Huon pine work benches; two large refrigerators and two large stoves each with utensils hanging above them on a wrought iron structure fixed from the ceiling.

Opening up the fridges that were brimming with food, of all descriptions, Rachael took some sliced ham and cheese and made the two stunned women a sandwich as the jug boiled.

They sat pondering, wondering what surprise Prudence would spring on them next.

Rachael informed them that, in fact, what Prudence had told Mr. Balsley about her fifty million was true. Mary had thought it was only a bluff and often laughed aloud to herself as she recalled the story. Causing both to sit in stunned silence again Rachael told them that the contents of the homestead, the safe and property added a further five million to Prudence's fortune. Sky laughed as she remembered Prudence telling her that she was impressed with the Big Sky. "Well, our little Prudence," she laughed, as the others joined in, "We are more than impressed also."

Rachael showed them to their respective bedrooms. Mary and Sky loved the master bedroom, it was huge; the ensuite boasted shower and bath facilities as well as a powder room; large white towels hung everywhere; the king size bed especially made for the colonel, sat at one end of the room. Sky sat on the bed, it was soft and inviting. The huge canopy seemed to make it peaceful but Mary intervened saying they had better return to the party as the three were half of the main attraction.

Mary retired at midnight, totally exhausted, she sank into the inviting bed. Sky placed the sleeping children in bed at midnight also, and both collapsed after playing well past their normal bedtime. AJ had wanted them stay up late as it was a special occasion. Sky, by one in the morning, felt exhausted and informed Prudence and AJ she was going to bed; both had fussed over her asking many times if she was ok. Sky knew both had old friends to catch up with and with that, she gave each a hug and went to bed.

The party continued until four in the morning and when the last stragglers left, AJ, Prudence and Michael sat in the kitchen having a cup of hot chocolate as the roosters started crowing in the chicken pens. They were glad to finally be home amongst family and friends.

Sky awoke the next morning to find herself in the middle of the huge bed with Prudence's arm over her waist.Gently lifting it off, she left the slumbering pair, showered, dressed and found her way to the kitchen where Rachael and Mary were tucking into bacon and fresh farm eggs.

She quickly checked on the sleeping children then joined in a hearty breakfast, laughing about the antics of the previous night, they'd enjoyed it, letting their hair down and as Mary described, it was good for the soul.

After breakfast, feeling great, the three decided to go for a walk. It was a beautiful morning and walking down the front stairs they were surprised to see Prudence's father and a few volunteers cleaning up the mess from the celebrations. The marquee ordered for the wedding the next evening would be there at ten and the lawns had to be cleared, so Charles informed them. It seemed that Isabella felt a bit precious as did others and would not be capable of helping them. The three volunteered and in an hour, they had the job finsihed.

Charles invited Sky to come for a drive to the tip with him so he could show her some of the property. Mary and Rachael volunteered to stay and make breakfast and to dress the children when they finally woke up. Charles immediately warmed to Sky, although he was not aware of the true situation, he was pleased the three who shared children seemed to be so close.

Sky fell in love with Forth; it was less harsh, green and softer than the Kimberleys. She loved her homeland but this was a nice change and the thought of spending the wet seasons here thrilled her.

Dropping off the rubbish in the huge pit set in a gully, two kilometers from the house, Charles showed her the shearers' quarters and shearing shed. Sky had to smile when she remembered Prudence's account of her experience there with AJ, in one of the rooms, and she wondered which one.

Sky loved the smell of the newly baled hay stacked neatly in the sheds; the beautiful hawthorn hedges and red and white cattle grazing on lush pastures. Charles saw the delight in which she was enjoying the expedition and suggested she come with him to move ewes and lambs onto fresh feed and she jumped at the chance. They collected three, energetic kelpies from the kennels. The two, now firm friends, rounded up a mob of ewes and chatted while the sleek kelpies, unaided, moved the bleating, confused mob, effortlessly onto a fresh paddock.

Sky absolutely loved the red and tan kelpie dogs, amazed at their willingness and training.

It was lunch time when she ended up back at the homestead, requesting AJ build a kennel for her two new kelpie pups, selected from a station litter by Charles, as a gift. Prudence was happy that Sky fitted into the life at Forth so quickly.

Hopping into the station ute, she drove Sky to where she knew a disused dog run sat and they loaded it into back. The two women found a nice spot near the homestead and with the help of AJ, they cleaned and repaired the run. Sky was now the proud owner of two boisterous kelpies.

Prudence announced to AJ and Sky she had something to show them and like two children, they followed her and jumped into the land cruiser. She drove them down to one of the implement sheds where two shapes, that appeared to be vehicles, were covered. Whipping the cover off one, both AJ and Sky shouted in glee; there stood the old Holden, gleaming with a fresh coat of paint; new tires; seats re-upholstered, as if it had just come from the factory. AJ was so overcome he grabbed both women and they all fell about and rolled around on the fresh grass. Not a worry in the world, Prudence thought of everything; life was perfect and he and Sky let her know by hugging her so tightly, she had difficulty breathing. Prudence also showed them the Snipe in all its glory, promising both they would go for a drive in it after lunch, to visit her grandfather's grave.

Chapter

20

AJ drove the land cruiser back to the homestead while Sky and Prudence followed in the Snipe. They were in great spirits as they bounded up the stairs making their way to the kitchen for lunch. The marquee was already up on the lawn, with men unloading all the tables and chairs to set up for the wedding, on the following day at four. The caterers would arrive early the next morning, on Christmas Eve, to prepare the feast for the guests and wedding party.

The house was empty, yet on looking out the kitchen window, they spied Mary, Michael, Rachael and the two children playing with Sky's two kelpies under a huge spruce tree. The three smiled at each other as they watched the happy scene before them. AJ, unable to control his emotions, gave both a passionate kiss as he told them how much he loved them both.

Prudence asked Sky what names she had called her two kelpies. Sky replied she had named them Billy and Sioux, after her father and grandfather. Prudence and AJ thought both excellent names.

Sky ran down the garden to fetch the others for lunch, while AJ and Prudence prepared some cold chicken and salad. They sat on the verandah, enjoying lunch and chatting about the coming wedding, as the two pups lay at Sky's feet; already she had a strong bond with her pride and joys.

Rachael and Michael decided to spend a quiet afternoon to let Mary, David, Little Mary, Sky, Prudence and AJ go to visit the Colonel's and Nanny's grave. After that they wanted to visit AJs parents.

AJ looked at Prudence as she knelt before her beloved grandfathers grave and he realized how much the old Colonel had meant to her. Both he and Sky stood beside her, holding her hands, as Prudence stood silently looking at the two gravesites, remembering the times she snuggled in between those two remarkable people; she missed them both terribly.

Prudence looked at her own son and thought how proud the Colonel would have been of David; she imagined his 'dash good show' with the old tap to the nose in recognition of her feat, in giving birth to such a fine chap.

Placing flowers on the graves, AJ and Sky told both children what a fine man their grandfather had been, and how Prudence loved him and Nanny so much. Mary was greatly taken with the obvious genuine love and respect Prudence had for her grandfather; she knew despite her bravado under the exterior, beat a heart of gold, and placing flowers on the graves Mary gave Prudence a quick hug. The group left in the Snipe to travel the short distance to AJ's parent's farm.

His parents greeted them with enthusiasm, glad to finally see their son safely home again. For good they wished, both wanted to retire and let AJ have the responsibility of running the small property.

David Wilson had been in poor health for some time, unable to do any farm work, he was more than ready to see the last of the property.

Agnes and Mary ordered everyone to sit on the porch and have a chat while they finished preparing afternoon tea. Mary wondered how many others must be coming as Agnes fussed about over a mountain of food. Later AJ informed her this was his mother's usual procedure, always providing twice as much food as needed in the spirit of old fashioned country hospitality.

AJ and the children went to check out the farm dogs and chooks, while Prudence and Sky chatted to David. Although Prudence was a favourite of his, he soon fell for Sky also; she was quiet and respectful. He also noted her beauty; he had been informed by Agnes of the situation and wasn't sure how his son had landed not one, but two of the most beautiful and eligible women he had ever met.

Sitting on the porch, eating the delightful treats cooked by Agnes, it was an enjoyable family afternoon. The children doted on by Mary and Agnes, David chatting to the two young women and AJ looking on contented at those he loved the most in this world; he wished the moment would last forever.

As evening approached, Prudence suggested they had better leave for home, not only to bath the children, but because the children had a late night the previous evening, thanks to their father; an early night was planned as the next two days promised to be hectic.

Agnes invited Mary to stay overnight and accompany them to Forth the following afternoon and realizing Agnes longed for female company, Mary agreed. She was tired also and thought a night apart from the energetic threesome may restore some of her energy.

AJ drove the Snipe home, dropping off his family at the homestead, he returned the car to the shed and carefully covered it up, patting his beloved Holden as he walked past.

Back at the homestead, Rachael had a roast meal cooked with the help of Michael. The old friends talked about how their lives had changed so dramatically over the past few years, and how they wished for the happiness they now had, to last forever.

Bathing the children, Prudence and Sky retired to bed also. When AJ entered the room, they were chatting away about the wedding; they would be leaving at ten in the morning to have their hair and makeup done. They were excited and warned AJ to have Michael and himself waiting at least five minutes before their arrival.

AJ undressed and showered and then settled in between his two loves, holding both to his chest he felt settled, happy and in love; it had been a perfect day.

He was awakened early to both girls chatting excitedly and kissing both, he felt his excitement start to rise. Prudence bounded out of bed, followed by Sky, shaking her finger at AJ smiling. She informed him that he missed his chance last night and that there was no time for sex today as too much needed to be done; but they both guaranteed him to make up for it after the wedding. AJ groaned, then smiled as he dropped back into the comfort of the bed, watching the two most beautiful backsides sashay into the bathroom.

AJ lay in bed until mid morning, contentedly dozing until the children burst into the room. Sky tossed them onto the bed, giving AJ instructions to look after his offspring as they were leaving to go to town to prepare for the wedding. Wrestling both children, AJ soon tired of the game and with his two energetic children in tow, went to the kitchen to prepare something to eat. Michael was already there munching on toast with a couple of slices ready for AJ.

"Looks like we're the babysitters," Michael exclaimed, a nodding AJ agreed.

Michael then told AJ he had better start to learn as Rachael was expecting. Like AJ, he too had begun the race before the starting gun. Congratulating Michael, AJ slapped him on the back. Michael limped off ,roaring like a lion at the two children while AJ munched contentedly on his toast. Yes, he thought, life is good.

It was decided, with the insistence of the children, to take Sky's pups for a run. As they passed the marquee, the caterers were placing white table cloths on all the tables; flowers were festooned everywhere. Walking along the willow-lined river, the two youngsters frolicked with the lively pups and for the first time Michael talked about Vietnam. "Look mate, I just want to thank you for saving my life back there. I'll never forget that," he said

"It was a bad time in both our lives. I've made it a point to try and forget the whole stinking mess. I lay awake of a night between two of the most remarkable women in the world and all I can think about is making them happy and leading a good life," said AJ.

Michael agreed, he told AJ he had nightmares still, the pain at times was almost unbearable but that he would always love Rachael, she was his rock and he would make her a good husband and father to his children. The men agreed that the five would always be close friends, in good and bad times forever; AJ thanked him for choosing him as best man and his two loves as bridal attendants.

"We'd have it no other way, mate," Michael said. He felt proud to have a friend like AJ, just as Rachael had Prudence and Sky.

Returning at two o'clock to the scolding of Mary and Agnes, the two friends with two children and two dogs soon found themselves ordered to take showers to be ready for the wedding. Guests would start to arrive shortly. The two older women took charge of AJs offspring, a job both lived for; it was their oxygen in life, fussing over the grandchildren and even though Mary was not an actual grandmother, she classed herself as one, wearing the title with pride.

Michael and AJ changed for the last time into their army uniforms. Both officially still served in the army, and as neither thought they would ever wear a suit in the future, the uniforms were chosen instead. The girls reckoned they looked damned sexy.

Isabella arrived and with Agnes and Mary, took charge of dressing the children who were to participate in the wedding.

Isabella had become a pillar of cooperation and patience, and Agnes noted her behaviour was far different from her own daughters wedding. Although she admitted when it came to her own wedding Prudence only wanted a smaller affair and seemed more concerned to get AJ into the sack than entertain a large number of guests.

AJ was far more nervous than Michael, in fact, Michael had to administer a stiff brandy to his best man. The more cars and people who arrived the more nervous AJ became. Michael was glad when four o'clock arrived and he and his nervous attendant stood before the minister waiting in the huge marquee for the bridal party to arrive.

The organist started the wedding march, AJ looked straight ahead in nervous expectation as Michael turned to see his lovely bride enter as she start walking towards him, in between the rows of guests. AJ also turned to look, he found it hard to believe the scene before him; his two children looked absolutely amazing and he felt so proud. But his two loves dressed in long pink full length bridesmaid dresses, following with the ruby pendants draped around their necks, was a sight that for as long as he lived, would remain etched in his memory. Even the guests gasped at the vision before them; all participants looked breathtaking. Always a bit emotional AJ had a job to control his feelings, he felt so proud of his family.

After the exchange of rings AJ stepped back between Prudence and Sky who were both aware he was nervous so they both clasped his hands. As he stood proudly between them, the wedding ceremony was soon over.

The newlyweds signed the papers while Sky and Prudence amused the children, then followed the married couple to the main table under a shower of confetti; AJ was glad it was over. He only had the speech to contend with then he could relax.

The guests were abuzz as AJ sat between the bridesmaids, both were glowing as was the bride. Agnes and Mary had collected the children with the help of Isabella; they would take them back to the house for bathing and to bed later that evening.

The master of ceremonies clinked his glass and called for the toast to the bridesmaids from the best man. Rising to his feet, AJ, nervous as ever, was surprised how easy it became once he started. He thanked both attendants on behalf of the bride and groom then requested everyone to rise to drink a toast to the two most beautiful attendants to ever assist a bride. A huge round of applause followed as glasses were raised and emptied. AJ then went on to wish Michael and Rachael all the best wishes anyone could bestow on two newlyweds; two amazing people and lifelong mates. He also wished to give them a gift from Sky, Mary, Prudence and himself, given with love and best wishes always, he then passed a small parcel to Rachael.

AJ was more than relieved that his duties had came to an end. He gulped another drink down as Prudence nodded well done to him. As Michael rose to make his speech Rachael opened the package. Michael thanked Prudence for putting on such a wonderful wedding and that they would be eternally grateful for it. Michael then went on, to AJs embarrassment, to tell all the guests how his friend had saved his life. At this stage no one apart from Mary and the two girls knew. He told of how ,under heavy fire, AJ had carried him in a super human effort to safety. He also told of how Mary and Sky had come to his assistance in Sydney and how they, along with Rachael and Prudence, had nursed him back to what he was today.

"I thank Mary for giving us a car and paying for the best treatment money can buy and for her benevolent friendship. A remarkable woman indeed and we love her dearly."

Rachael, looking a bit shocked, shook his arm and passed him the title deeds and key to a house in Campbell Town. In a wavering voice, holding Rachael's hand, he continued, "And now these four generous and kind hearted friends have given us a house as a gift, what more can I say but thank you?"

Michael sat down stunned and bewildered but happy, they thought they would have to find a place to rent on their return to Sydney.

The whole marquee exploded in whistling, clapping and shouting as the band struck up and the food and wine began to flow. People came forward to hug and congratulate the happy couple. Sky and Prudence got so many slaps on the back, along with congratulations on their kindness, that both became more than a little embarrassed.

The now married couple mingled with the guests, as did AJ and Prudence. Sky was escorted about by Charles and introduced to every guest; he was impressed with her beauty and poise and it made him feel important to have such a looker hanging onto his arm.

After the official photos had been taken Prudence rounded up her little family as she grabbed the photographer and escorted them to the library. There in a big leather chair she sat AJ in with the two children, one on each knee; Prudence and Sky stood on either side, hands on AJ's shoulders. Under strict instructions from Prudence a number of photos were taken. Later Prudence had a photo painted by the best artist she could locate. Framed, it was proudly placed in the dining room between one of the Colonel as a dashing young soldier and the other of Charles and Isabella's wedding. The Colonel would have been proud of his granddaughter and perhaps not alarmed at her unusual family; he always knew Prudence was different yet he knew the dynasty he wished to leave was in capable hands. His expectations would later prove to be right as his granddaughter would, in fact, leave a vast rural dynasty, one of the largest in Australia's history, spanning the continent.

Guests started leaving at ten that night when the band stopped playing and this was a sign that the celebration had finished. AJ checked on his children to find them asleep along with Mary and Agnes who had tucked in with them. His father had also retired with quite a few others to the shearer's quarters for the night, ready for the next big event - Christmas day at Forth with presents and heaps of food for everyone.

Showering, AJ dried himself off and jumped into bed; nearly asleep he heard the two girls enter, giggling as they undressed in the powder room. Both came out wearing crotchless panties with nothing covering their breasts. Wiggling their backsides as they jumped into bed, it was a long night for AJ; satisfying both of them proved to be a bigger task than he had anticipated.

Chapter

21

The three lovers were abruptly woken in the morning at daylight by the two excited children accompanied by their grandmothers, Mary and Agnes, carrying heaps of presents. Prudence and Sky made a dash for the powder room to dress while AJ made some attempt at modesty in the confusion and laughter that followed.

In ones life perhaps we all remember certain events; this particular Christmas day was one the three young lovers never forgot during their entire lifetime, often fondly remembering it. Young and in love their small part of the world was in order, happy and contented amongst family and friends, the problems of the world forgotten as they all united together; the day was one of laughter, love and sharing.

After presents were exchanged everyone shared a magnificent Christmas dinner. All had pitched in to help prepare the meal which lasted over two hours, the finest of wine and food was on offer as usual. Prudence, with the help of her mother had stocked the kitchen with a smorgasbord of delicacies, it was indeed a special day shared with family and friends.

The children were exhausted after all the excitement, they had a sleep about mid afternoon, the adults decided after cleaning up to join them for a snooze; it had been a hectic two days. AJ dropped off to sleep, snuggled in the middle of his two loves, contented, happy, and totally dedicated to both. The sun shone from the two girls, it had been the best time of his troubled life and events that had caused him heartbreak and sadness, but since stepping off the plane in Sydney life had taken a full turn for the better.

That evening everyone was too full to eat much so they gathered in the kitchen making coffee and tea, picking a few leftovers before heading to bed for an early night.

As was to be her usual habit in the mornings Sky rose early to take her kelpies for a walk. Feeling happy and refreshed she watched as the two half grown pups frolicked about; whistling them, she smiled to see their ears prick up and then run back to her. She was pleased to see they already had started to learn simple commands; Charles had informed her he would help her break them in.

Sky hadn't realised she had walked nearly two kilometers along the willow lined river when she saw a herd of deer standing on the rise to her right. Spellbound she watched the magnificent stag snort then gracefully bound off with his harem of does and fawns. Always one to appreciate the earth and its creatures she fell in love with the magnificent animals. It was later, through Sky's intervention, that hunting was banned on Forth.

Returning to the house for breakfast she fed her dogs before joining the others breathlessly telling them about the beautiful animals she had just seen. Prudence and AJ never gave the deer much thought; they had grown up seeing them on both properties where they were raised, however, both appreciated Sky's love of wild animals.

Boxing Day was the annual day for a local picnic. All the residents of Forth attended for a few hours before escorting Michael and Rachael to the airport for their return to Sydney. They had to pack their belongings and then travel back to Tasmania to their new home in Campbell Town. Rachael was going back to work for a short time until the birth of their first child and Michael would be on an army pension. Prudence and

Mary would always make sure, without being intrusive, that money was never a problem for their friends.

Over the next few days Agnes and David returned home with sadness, they missed the atmosphere and family at Forth.

Sky and AJ were busy helping bale the lucerne and jetting sheep against fly strike; it was great to be back in the fresh air working together.

Mary and Isabella looked after the children while Prudence sat in the office catching up on correspondence and farm accounts; she visited the accountants and solicitors between Christmas and the New Year.

Prudence realised both AJ and Sky loved the outdoor and rural life, neither seemed interested in the bookwork and finance; Mary also noticed this and told Prudence they made a wonderful team. She told Prudence that she was the leader of the pack, the decision maker,. Even in discussion during the evening both AJ and Sky told her that only one person can be a team leader, they both viewed her as that person. They had the utmost respect and admiration for her ability to organize and plan, totally supporting her in every decision she made, assisting her in what ever direction she chose the family to take.

Mary had several discussions with David and Agnes: surprisingly both agreed with her and Prudence's plan. Prudence called a meeting New Years Eve and they all sat around the huge dining table to hear her outline the plans. David and Agnes had agreed to sell their farm to Prudence, Sky and AJ for a reduced sum of course as AJ was to inherit it anyway. However, the couple needed retirement money and this seemed a fair solution. David and Agnes had agreed at Agnes's pleading to go and live with Mary in Sydney, both women would be company for each other and David would potter in the garden with the gardener, fussed over by two women. Mary and Agnes had both endured loneliness and lack of female company, they looked forward to their last years with the company of each other. Also the children would be educated in Sydney when old enough to attend high school, with both grandparents supervising them.

Prudence's father was doing a magnificent job of managing Forth, the new farm would be de-stocked of sheep and Charles would use it to run heifers for re-stocking Forth as well as fattening steers. Lyndon Fish was looking for a house, he gladly accepted free rent to caretake David and Agnes's old farm, now part of Forth.

Prudence and her family would stay at Forth for six months of the year and hopefully Mary, David and Agnes, would visit whenever possible for as long as possible. The family would visit Sydney as well if they had time between their journeys to the Big Sky and Forth.

Prudence announced that she and AJ had been appointed trustees of the Big Sky. She also stated that in her view the Kimberley area of Western Australia was a sleeping giant, raw and untamed, open to those brave enough to tame it; she intended to make her little family one of the largest cattle enterprises in Australia. Her fortune was growing at several million per year but she found it boring to watch investment grow; she would keep a certain amount invested and purchase several cattle stations with the returns and with a seed of ten million she had just released for the purpose, a company had been formed with AJ, Sky and herself as shareholders. The partnership would manage Forth and the Big Sky as well as hold all further acquisitions they would make. Stunned, everyone in the room was silent apart from AJ and Sky who had previously discussed and agreed to her plans. They were proud and confident of her ability to plan and organize and to then promptly take action.

Prudence informed them that they already owned fifty one percent of the largest freight company in West Australia with the proposed expansion of the Ord Scheme and dam construction; this would also grow as the region expanded. Prudence then told them she had appointed a full time accountant to run the office which would be at Forth as the proposed headquarters of the intended operation, and that they would also be advertising in Sydney for a nanny to help with the children, accompany the family on trips and to also school the children.

Mary immediately stood up and clapped, she had seen Prudence in full flight before and told the audience she was one hundred percent behind her as were the other members of her family. She would guarantee Prudence and family would be one of the biggest cattle companies in Australia if not the biggest.

The stage had been set, lines of responsibility drawn, everyone was happy. Sky and AJ were relieved again that Prudence had made the hard decisions for them; both loved the free outdoor life never having been skilled in bookkeeping or business practice, and as David told them, too many cooks spoil the broth.

Prudence was also relieved, she loved both AJ and Sky but knew they were free spirits, she did not want to clip their wings, she loved to see them free and happy; too much decision making would worry them, even destroy them, and she did not wish that, just having their support and comfort around was more than sufficient.

For the next few weeks Sky and AJ spent many happy hours working at Forth often joined by Prudence who always made them laugh. When moving sheep the children accompanied them. Order had come to their lives, all three thrived on each others company.

Mary and Agnes, along with David, went to Sydney leaving the different little family to become the sole occupants of Forth homestead. Family evenings were cherished, love oozed throughout the home; Forth would become their sanctuary in the future when all business took a break for several weeks of the year.

Prudence made a wise choice appointing a full time accountant and book keeper; it freed her up and proved cheaper than the two firms handling the growing business. Her choice was also better than expected, William Browning was young and keen, he soon found many methods of streamlining and saving the payment of tax, other than what was necessary. Prudence cleaned up and renovated one of the farm cottages, the accountant and his wife loved living in the quiet surrounds and they also looked forward to the travel the position would bring.

Sky settled well into life with AJ and Prudence. She found it humbling to think she may now keep her promise to Bradley Jones, she felt secure with Prudence and AJ around.

As she bounded along with her beloved dogs, looking for the wild deer, Sky smiled when she saw the beautiful beasts that had become used to her morning walks. She seemed to have an affinity with the sleek, agile animals who shared her love of freedom.

AJ on the other hand expected no less from Prudence and was happy to just have the company of both women. Whatever made them happy made him happy too. Prudence had seemed to, once again, make plans in which everyone would be content, plus it allowed Prudence to follow her path. Natural to her drive and organizing spirit, AJ knew Prudence would only ever be happy as the head of her little family, she thrived on the challenge of any event, he had every faith she would do as she planned and he was excited at the future, life would never be boring, of that he was sure.

Chapter

22

It soon came time for their return to the Kimberleys. Prudence arranged for the placing of an advertisement in Sydney newspapers to acquire a nanny to coincide with their arrival. Sharing a farewell meal with her parents, she arranged for the station workers wives, who looked forward to the extra money, to assist her mother in the job of maintenance of the homestead.

William Browning, and his wife Anna, promised to keep an eye on things between business trips, on behalf of Wilson Pacific Pty Ltd, the company formed by Prudence. A telex machine had been set up in the office at Forth and Prudence intended setting one up also at the Big Sky and it would be their northern headquarters.

Mary had arranged a hire car to pick the family up at the airport, the driver was surprised when two women, one man, two children and two dogs piled into the vehicle along with a boot load of luggage. Mary and Agnes missed the children; in fact, their motherly instincts had turned to David Wilson, he was glad to have a reprieve from the constant attention.

Sky's two dogs, now nearly full grown, and well trained, deposited themselves on the front porch of Kimberley Cottage. As the surrounds were well fenced, Sky left them there with food and water; they wouldn't go anywhere anyway, but would sit and wait for their mistress, no matter where they were.

Maria and Giovanni loved the intelligent dogs and overfed

them on the two week stay at Kimberley Cottage. *If this goes on for an extended period, both animals will die of obesity,* thought AJ

On the second day, phone calls started to come in about the position of nanny for the children. It sounded very exciting to many, the prospect of spending time in the Kimberleys and Tasmania on such large stations. One of the applicants who sounded interesting to Prudence was Annie Rowlands. Annie was the child of two high profile solicitors in Melbourne, who only had Annie as a status symbol, as they thought the appearance of a beautiful child would boost their status in the circles they moved in. To their horror Annie turned out tall and skinny with no breasts and eyesight that needed thick glasses: to top it all off she was knock kneed and awkward. Sent to Sydney for education so as not to embarrass her parents, Annie spent every spare moment studying, she was a brilliant student scoring straight A's in all her subjects. She graduated as a teacher, with excellent marks, and was blessed with the ability to pass on her love of learning to her students. Living alone, she never went out like other youngsters her age, but read books and marked her students papers, taking a personal interest in each one, However, because she did not have the confidence to promote herself, she never taught higher grades than year seven, unfortunately for higher grade students with inquiring minds.

When Annie read the advertisement, she immediately dreamed up images of the outback: dashing cowboys flashed before her. She felt that she would be unhindered in improving the minds of two children while imparting her knowledge to them.

The interviews took place at Kimberley Cottage; Annie was a late inclusion, in fact the last of six chosen to be personally checked out by the two grandmothers and parents of the two siblings. By the end of the afternoon all had basically chosen one bright young girl who seemed to have all the attributes needed for the job. The last two were only interviewed because it was deemed necessary to do so since they had made the effort to attend.

When Annie entered the room, the difference physically to the others, was apparent, but it was her credentials and sincerity that caused Prudence to cast aside the other applicants. Annie Rowlands was informed on the spot to pack her bags, she was now part of the family.

Annie in her glee, phoned her mother and gave her the news of her change in position. Shocked, her parents immediately flew to Sydney for the purpose of checking out their daughter's new employees. Picking up Annie, they drove to Kimberley Cottage where Prudence welcomed them as she ushered them into the lounge, offering coffee. Taken with the surroundings, their impression soon changed when it appeared that one male actually shared two females, who had one child each to whom Annie would tutor. They also noticed Annie looking moon eyed at AJ. Annie considered any man who would maintain the love of two women must indeed be some Casanova.

On the way back to Annie's one bedroom flat, where she had lived a quiet existence, they tried to talk her out of the position that she had accepted. Annie would not be moved, her excitement at the opportunity to change her life was so obvious, both parents gave up and went home. They agreed with each other never to discuss the embarrassing situation and on their return home, they discovered that one of their wealthy clients was suing her ex husband, the thought of the remuneration eased their pain.

Nanny Annie soon formed a happy relationship with Mary and David, she too joined the growing family, it did not take long before she was able to impart her wonderful world of knowledge onto her two new charges. Her ability to tell stories was awe inspiring as she explained the wonders of the world that she had read about. Her voice kept the children enthralled, listening to her with wide-eyed amazement.

Prudence, in her wisdom, summed up the transport difficulties for the family fairly quickly. She purchased a new Cessna, six-seat aircraft in Sydney, and part of the deal was it had to be sitting in Kununurra before the arrival of the family. The old four-seater would still be maintained for station work and the odd trip into Broome for business reasons, when the new plane was unavailable. The new aircraft also had larger fuel tanks and could carry more freight, with longer distances between refueling.

Two weeks soon passed and it was time for the ever growing family to bid sad farewells to Mary, Agnes and David. As they piled into two taxis for the airport, and the long trip to Darwin, Prudence decided that Sky and the two children, dogs and Nanny Annie would continue on to Kununurra on a connecting flight. The logistics of staying in Darwin, especially with dogs, was a little daunting; Sky would pile her charges into the new aircraft already waiting for the final leg to the Big Sky.

Prudence and AJ helped Sky, and her group, onto the flight an hour after arriving in Darwin for the trip to Kununurra. Knowing Sky's flying abilities, Prudence knew they were in safe hands. Nanny Annie had already proven to be a dedicated and responsible carer for David and Mary. Waving the little band off, Prudence and AJ felt a pang of emotion, having to part with other members of the family. Taking a taxi to the airport they booked into the hotel, again asking for the room they had all previously used. The next morning, they would sign the documents making them trustees and benefactors of the Big Sky.

AJ and Prudence had a nice meal, then went out for a walk. Prudence wanted to take in the harbor, and she loved the beautiful color of the tropical water and the smell of frangipani. They returned at dusk to phone the station, glad to hear the balance of the family had arrived home safely. Sky was impressed with the new aircraft, the extra power and improved controls made flying it easier than the older plane; the extra baggage area made it more comfortable. Wishing the children good night, over the phone, they retired to bed.

As they snuggled into each others arms, it seemed strange without Sky and both mentioned it, but AJ, although tired, could never resist the allure of Prudence. He seemed unable to get enough of her, she drove him wild and he often felt ashamed of the lust she stirred in him, her energy was infectious and unquestionable.

The following morning found them both at the station solicitor's office. The senior partner had not forgotten Prudence and after signing the document regarding the Big Sky, Prudence informed him of her plans to expand into cattle in the Kimberleys. She showed him the financial plan and company setup, his opinion and demeanor changed immediately, her fortune would have been in the top few percent of Australian residents. He informed Prudence that his firm would be available at all times, he even gave her his own after hours number and requested they join him for dinner, but Prudence and AJ declined as they had an afternoon flight to Kununurra and were anxious to get home to the Big Sky and their family, but Prudence gratefully accepted a rain check.

Prudence Forsyth-Wilson, with her private school background, had the ability to mix it with the best and hold her ground with the rest if she had to, confident of her own ability it rubbed off onto all she had dealings with and they soon admired her.

The visit to the accountants office was not as friendly, she informed them that her own accountant would be calling within the next two weeks and to please hand over all documents to him, plus a final account, which he would pay after checking all was in order. Mary had even signed a letter asking for her file to be passed over also; she decided to pay her share, and place all the family business in one basket under the stewardship of Prudence, who she held in high esteem when it came to business matters.

Boarding the flight to Kununurra, the excitement grew. AJ was anxious to see the Big Sky he had heard so much about, as well as the red and the white Brahman cattle both the girls raved about. On the flight, they discussed the plan to turn the Big Sky into a breeding operation, to stock any further acquisitions they made. AJ also placed an idea in Prudence's mind, he thought helicopters, with their ability to fly low and maneuver, may be the future in mustering large areas like the Big Sky, cutting back on already hard to obtain manpower. Prudence and Sky were aware many of the young aboriginals were succumbing to growing Kimberley towns with the allure of alcohol, gambling and other white vices.

On landing in Kununurra, AJ was a little apprehensive as he helped Prudence push the little plane out of the storage hangar. Sky had shown Prudence how to check the oil and controls, get seated and belted. AJ was impressed as Prudence started the little machine then taxied to the end of the runway, all lined up for the takeoff. She gunned the engine and hurtled down the runway lifting off into the clear, blue Kimberley sky. Prudence and Sky never ceased to amaze AJ. Ever confident, Prudence chatted away, pointing out the sights below, including the diversion dam and the little, yet growing town, of Kununurra.

Prudence tracked west over Wyndham to show AJ the range Sky had taken him to, then swung south following the Gibb River Road until she struck east and onto the Big Sky. The wet season had lasted longer than usual, Gieke Gorge was still running well up the magnificent cliff face. AJ was in awe of the scene, he'd admired the harsh landscape on his earlier visit years ago, but from the aircraft it was awesome, giving a different perspective altogether. He understood why Sky loved the place, and Prudence viewed it as a challenge with ambition to raise cattle, the potential was unlimited.

AJ held his breath as Prudence eased the aircraft down to demonstrate a perfect landing. Prudence put an offer to AJ, that she and Sky would teach him to fly as soon as practical, it was almost necessary being so isolated on the large property. She also mentioned that learning to fly a helicopter would be worth looking at.

That evening, AJ checked out the station homestead surrounds and the vast cattle handling facilities. Sky's family were overjoyed to see AJ and he met Sky's mother for the first time; he was surprised to see how young she still looked, her good looks shone through and he took a liking to her at once. It was great to have all the old friends he had made, together again.

As the wet was still hanging on, and repairs had been done, the men fished and supplied the station with fresh fish, while waiting to begin the muster.

Prudence was again highly sought after by the women. The first she week took six ladies to Broome for the customary shopping expedition. Mr. Fong was excited to see Missy Ploodence again; business had been a bit quiet during the wet season and he had hoped Missy Ploodence would return.

AJ was amused at how 'Auntie Pruey' seemed to attract a such a large mob of excited children wherever she went. Even in the office, they hung about waiting for her to go swimming or organize some mad game. Sky's dogs fitted into the station life like ducks to water, they followed their mistress everywhere, even flying in the plane, checking out where the main herds of cattle waited to be mustered.

AJ often went with Sky, he was her second student, she was

a good, calm pilot and natural instructor. The two dogs sitting in the rear seat looked below whining when they saw cattle, keen to help with the muster.

Prudence arranged for the pouring of the cement as soon as it was dry enough to bulldoze the river bottom and exits. AJ started the machine and began to make cuttings for the new crossing, it seemed like everyone was poised to spring into a flurry of activity as soon as possible.

Nanny Annie settled in well, and fell totally in love with the station life. She chose to copy Prudence and Sky, wearing shorts, shirt and boots. She looked an amusing figure as she even copied Prudence's movements, sashaying along with her skinny legs going flat out. A school was started for two hours a day. Nanny Annie and Prudence had many difficulties rounding up the students as it became a game of hide and seek, until Auntie Pruey made out she was going swimming. After they'd all madly jumped into the back of the ute, she deposited them at the school room, with her typical Prudence logic.

She had the workers extend the aircraft hangar to accommodate the new aircraft. She was hooked on the new machine, it had more grunt than the old plane and it absolutely thrilled her. Out of the blue, she announced to a surprised AJ and Sky that she had arranged to buy a secondhand helicopter to try out for mustering. Part of the deal was the owners had agreed to deliver it, and stay a few weeks, until all three were proficient in its operation.

Prudence also inquired whether any stations were available in the Kimberleys; she was surprised that one, adjoining The Big Sky, was, and had been for sale for some time. It covered eight hundred thousand acres to join the Durack River, on its northern extremities. Badly neglected, it had a lot of fertile black soil plains, a few thousand shorthorn cattle still ran on its runs, though no muster had been carried out for two seasons. The homestead and facilities needed attention as well.

The three partners flew over it the following day and were equally impressed that it would be a good addition to the Big Sky, as many of their cattle often strayed onto the property known as the Plains, during the wet season. That evening they made the decision to purchase the property, and it was agreed that in order to expand, they needed more station hands. In an attempt to find some, they planned to fly to Kununurra to try and recruit any who may be waiting to start the mustering season.

They arrived in Kununurra the next morning, keen to find a few station ringers. Kununurra was a frontier town, conditions were tough and tougher men and women lived there, all anxious to carve out a new life with the promised Ord scheme.

Only one wet canteen existed and the owner had employed a brutish, giant of a man to try and at least stop some of the constant fisticuffs, a favorite pastime of many of the workers and ringers. Only the evening before, he had hurled a very drunken Snowy Figg, and a couple of fellow guzzlers, onto the dusty street. As the three drunken men crashed onto the dusty street, along with the empty fruit tins that had held their liquid, Snowy slowly drawled, "You shouldna done that. I'll see ya here, morrow morning at nine o'clock, when I'm sober."

Snowy was about thirty five, bow-legged from years in the saddle, and like many others, years of living in the open, sleeping under the stars made him as tough as old boots, no fat on Snowy, just lean muscle.

The bouncer was twice his size and turned up at the appointed time, confident to finish the job quickly to maintain his reputation, and go grab a few more hours sleep.

Prudence and her two confidants left the Big Sky at daybreak, parking the plane in Kununurra, they hitched a ride into town, in time to see the crowd gathered to watch the spectacle. They found a good spot to sit under a tree, the heat was starting to rise as a circle formed. Not knowing what was taking place, they asked the waitress, already with a bottle of beer opened, who informed them a ringer was about to be killed by the pub bouncer. Both girls became a bit alarmed as the waitress, without asking, plonked three opened bottles on the table. The two combatants entered the ring. Sky told the waitress she didn't drink beer and to have hers if she wanted it; picking up the bottle of beer, the waitress skulled the contents, gave a belch, and said, "Ta, thanks," as she walked off.

The huge bouncer had a smirk on face as he made a rush at the little ringer who gracefully danced aside, and in three minutes pulped the monsters nose, broke his jaw and two ribs. The bouncer left town that night, his position destroyed, the pub owner having to search for some other method of crowd control.

Prudence, Sky and AJ had found a new station manager, who promised to turn up within the next few days with five of his fellow workers, who just happened to be in town looking for work for the mustering season. Snowy Figg liked the 'no nonsense' way Prudence had bounced up to him and said, "Are you as good a cattle man as you are a pugilist?"

"What the fuck is pugilist?" asked Snowy.

Bursting into laughter Prudence said, "A fucken brawler!"

Snowy immediately liked Prudence. *Here was a woman who would take no shit,* thought Snowy. Sitting under the tree with Prudence, Sky and AJ, he immediately took a liking to the three, and an even bigger liking when Prudence explained that she needed a good supervisor for her expanding cattle operation. Snowy did not know what supervisor meant, but guessed it was either boss or drover, and the pay was the best he had ever been offered.

Chapter

23

Sky, Prudence and AJ did a bit of shopping at the local store, amused at the bureaucratic bullshit that made the store owner place the verandah back off the footpath, causing red dust to go swirling everywhere; luckily commonsense and local anger changed the ludicrous regulations the early settlers of Kununurra had to face.

Catching a ride back to the airport, they talked about the morning's events. They felt sorry for the one police officer trying to maintain law and order in an area the size of Tasmania. On the return trip, they checked out the station on the eastern boundary of the Big Sky. Prudence in her research heard that perhaps the owners may be persuaded to sell, the acquisition of this would indeed make the Big Sky the biggest operation in the area.

Landing the plane, after a long day, the trio drove to the river and decided the works on the crossing could start straight away, the flow had stopped, and the area chosen was solid enough. Prudence phoned Bill Balsley that night and he promised if the main channel for the bridge was cleaned out within a week, he would have trucks and men ready to start.

Prudence informed everyone at dinner that evening about Snowy Figg and the events of the day. Nanny Annie and Rose were looking forward to meeting the little ringer.

The following morning, AJ started work on the river crossing, while Prudence and Sky started the muster with the aboriginal stockmen, keen to start the annual muster. True to his word, three days later, as AJ was working at the crossing, he saw an old Holden ute trying to cross upstream. Several ringers, in various positions, lay in the back. Snowy was making wild charges trying to cross the soft sand, causing his rear passengers more than some discomfort in the condition they suffered due to a week of hard drinking. Helping the new recruits across, AJ was a little perturbed at the look of the bunch that fell out of the back of the old ute, however, his concerns were unfounded as the group turned out to be hard working and became the foundation of station managers for the future.

The new ringers, under Snowy, started work the following morning. They soon proved to be loyal and hardworking, especially when there was no access to liquor. Prudence and Sky insisted the station was a dry area and that alcohol was forbidden, and even the owners had to comply by the rule to make it fair to everyone.

The helicopter arrived two days later, much to their excitement. Having just finished the crossing, AJ, with the instructor, took to the air. Even Snowy, an ardent supporter of mustering on horseback, had to admit that days, even weeks, would be saved by pushing the small groups into larger mobs by the helicopter.

AJ loved the chopper and soon grasped the fundamentals of helicopter control. Sky, once again, proved to be a natural. Prudence also insisted, being Prudence, that she not miss out on instruction. Six weeks later the instructor left the station satisfied with the ability of the three to fly the chopper. Prudence asked Snowy to learn and fly, but Snowy insisted if he was meant to fly, he would have feathers.

Snowy and his group also had another talent which made many a happy evening on the porch of the homestead. Snowy played the guitar as did another ringer: one played the violin, another the squeeze box as he described it. Sky loved to sing along with one of her relatives and she surprised everyone by picking up a guitar and playing well. AJ remembered Sky singing, when happy, years ago and loved to listen to her dulcet voice wafting in the still Kimberley evenings.

These evenings became a regular event when circumstances allowed, and often, AJ would grab Prudence, to the delight of all, and waltz on the lawn.

The crossing took over four weeks to construct but the benefit was immediate as the trucks never again were held up. Even cars now had easy access to the station after regular grading.

With the new ringers, the mustering stage was so advanced that Snowy and a crew decided to go to the new station, with the help of the chopper, to round up all the stock if possible, and bring them back to the Big Sky for loading, as the facilities on the Plains were unusable. Prudence and AJ, along with Sky, formed a plan that with each purchase, unless the stock was Braham or Santa Gertrudis, to clean out all cattle on the Plains property, do all repairs, then restock with yearling heifers from the Big Sky, now the main stocking point for all stations in the initial period.

All at the station were shocked when Rose decided to go with Snowy to the Plains during the muster. They had observed the two as friendly but did not click that more was happening. Rose and Snowy both longed for company of the opposite sex, and although Rose was five years older than Snowy, he seemed happy that Rose had agreed to go with him. As Nanny Annie looked after the children it would cause no problems. No one was happier than the ringers, as Rose was a good cook, and after eating so well at the Big Sky, they didn't look forward to meals of cold baked beans after a hard day in the saddle.

The bulldozer, now available, had been used to construct internal roads to join both properties. Prudence's presence insured no person didn't know what their duties were, at least a week ahead; the station was now in full swing.

Prudence waved farewell to Sky and AJ as they took off in the little plane and chopper, at daylight every morning, rounding up and spotting cattle, they worked well as a team, and everyone admired the skills the two had in the operation of both machines.

Prudence had been negotiating the purchase of the adjoining property to the two they now ran. After a few weeks of offer and counter offer, Prudence won. Another six hundred thousand acres was added to the growing enterprise, the present owners would leave the station de-stocked and sell off all plant as their muster was half over. This suited Prudence as she decided not to add any additional property at this stage, until they had settled down, what had been acquired. Prudence, along with the expert opinion of Snowy, who in fact had worked on the new addition, calculated they could now run sixty thousand cattle, once repairs and the old scrubbers still left were rounded up, or shot.

Sky became an expert at shooting injured or old culls too diseased or cunning to be rounded up. AJ would maneuver the chopper and Sky would dispatch the hapless victim, often an act of kindness for poor, old and injured animals.

On the completion of rounding up the ragged bunch of inbred cattle left on the Plains, Snowy and crew drove them on the new road back to the Big Sky yards, with Rose driving the truck loaded with kitchen and supplies following, as was to be the case in the future.

On the return trip, Snowy decided his partnership with Rose was bliss after a life of loneliness. He proposed to her, a stunned Rose accepted. Without blinking an eye, Prudence, with the help of Sky, excitedly arranged a wedding and big bash at the Big Sky, both even allowed a few drinks, which unfortunately got out of control, with one day allowed off, to

Prudence's annoyance, turning into two, as the guests sobered up.

Rose, to AJs amusement, insisted Snowy swear off drink, which he dropped on his knees and agreed to. Also she stipulated to Snowy's disgust, that he take his boots off in bed. Snowy tried to argue that men always wear their boots to bed and he would be the laughing stock of the Kimberleys if people found out, it would ruin his reputation.

The running of the Big Sky that season ran like a well oiled machine with the service received from their partner in transport, Bill Balsley, who gave his partners first preference. He personally supervised the removal and transport of the season's livestock.

The weeks and months flew by, time for departure soon arrived, and Snowy and Rose agreed to camp in the homestead and supervise the ringers who had been given full time jobs doing repair work on the new stations. Snowy never had to repeat an instruction more than once; several of the ringers had viewed his work in Kununurra, and his reputation as an easy going, but dangerous individual if insulted, was well known. He was assured full cooperation at all times.

Sky and Prudence organized the first annual Big Sky end of season bash a few days before departure for Tasmania and invitations were sent out. On the afternoon of the event, planes and vehicles started arriving early: truck drivers, local aborigines, station owners, ringers and even a few tourists. AJ was amazed how the word had spread, and surprised how many uninvited guests appeared.

Sky and Snowy, along with Rose and the other musicians, struck up on dusk. Prudence and Sky had again allowed alcohol for the event, which was just as well as visitors arrived with ute loads. AJ would remember the night for the good behavior of the crowd, no doubt helped by Snowy, who now reckoned over-indulgence of the evil drink was uncivilized, and threatened anyone who looked like causing trouble.

Prudence and AJ loved dancing around to the beautiful voice of Sky, whirling around amongst the other guests, having a wonderful, carefree time, after all the season's hard work. The initial season at the Big Sky, that the three lovers had run, was so successful with the inclusion of two other stations, even Prudence who had eased off on the alcohol, let herself go and held her own with the others. Much to the surprise of some of the ringers, Prudence's reputation again rose in their eyes, she mixed it with the boys as well.

Snowy and Rose seemed thoroughly infatuated with each other. Sky was thrilled as Snowy treated Rose like a princess. He thought she was something special and told everyone. In turn, Rose fed and looked after Snowy more than she had any one previously, so grateful for the way he treated her after the often drunken and violent relationships she had experienced in the past. Snowy even found it more comfortable to remove his boots before bed, he turned into a perfectly civilized married man.

AJ, Sky and Prudence decided to fly the new plane back to Tasmania, all three were capable pilots and they did not plan on going to Sydney as Mary, Agnes and David had agreed to go down to Forth early to meet them there. The thought of airports and changing planes made the decision easy, with four adults, two children and two dogs, to travel commercially was becoming a logistical nightmare. The plan was to fly to Alice Springs across the Tanami desert, refuel, follow the Stuart Highway to Port Augusta, swing right, follow the Nullabor along the great Australian Bight to Adelaide, onto Geelong, track right over King Island onto Tasmania, then follow the Midlands Highway down to the Forth airstrip, used by planes to spread super phosphate but capable of landing the Cessna.

They were to leave at midnight as Sky was trained in instrument flight. The other two would take turns when they left Alice Springs, as the Stuart Highway would lead them to Port Augusta, then refuel and onto Adelaide. It would be a long trip, but the new plane was comfortable and fuel stops would allow for toilet breaks and to stretch their legs. So excited were they that in fact, no one thought of sleep. The little plane powered into the air at midnight, Sky glad of the modern instruments tracked directly east, it was so moonlight they saw the landscape below, it was an awesome sight at three thousand feet as Sky piloted the little family through the night sky towards Alice Springs.

The children soon dropped off to sleep, unable to stay awake any longer. Annie covered them with blankets and she also settled down for a few hours sleep before landing in Alice the next morning. Prudence also dropped off in the rear seat.

AJ talked to Sky to keep both well awake. The responsibility of their position kept them both alert. Time and distance soon passed, as daylight came about five that morning, and soon after, they saw Alice Springs on the horizon.

AJ left landing the plane to Sky, he was more than happy to let her take control as her ability as a pilot was, in his opinion, better than his own. The sleepy passengers, pleased at the opportunity for a toilet stop and walk, had a coffee while the plane refueled. They were all keen to continue as soon as possible due to the long flight ahead of them. Sky went to the back of the plane for a rest while Prudence and AJ sat at the controls. As Prudence took off, she banked right, picking up the Stuart Highway and settled into the next phase of the trip.

By late afternoon, the aircraft approached Port Augusta. It was decided to break the journey here for the night, the children were bored and tired. Luckily, a local gave them a ride to a caravan park that signed them into two chalets and reluctantly let Sky tie her two dogs up in front of their accommodation.

It had been a long day, the showers felt excellent which refreshed the family. AJ and Nanny Annie called a taxi to go out and buy dinner, and on the driver's advice, purchased some fish and chips at a local takeaway, as well as several bottles of cordial. After a meal enjoyed by all, they collapsed into bed. It had been a long, tiring day.

Anxious to start before daylight to finish the trip, all, including Nanny Annie, looked forward to the comforts of Forth, catching up with family and Christmas celebrations.

Daylight found the family taxiing down the runway, AJ and Sky at the controls, churning up the dust as they rose into the air for what they hoped was the last leg of the journey. A tail wind gave them good air speed as they cruised down the coast, all excited at the scenery of magnificent cliffs and blue sea, the children even spotted whales blowing twice.

The time seemed to fly by and next thing they were landing in Adelaide. The excitement was growing as they were cleared from the tower after refueling, flying slightly inland, clearing Geelong. It was about two in the afternoon when they crossed the Bass Strait on their final leg to Tasmania.

Chapter

24

Mary was beside herself with worry waiting at the airstrip on Forth with Agnes, David, and Charles, pacing madly about. Isabella, sitting on the ground, also worried with Michael, Rachael and baby Susan who was only a few weeks old. Mary was trying to calm everyone, telling anybody who would listen, that Sky was an experienced pilot and along with two others capable of flying, they would be ok. Hoping madly they would, as the plane was over an hour late. Tensions were rising with Isabella wailing that if Prudence was not so headstrong this disaster would not have happened.

Michael was the first to hear the drone of the approaching aircraft; slowly it came into view, immediately spirits rose. As they watched, they recognized Sky and Prudence both in the front two seats. As the plane descended with Sky in control, the waiting crowd cheered as she made a perfect landing, and followed by a mad convoy of vehicles, the aircraft came to a stop. Sky immediately cut the engine, leaving the craft at the end of the runway. Exhausted, she decided to move it the following day. The passengers, with the help of the exhilarated ground crew, disembarked to hugs, tears and excited chatter by everyone, even the dogs, cramped for so long, recognized home and proceeded to piddle on every wheel, yapping madly. Sky let the two dogs run back to the homestead following the convoy.

Agnes and Mary had arranged a cold meat evening meal, everyone sat on the porch of the Forth mansion taking in the peaceful spring evening, ewes and lambs fussed about on the green lush pasture below the homestead, and it was a relief to be home.

Agnes, Isabella and Mary insisted on cleaning up and giving the exhausted Nanny Annie the night off; never complaining, Annie was extremely tired. Showering after the meal she made her way to the bedroom that she and the children were to share. On the way she was interested in the huge room at the end of the hallway, although tired she decided to explore, entering the giant library Annie stood spellbound at the rows of beautifully bound leather and hardcover books. The magnificent old masters hanging on the walls; she was perhaps the only person in the house conversant with many of them. To Annie she had entered nirvana, making her way to the bedroom she decided to make the library her pupil's schoolroom to instill as much knowledge as possible from the literature she was yet to explore.

Over the meal the trio caught up on all the news. AJ decided to go and have a bath first; he hadn't had one in many months as the Big Sky only had showers. He missed the beautiful huge bath the Colonel had installed, soaking in it was one of his greatest pleasures. He had just finished filling the bath and sank into the warm water when Prudence entered, stepped into the bath and sat at the other end. Sky came in naked, sitting herself between his legs to lay back in his arms. AJ rubbed her belly which he noticed was getting a bit potty; he then noticed Prudence also seemed to be expanding around the middle. On feeling him rub her stomach, Sky casually informed him he was about to be the father of two more children; in only five months time, both would be born in his own land Tasmania.

AJ was absolutely thrilled. Sky turned to him and he kissed her, with Prudence smiling and blowing kisses, scolding them for not telling him earlier. Prudence said he would not have allowed them to fly home in the little plane or indeed worked so hard the last couple of months so they decided to keep it a secret until they came home to Forth. Prudence laughed and told them they were all completely crazy for flying home in the little aircraft anyway, in fact, they would be going back by commercial flights; she would pay a couple of young pilots who wanted to get their hours up to take it to Broome for them in the next six months. Sky agreed it had been a crazy scheme and that they had stretched the boundaries of both the capabilities of the aircraft and indeed the pilots. They all agreed it was indeed a crazy bloody flight and in future would not risk the lives of their children, all four, with such stupid schemes.

Sitting in the bath they discussed and decided not to head back north, at least until the new arrivals were about three months old. They had no doubts that Snowy was more than capable to muster the stations along with the crew he had: a helicopter pilot was easy to find with many young southern pilots wishing to get flight hours up and they often rang the station for work.

Soaking in the bath the trio chatted about the future and agreed to slow down a bit to enjoy each other more and spend time with the children.

William Browning had been a great addition to the staff; he stayed at the Big Sky for three months sorting out the station books and setting up the running of the two new stations. He had indeed made them more money on the investments than ever; the seed money for station purchases still sat in an interest bearing account at eight million plus. Prudence had purchased well and her initial inheritance had increased markedly.

The three agreed that with a growing family they would still need to look at better forms of air transport in the future. Nearly nodding off, Prudence stepped out of the bath, wrapped a towel around herself and asked the others not to be long. She went out, leaving AJ and Sky alone.

AJ had become a little aroused by the closeness of Sky laying in his arms. Turning around he slid further into the bath, Sky slowly sat upon him, he felt her warmth as he slid into her. She kissed him passionately while he held her close and they made gentle and passionate love. When they reached the bedroom, there in the huge bed they found Prudence asleep, she looked angelic and peaceful, so unlike the Prudence that she was capable of. Sliding in quietly either side of her they snuggled together, falling into a deep sleep.

AJ was woken by Prudence fondling him at about seven in the morning; he had slept longer than usual. Sky had already gone to take her beloved Billy and Sioux for their morning walk and to no doubt look for her deer. Prudence started to kiss him passionately which he returned and soon they became entwined in passionate lovemaking. He found it hard to believe the passion he felt for both Sky and Prudence; life would be unbearable without either and the two beautiful children they had produced. Exhausted, he lay with Prudence snuggled in against him, rubbing her growing tummy and breasts; Prudence loved him caressing her and without realising, they both drifted off back to sleep.

In the next few weeks everyone settled down to helping on Forth, attending shows and picnics with the children, as promised; they became an even closer and happier family, indeed soaking up the love of each others presence while the two babies grew inside both mothers.

Sky and Prudence had been informed that the expectant birth dates may even be in the same week. Prudence seemed to slow down; pregnancy had indeed put her ambitions on hold. Her grandfather had instilled in her a strong sense of family loyalty that must always come first, as ones main focus in life; any other matters, including money, were secondary. Prudence agreed, even though her family relationship was certainly different, she was unable to comprehend life without her two soul mates. Perhaps it was the pregnancy of both that strengthened the bonds between all three to a greater height than before. They often lay on the lawns of Forth homestead watching Nanny Annie and the children playing games in total contentment, soaking in the presence of one another.

Mary, Agnes and David noticed the close relationship and passion between the three. It seemed many times they sat together relaxing, totally oblivious to all around them, gazing at each other in a world of their own; even Michael and Rachael commented that, if possible, the passion between the trio was greater than ever.

Christmas and the New Year arrived and passed with the usual feasting and exchanging of presents.

Prudence and AJ gave Sky a beautiful Gibson guitar, to her delight, amongst other gifts. It was a magic time at Forth, even Annie enjoyed the family atmosphere where she had a feeling of belonging to this extraordinary family group.

The weeks flew by and in the middle of March, Sky gave birth to a bouncing baby boy, William Anthony Wilson. Three days later, Prudence joined her in the opposite bed, arranged by Rachael, holding a small bundle of squirming daughter, Sky Agnes Wilson.

Both women advised AJ that they had discovered the pill and their child producing days had ended; AJ smiled and nodded his agreement as he watched the two older children, so taken up with the two new additions to the family, reveling in the situation.

AJ collected both his loves on the same day and with two children climbing over their mothers trying to look at their new brother and sister, it must have looked an extraordinary sight to anyone traveling that day.

Life became hectic at Forth homestead with Agnes, David and Mary, who had stayed for the birth. Even though the house was huge, it seemed to be frantic with people running everywhere, napkins being washed and two infants constantly suckling at their mother's breasts.

AJ had been helping Annie with the babies as well as assisting on the farm. Two rural exchange young men had arrived from Germany; they moved into the shearer's quarters for a week. One of the men, Albert Goring, a tall boy, quiet and wearing heavy spectacles, did not seem all that keen on the farm but instead offered to cook some German cuisine for his guests. He was happily cooking in the kitchen when Nanny Annie walked in; it was love at first sight. Annie swooned and Albert found himself unable to talk in English, but followed her around the kitchen, burning the meal in the process.

Prudence took over and suggested a walk around the gardens for them might be in order. Annie and Albert soon walked hand in hand from the homestead down the willow-lined river; within the hour, both were undressed, making awkward love on the fresh green grass; something they continued to do quite regularly for the next week until Albert was supposed to leave. Both were heartbroken at the idea. Prudence arranged for Albert to stay on, even jokingly suggesting she would arrange a wedding for the couple if they so wished and to her surprise, both eagerly accepted the idea.

A small wedding was arranged for the infatuated couple: Annie's parents arrived from Melbourne, more than impressed with the Forth homestead, but alarmed at the rush Annie seemed to be heading into with marriage.

Two weeks later Mr and Mrs Albert Goring boarded an aircraft bound for Germany on a month long honeymoon as a gift from the residents of Forth. The couple would return to Forth, one as a nanny and the other as cook, to the ever growing family. Prudence hoped the lovemaking would become less frequent on their return so both would settle down to again helping around the homestead; the children missed

Annie's spellbinding stories and attention.

The month soon passed and all greeted the couple on their return; it was great to have Annie back. Albert was a wonderful cook who loved cooking up huge family feasts.

Agnes, David and Mary returned to Sydney and once again life at Forth settled, even though more participants had now joined the family.

Chapter

25

And so the seasons went by with the trio always spending the spring and summers at Forth; it was their time out, time they spent together away from the cut and thrust of business.

The big bath at Forth was christened their 'think tank' and many an evening they lay soaking in the huge bath discussing new plans and reminiscing, or just soaking up the strength they gathered from each other.

Young Mary graduated from law school, a brilliant student with a thirst for knowledge instilled by Annie Goring during her happy childhood; she settled into a good position with one of Sydney's top law firms. She lived in Kimberley Cottage, left to her by her beloved Grandma Mary; Mary lived to see her namesake graduate proudly, watching her receive her honors.

One evening, arriving home a little later than usual, young Mary, as always, went to check on her beloved grandma and was shocked to find her dead; a look of contentment on her face.

Mary had simply drifted off to sleep never to wake again. She had requested to be buried with her family stating in her will the thought of returning to the harsh Kimberleys frightened her, although she loved Bradley Jones, the main focus of her life had been her new family; they had been the best years of her life. Grandma Mary Jones was buried in the Colonel's family plot in Tasmania surrounded by her grieving family at the age of ninety one.

Ten years earlier, David Wilson, at Prudence's insistence, had been buried there also.

Agnes now lived with her granddaughter, looked after by Sue Davis; Sue had came into their lives during a bull sale at Rockhampton in Queensland. During the sale, a young Edward Davis, only seventeen, had approached AJ to shyly ask for a job on one of the twenty three stations the company had owned at that time, explaining that his father had been killed in a station accident and his mother, brother and sister were reliant on his meager wage for a living. Prudence and Sky took a liking to the young lad and he and his family found themselves, at the conclusion of the bull sales, on their way to Sydney with the family.

Sue and the two children stayed in Sydney. Sue gratefully accepting a job to housekeep for Agnes and Mary and the two children were enrolled into school there, with young Edward placed under the care of Snowy for education in the running of the cattle stations owned by the company.

Australia had changed remarkably in three decades: Whitlam came to power and the war in Vietnam had ended, but it seemed conflict still raged in many parts of the world.

The Ord Dam was built and Kununurra flourished: civilisation came to the north, new sealed highways snaked their way from Perth to Darwin, the abattoir at Wyndham closed and the live cattle export business bloomed.

Young David Wilson finished his education at agricultural college and under the guidance of his parents and Auntie Sky, started to take over the cattle empire. He had become an astute and quiet young man. He and his sister Mary formed a close relationship, constantly on the phone to each other as they had during their earlier years of education, always fiercely coming to each others assistance in the crisis's life makes one endure.

Young Sky Forsyth-Wilson turned out a clone of her mother being kicked out of several schools. She was the apple of her father's eye and along with Auntie Sky, was unable, no matter what the indiscretion, to do any wrong.

Always there to pick up the pieces, Prudence was reminded lovingly by AJ about a young free spirit he once knew named Prudence Forsyth and a grandfather who doted over her. Sky eventually finished her troubled education and came home to Forth, helping her grandfather, bouncing about like the young Prudence years before, drinking local boys under the table and roaring about in a Hilux ute with numerous aerials protruding from it. She even once flattened a strapping, six foot farm worker in the pub who had made a sexist remark to her; spitting out teeth, the recipient promised to sue her for damages until the rest of the bar called him a bloody woos and told him not to come back if that was his reaction.

William also attended agricultural college and he then moved into the Big Sky homestead with his grandmother Rose and Snowy. Snowy no longer rode horses, preferring instead to drive around the properties in his air-conditioned land cruiser supervising, keeping an eye on all the station managers. He still refused to fly. He and Rose chose a caravan to visit all the stations with and this turned out to be a great thing; no one ever was sure when Snowy and Rose would turn up for inspection, all the managers kept themselves at the ready.

Three of the initial ringers now were station managers as was young Edward Davis. Edward had met young Sky at the annual Big Sky bash and they had formed a love, hate relationship. Edward drove Sky mad with his apparent indifference to her approaches and she in turn goaded him at times, but the easy going Edward just smiled after each assault which pissed Sky off more. However, Sky always made sure Edward was invited to the Forth Christmas celebrations; she even phoned to make sure of his attendance.

In nineteen seventy two, the company had purchased a Cessna Citation, a twin engine plane with seating a capacity of twenty two which made life easier for the company directors and accountant to visit all the stations and commute back to Tasmania. The plane was based at Broome and Launceston airports. Surprisingly it always seemed to be in use: two pilots had been recruited to fly the sleek machine as the three owners had no desire to train up to a jet engine rating, as acquiring stations and running the Cattle Empire was a full time job.

Prudence and Sky always insisted on never parting the trio; if one was unable to go then the other two would not even think of going. The two occasions that demanded every member of the family must gather was Christmas Day and the Big Sky bash. The Big Sky bash included station managers and workers, who all flew in to the station by plane or helicopters owned by the company.

Snowy would stride to the station verandah and proudly give his annual speech, older, more bowlegged, but still receiving awesome respect. If any young ringer made a noise during the speech, he was quickly hauled aside and told the story of Snowy and the bouncer, which was added to over the years to legendary status, this always had the desired effect.

Then Sky and her mother would stride to the stage to lend their beautiful voices, the beer would flow, and AJ and Prudence would lead the dancing under the stars on the green lawns of the Big Sky. The one day event had stretched to a weekend event in the first few years; it became famous, and invitations were one of the areas most sought after acquisitions.

Both of Sky's grandparents passed away in the one dry season. Prudence and AJ left Sky, along with her people, alone to wail their traditional death ceremonies, giving her love and support when needed, but respecting her aboriginal heritage and beliefs. Both were interned in the gravesite above the homestead with Bradley Jones and his ancestors. The site was always cleaned and taken care of each season, a task Sky personally attended to.

The company had purchased stations in the Kimberleys, two on the Tanami Desert, several in the Northern Territory and Queensland. In all, at the end of three decades, thirty five stations, running three hundred thousand cattle.

Nanny Annie and Albert produced two beautiful children, both girls named Helga and Lorraine who became much loved members of the family. Annie had opened up for them, along with the Wilson children, a wonderful world of knowledge. Both had followed in their mother's footsteps and taken up teaching careers.

Annie and Albert stayed on after all the children left their loving stewardship. Annie so loved the Forth library, with additions made over the years, she would not ever consider leaving her wonderful world of literature and the memories of Forth. They both now acted as caretakers of the homestead, looking after the family when in residence. Their children became part of the life at Forth, returning to spend Christmas and holidays with their parents and extended family.

William Browning and wife Anna eventually had three children and again, all three were welcomed as part of the Forth family; they all followed commercial careers. William became overwhelmed with the accounting workload as the years passed and the empire grew and it was handed over to a large Sydney firm. William attended to the day to day bookkeeping and advising Prudence on business matters; he was always considered a loyal and trusted member of the family.

The fortunes of Prudence and the company, under his stewardship, grew in the decades to one of the largest pastoral companies in Australia. It was on William's advice that Prudence sold her share in the freighting business back to Bill Balsley so as to concentrate on rural matters, the core business and expertise of the company. Bill Balsley was always grateful to Prudence for her assistance in the growth of his own company; his two sons jumped at the opportunity to buy back the business and Prudence let them have her share at a more than generous price. She was always first on the list of customers thereafter, and no matter where or when, if cattle had to be moved, her jobs were attended to before all others.

One of Sky's greatest misgivings was the moving of the last of the aboriginal stockmen into town, lured by social security money and the excitement of town life, the old ways soon disappeared. This was replaced by alcoholism, gambling and drugs. Fitzroy Crossing turned into a large town based on different aboriginal communities; the old customs disappeared forever much to the sadness of the older members of the aboriginal community. The skills of the aboriginal stockmen were replaced by helicopters and contract mustering gangs.

Communication improved along with health services as predicted by Prudence. The sleeping giant, The Kimberleys, had stirred to life: mines opened up, the Argyle diamond mine turned into a huge enterprise, the Ord scheme after many failures boomed into a huge oasis in the desert. The trio often flew over the green fields of sugar cane and tropical fruits marveling at the changes since they arrived three decades ago.

Despite all the changes and size of the company's holdings, nobody ever questioned the directions of Prudence; all who worked in the enterprise respected both her and the other company directors, AJ and Sky. The respect, loyalty and dedication of all those who were employed by the company was unquestionable. Prudence always insisted good performance was rewarded with bonuses and recognition, workers always had good clean accommodation as well as reliable transport. The three directors made sure all events such as birthdays and anniversaries were remembered and honored; the advice of Colonel Charles Smythe was ingrained in Prudence, *Happy troops mean an efficient army.*

David spent a great deal of his time involved in the marketing and transport of cattle. Snowy, along with William, his student, ran the overall day to day operations of the stations, insuring the smooth running of the entire enterprise. William respected his tutor and grandfather, as he called Snowy; both Snowy and Rose doted on their grandson, he was their favorite and the natural successor to Snowy.

The trio had eased back on the day to day operations. Slowly they were passing decision making over to the two boys and the younger Sky; Mary helped with any legal advice and was the hand that held the other three together, sternly rebuking any dissent if it even looked like fermenting. She informed her brothers and sister that family comes first, always, that nothing else matters, and to remember their parent's advice and the marvelous upbringing they had experienced in a different but loving family. "All you are and have, is the result of our magnificent parents," were her often spoken words.

Chapter

26

Getting out of the bath, drying each other, pulling dressing gowns on, the three made their way to the kitchen to join Annie and Albert for the evening meal. Christmas was only nine days away. This year's celebration was to be bigger than ever with all the family arriving over the next few days.

Prudence and Sky arranged a large marquee and a catering firm to prepare all the Christmas Day food so the whole family would be able to relax and enjoy the day. Chatting over the arrangements and accommodation for all the families everything seemed in order, several of the now disused workers cottages had been repainted, new beds arranged in all the rooms for what was now a huge family that were to arrive for the festive celebration.

Retiring to bed the three had just settled in when in burst young Sky having just returned from a girls' night out at the local pub. Slightly intoxicated, as usual a friend had driven her home as she'd been well warned by her father of the dangers of drink driving. Prudence was a bit ashamed to pick up her daughter on this point, thinking of her own exaggerated driving as a young girl, boosted by copious quantities of alcohol. Flopping into the middle of the bed and kissing everyone, she excitedly announced that Edward Davis had just phoned for her to pick him up at the airport and what an absolute nuisance this would be, she did not see the reason he even came to Christmas at Forth.

That was enough for Prudence, she pounced on her daughter

tickling her all over with the help of Sky and AJ, holding her down as they used to when she was a little child.

"Listen my daughter, the light of our life, stop this absolute bullshit. I will hear no more of it; you have been madly in love with the boy for bloody years. When I was your age I had two children, the oldest ten. This coming year I am having two weddings at Forth, one being you and Edward, the other William and Susan Webb," said Prudence. "William proposed to Susan when he was twelve. And it's time both of you were married." Then she added, "I often wonder if Sky and I used up all the sex genes in this family; I want grandchildren running about and that is that!"

Young Sky looked a bit stunned at her mother and started to sniffle. "Its not my bloody fault the useless prick won't ask me. I have trapped him in the sack a few times but he has no bloody romance whatsoever, the barstard's useless."

"Well my baby, let me tell you this, time flies. Both your Auntie Sky and I made the decision for your poor father, sometimes love needs a bit of assistance. We've enjoyed a wonderful life together, successfully you will note, your grandmother Agnes proposed to your grandfather and had a happy marriage, just look what they produced," Prudence said as she hugged AJ.

"When Edward steps off the plane tomorrow, just inform him you will be married here in a month. Do you really love him?"

"Oh mum," Sky replied, "ever since I met him, I have never looked at another man. I feel I've wasted years waiting for him to make a move."

"Well that's settled then," said Sky. "If you don't make a move then we will on your behalf, besides we have discussed the future of Forth, it lies in your hands, your grandfather Charles should retire soon, you and Edward can take over."

Sky then went on to tell her mother she was only unhappy

once before when the two of them pulled her and William out of the local school in year three. Prudence burst into laughter.

AJ looked at his daughter and said, "Did we never tell you why we stopped you attending school?"

"No, not really. I just know mum had a fight with Miss Pringle-Jones and we never went back," Sky replied.

Auntie Sky broke into a grin and urged AJ on to tell Sky the full story while Prudence covered her head with the pillow.

"Well Sky," AJ went on to explain, "it appears at Show and Tell, either you or William told the class that you had two mummies and you often played in bed with your daddy and two mummies. Well, Miss Pringle-Jones was mortified and called both the mummies in to give them a lecture on child raising. They had to sit in front of Miss Pringle-Jones and were given the lecture on the finer points of what she required, as your teacher, from parents of those lucky enough to enter her classroom.

"The only reason you were there is because Annie thought it a good idea you mix with other children in the first place.

"Well poor Auntie Sky was looking at your mother calmly, listening to Miss Pringle-Jones, waiting for the response; it soon came as Miss Pringle-Jones started into bureaucratic gobble gook and then your mother waded into her and Auntie Sky has relayed to me the following conversation."

AJ smiled and looked at the two women, then continued, ""That will be enough thank you Miss Pringle-Jones. As to whom Sky and I fuck is no business of yours and if you had taken the time to find out the full extent of the knowledge of both these well adjusted children, you would have found them far ahead of their age group and indeed conversant with a wide knowledge of our history and in fact, even our constitution.""

"Then the teacher said, ""Really Mrs. Forsyth-Wilson, how dare you talk about bodily functions and use such inappropriate language in my presence.

""Well, Miss bloody Pringle-Jones," Mum shot back, "it shows your education when you think our constitution has something to do with bodily functions. Further, our children come from a very loving family environment, something I am immensely proud of. We may not be what society calls a normal family but I suggest the bond and love within our family unit far surpasses in many instances what you call a normal family.""

"And that is why you came home to be educated by Nanny Annie," said AJ.

All four were roaring with laughter, recalling the event so long ago.

"Bloody hell mum," Sky exclaimed "you were worse than I ever was."

"It's not the end of the story," Auntie Sky explained, "the education department, no doubt informed by Miss Pringle-Jones, wrote to your mum and informed her that to home educate she must get permission from the department. Well Prudence wrote a lovely letter back, thanking them for their concern and informed them that the children were being educated at a West Australian approved school on the Big Sky station and she also informed them that the teacher there was, in fact, educated and could spell and do maths as well as having a thorough grasp of Australian history and suggested perhaps it would be a good idea if such ideas caught on with local education here.

"Fuelled by this letter, and in discussion with Miss Pringle-Jones, no doubt, the education department fired a letter back stating that, *Last weekend the children had been seen in Tasmania with both the parents,* and Prudence fired another letter back stating, *Why yes, thank you again for your concern, but is it a fact that most parents have their children home weekends in fact, if you wish to check at the Launceston airport you will find a sleek twin-engined jet aircraft with*

Wilson Pacific in gold lettering on the side of it. This was in fact the school bus used to transport the two children.

"Prudence, after that round, heard no more. Bureaucrats know when they are beaten."

"Bloody hell mum, you're a legend!" Sky told her mum as she leapt off the bed and ran out, calling back over her shoulder, "You're unreal."

"One down, one to go," muttered Prudence as she dressed.

William and Susan Webb had kept in contact since childhood and Prudence knew both loved each other. Susan had been waiting for William to name the date since he proposed as a twelve year old, but being apart while William learnt about the cattle trade meant they only caught up to each other at Christmas and the Big Sky bash.

William was a bit shy like his mother, Sky. Prudence again was tired of waiting for the union to formalise and produce some children. She intended talking to Rachael and Michael at lunch; both would be coming over for the day.

Knowing Mary and David had no love interests, all being work, the two younger siblings seemed the only hope of grandchildren at this stage. Prudence intended to have grandchildren, one cannot leave an empire to nobody. *Just ask Bradley Jones,* she thought.

During the morning, all three helped the ageing Charles muster for crutching. Young Sky had left for the airport to pick up her, *Husband to be,* thought Prudence.

Filling up the forcing yards for the rouseabout to pen for the shearers, the three decided to join the gang for a cup of coffee as it was morning tea time. Sitting on the wool bales they chatted to the shearers: one a middle aged man from New South Wales, the talk was about finding workers as the industry was not attracting newcomers; all involved seemed to be getting older and therefore the skills of the trade were becoming lost. The shearer from New South Wales said he once worked for a contractor, Smiley Foster, who had always raved about a girl he had working for him once. He described her as the ultimate shed hand, in fact, Smiley had made her a legend in the outback shearing sheds; all had heard of Sky Brown from far and wide.

Prudence always quick off the mark, informed the stunned shearer he had met Sky Brown and that she sat before him.

Jumping to his feet he shook Sky by the hand, "It's a privilege," he told her. "What I said is true, old Smiley told your story in every pub and shed in New South Wales, and I guess this must be the two-headed Tasmanian prick who put you up the duff and abandoned you?" he laughed, grabbing AJ by the hand, "So you was a shearer too," he said.

Sky found out old Smiley still lived, he had retired to Longreach with his long suffering wife and lived in a cottage there. Prudence and Sky agreed they'd all go and visit the old bugger on the way north.

"Better not take AJ," the shearer laughed, "he blames him for the loss of the best rousy he ever had."

The three talked about the event after lunch on the way back to the homestead to prepare for their visitors. *One never knows the direction ones life can take, bloody old Smiley,* AJ pondered and even looked forward to taking the risk and seeing him again.

Michael and Rachael had arrived, anxious to catch up with their old friends. AJ was sorry to see his friend's health had deteriorated since they last saw Michael a few months before; he was drinking heavily.

Prudence suspected Michael was giving Rachael a hard time, although Rachael always remained loyal and caring of her husband, she had often said to Prudence that 'sometimes we hurt the ones we love the most'.

Prudence noticed in the last few years that Rachael seemed to carry a heavy load, her young vibrancy gone, a sad and worried woman replaced her beauty and love of life. Prudence and Sky, in their women to women talks, never intruded on Rachael to extract the truth, but always informed her they were her friends, always, and if she needed anything at all to just let them know, if it was in their power it would be a privilege to help their old friend.

Prudence raised the subject of Sky's son and Rachael's daughter; Rachael agreed she felt sorry for her daughter who had waited patiently for years. She, like the others, had noticed the love Susan held for William and it was obvious they were always going to be a pair.

Once again, Prudence advised her friends, "Leave it to me. I will have them married within the month."

AJ and his old friend talked for hours. Michael knew he had a drinking problem, he knew he hurt his wife, often in his drunken rages. He admitted to AJ that he was ashamed of himself but the pain and terrible dreams were like a dark cloud that enveloped his soul. His only relief was alcohol; he felt he could not carry on suffering and hurting the one person he loved most. His daughter, whom he loved dearly had left home to work in Sydney and did not return home very often, as he knew it upset her to watch both her parents suffering.

"I feel like a ship out of control on a chaotic sea," he told his old friend, "sometimes I feel you shouldn't have risked your life to save me."

AJ tried to console his friend, informing him that his daughter and William were on their way home for Christmas and that Prudence would have them married within the month; this cheered Michael up, he looked forward to the event. Michael thought the union of the two young adults would be the second best event of his life, the first being his marriage to Rachael.

That afternoon, while AJ and Michael sat on the porch talking about old times, AJ tried to cheer his friend up, but it was hard work. He was worried about Michael's mental condition and intended to talk it over with Rachael; perhaps help could be found.

Sky and Edward turned up and immediately Prudence rushed down the verandah to meet them.

"Well," she exclaimed, "come on you two, let us in on what is going on."

Edward smiled and grabbing Sky exclaimed, "Sky has agreed to marry me." It appears that at last Edward had gained the courage to pop the question saving Sky the trouble.

"Now Edward," Prudence said, "why the hell did it take you so long?"

"Well," he drawled, "I always thought even though I've loved her for years, she wasn't too keen on me."

"You stupid bloody drongo," Sky informed him, "I've been waiting eight bloody years for you to ask me!"

Prudence was at her best; the wedding planned for three weeks away she informed all within one mile. Albert and Annie appeared with the Christmas bubbly; celebrations started early.

Christmas day was, as usual, a mad event with people running everywhere; presents were piled up under the tree placed on the verandah of Forth homestead. The tables in the marquee were groaning under the weight of food and drinks; even Annie and Albert, boosted by the presence of their children, absolutely beamed. Annie had become a little tipsy by mid afternoon.

Prudence, making sure all were present, rose to her feet for a speech. AJ knew what was coming and called for quiet and a hush fell over the marquee as she announced, "There will be a wedding on the twenty first of January, of Edward and Sky. No long engagement please or they'll be of pension age, with her parents and Auntie too old to enjoy grandchildren."

"On the same day," she continued, "and again, no need for

long engagements, the wedding will be a double one with our son William and the daughter of our great friends Rachael and Michael. Susan is a lovely girl who, like Edward, we love dearly."

"Please raise your glasses for a toast," Prudence beamed, noticing Susan and William, both with a big smile on their faces, leaning towards each other to kiss. *Sometimes,* Prudence thought, *love needs a little assistance.*

Mary and David clapped and whistled, sitting together as they always did at family functions, it pleased them both to see their younger family members happy, especially their beaming mothers.

Mary joked to David, "I bet the pressure will be on for grandchildren, just look at the two of them scheming already."

Prudence made sure, with the help of Sky, that the double wedding was an affair to remember always. Held on the lawns of Forth in a huge marquee, there were: two bands playing, mountains of food, the entire families of the participants, with so many workers from near and far, the pilots had to call for help and chartered extra planes to ferry all the guests in from most parts of Australia.

The entire week was taken up with people coming and going. Prudence and Sky looked radiant both in full flight, beaming with motherly pride as they waved their two married children off on a honeymoon to Bali; both young couples had decided to go to the same destination.

Always being Prudence, she solemnly informed both brides to come home pregnant or else, exhausted with the effort of getting them married she required quick results.

Chapter

27

Once again things settled at Forth. Agnes did not wish to return to Sydney and Sue Davis stayed on with her; she had witnessed the last event in a momentous life since her son had met and married Prudence. She then witnessed AJ finding Sky again and the union of the two astonishing women with her son, had made her later life a most satisfactory one, never having a dull moment. Along with Mary Jones, she had educated her grandchildren in Sydney, watching their individual growth into fine young men and women. Mary had, every morning, come into her bedroom before work to check on her grandma Agnes; a kind and loveable grand daughter. David had visited her frequently, staying with her and his sister whenever possible.

AJ and his two loves had burst into her life at least twice every year for a few weeks. *Yes, her life had been great,* she mused as she lay in her bed..

Sue Davis found Agnes lying dead in her bed the next morning, a look of peace and contentment on her face. Agnes had known that returning to Sydney was a waste of time.

The family all returned home again and laid their grandma Agnes beside her husband in the old Colonel's family plot. Prudence was sure he welcomed them with '*Bloody good show, fine family at that*'.

Perhaps family tragedies happen in a sequence in life as the following week, Rachael came home to find Michael had taken his life; she found him hanging in the garage. Horrified, she had phoned her old friend Prudence, the trio rushed to her side, trying to console her in her grief.

AJ had seen his friend still hanging, moments before the police and ambulance officers arrived; it was a heart wrenching sight, one he would never forget, though he told Sky and Prudence his lifelong friend looked like he was at peace with his troubled soul set free.

AJ never, ever, could forgive himself for not realising his friend needed help. Caught up in family celebrations, he knew he should have taken time out to seek help for Michael.

Prudence insisted that Michael be buried in the family plot, being the lifelong friend and father of her daughter-in-law, and husband of her best friend, he was indeed family.

As they lay him to rest, AJ could see Michael, the happy go lucky comic, as a youth flash before his eyes; all the good times they shared, secrets they told each other, fears and hopes.

Michael was buried next to his dear friend, Mary Jones, and once again, Prudence suggested the old Colonel would have been pleased his troop was growing all the time, with a *'dashed fine show old chap'*.

The decision had been made between the old friends not to spoil the happiest time in both their children's lives; nothing would be achieved by spoiling the honeymoon and the bad news could wait until their return.

Prudence insisted Rachael stay at Forth and, in fact, accompany them on the next trip north; she refused to have her friend stay alone.

After the return of the newlyweds and having told them of the bad news regarding both Grandma Agnes and Michael, they waited until things settled down.

The trio, along with Rachael, William, Susan and Sue Davis, who was returning to Sydney, bid a fond adieu to Annie, Albert, Sky and Edward as they flew to Sydney.

William and Susan caught a commercial flight on to Broome for the return to the Big Sky while Rachael and the others stayed in Sydney for a couple of weeks with Mary and David who had flown down to meet them.

Prudence had been a bit shaken by the death of two of her family so soon and it dawned on her death comes to all. She again seemed to rejoice in the bond the three had formed, cherishing every moment they shared together, trying always in her own unique way to protect Sky and AJ and striving to make them happy.

David and his parents had decided to sell some of the more marginal stations, even Prudence realised in her quest, she had made a few mistakes. The Tanami stations were prone to drought, the windmills had to be kept maintained all the time to supply water to thirsty cattle. They decided to sell off nine stations and keep the ones further north, where the wet season guaranteed fresh grass every year. Improvements had been made to run as many cattle on the remainder. Station managers were hard to find: Edward Davis had been lost to Forth, and even old Snowy reckoned he was knackered, passing his job over to William. The winds of change were in the air, the old guard was slowly passing over to the new young bloods.

William and Anna Browning stayed for two days with the family in Sydney before David and the couple flew to Darwin, for the purpose of selling off the nine chosen stations.

Prudence decided to accompany Sky and AJ to Longreach, then go on to Darwin to have the yearly meeting of the trustees of the Big Sky.

They had decided to relegate the authority of the positions over to Mary, William, Sky and David; this was to be, in fact, their last meeting as trustees of the Bradley Jones trust.

Landing in Longreach they found a ride into town to look up the cottage of old Smiley Foster. Sky knocked on the door first, it was answered by Mrs Mancey. Shocked, Sky never had a chance to ask for old Smiley as Mrs. Mancey grabbed her in a bear hug and yelled, "Guess who's here Smiley?" as old Smiley came shuffling to the door.

"Bugger me dead," he said. "I'd remember young Sky anywhere. Come in Sky and tell us what happened to ya. I always wondered what happened to the best bloody rousy I ever had. Isn't that right Mrs. Mancey?"

"Mind if I bring in my two partners? I think you know one," Sky said.

"No problems," yelled old Smiley, and strangely enough old Smiley never recognised AJ, but Mrs. Mancey did, hugging him and telling old Smiley this was AJ, the boy who went off with Sky.

Old Smiley did not react in the way Prudence thought he would but said, "Bugger me dead. I thought you had abandoned me favorite rousy, young AJ."

Old Smiley had mellowed since he retired. His wife had died years before and as Mrs Mancey was also on her own, so both teamed up,. Smiley reckons now he not only has the best cook, but also sleeps with her. They insisted that the trio stay overnight; Prudence told the others if they wished to she was agreeable. Smiley did laugh when he told them he only had one other double bed and Prudence informed him they had shared the same bed for thirty four years, so one night wouldn't matter.

Prudence listened as old times in the sheds were discussed until late in the evening. Sky had worked for nearly two years for old Smiley and both he and Mrs Mancey reckoned she was the best. Sky never drank alcohol, worked hard and caused no trouble. He told Prudence about not employing Tasmanian shearers after the phone call to Mary Jones, but in hindsight, old Smiley chuckled, it was all a bloody waste of time.

It was a sad farewell for old Smiley and Mrs Mancey; Sky had been their favorite and one of the best if not the best worker. Old Smiley had never forgotten Sky, in fact, he sung her praises often. Mrs Mancey informed them that Smiley reckoned now he would die happy, he always wondered what happened to his Sky; he was glad she was having a good life. Prudence had told them about Sky's life and old Smiley just nodded.

"Best news ever,' he kept saying 'Sky deserves it, she was the best."

The trio flew directly to Darwin and stayed in the same hotel they had used since Mary Jones booked her and Sky in all those years before. Darwin had changed from a frontier town to a bustling city; all three decided to stay for a couple of weeks and enjoy the beautiful dry season climate and to check out the markets and relax. The running of the company was in good hands and after years of hard work, they all agreed to slow down and enjoy life.

The final meeting they had to attend came to an end and signing over to the children was a relief, even Prudence seemed to be tired of the whole thing, being just happy to enjoy the company of Sky and AJ.

Both women enjoyed shopping and attending salons to pamper them. Sitting under the palms on the foreshore, soaking up the beautiful waters of Darwin Harbor, all three relaxed on the lawns, watching the ships come and go. They swam at Mindil Beach and enjoyed meals in the multi-cultural city. Every morning they would lie in bed until late, reading the local newspapers, enjoying each others company with always a kiss and cuddle. Young at heart and still very much in love, even after thirty four years, the passion and lovemaking was unabated.

David and William Browning dined with them several times and negotiations for the sale of several stations proceeded faster than expected. David requested them to stay a little longer and all three accepted, enjoying the relaxing time.

Several companies had now extended their investments into cattle stations, prices were higher than expected and although David had authority to sell, he still sought the advice of his parents and sister Mary, whom he was always trying to talk into joining them in the running of the family company. Mary always replied she would one day, but for now, enjoyed the cut and thrust of representing corporate clients in court; at the moment it was a challenge and she loved every minute of.

It had only taken two months for the first of the stations to sell. With that sale and those also expected of the rest, the cattle enterprise would be debt free and the company would be well cashed up.

Mary and David talked about spreading their investment into other enterprises. Prudence was not too keen but informed them they were now much older than were herself, Sky and AJ when they had first launched into expanding the cattle business. She would, along with the others, stand by any decisions 'the children of Kimberley cottage' as she called them, entered into.

They all stayed in Darwin much longer than expected and were looking forward to traveling to Kununurra to be picked up by the Big Sky plane; the jet, unable to land at the Big Sky usually dropped them off in Kununurra and then returned to Darwin for use by David.

William and Susan picked them up at the airport, all were glad to see them well, in love and happy but to Prudence's annoyance, no sign of pregnancy. The season was near completion and William had as usual, under the watchful eye of Snowy, kept the muster at full speed, running like a well oiled machine, so Prudence and Sky started to plan the usual Big Sky bash. As they started sending out invitations the excitement grew, faxes and phone calls were made from the office, it would be bigger than ever. Snowy excitedly practiced with Rose and Sky, ready for the next event.

Prudence had been feeling a little unwell and at the insistence of Sky and AJ, decided to go to Broome for a check up. In fact, she had been to a doctor only a few times in her life; once when pregnant and then to get a prescription for the pill, she was usually a ball of energy.

Sky and three aboriginal women went with Prudence, intending to do some shopping. Mr. Fong and his shop had long gone, since replaced by modern shopping centres.

While the aboriginal ladies shopped, Sky accompanied Prudence to the doctor's surgery. After what seemed a long time, a concerned Sky was glad to see Prudence come out of the surgery, questioning Prudence about what was wrong with her.

Sky was relieved when Prudence said, "Nothing really, just one of those silly viruses. Let's pick up the girls and head home, we have a bash coming up and I intend to make it a good one."

The Big Sky bash was drawing near when Prudence received a call from her doctor, results had came back. When she put down the phone, Prudence as usual, brushed off the call.

"Nothing really," she said, as expected, and changed the subject.

However Sky and AJ had concerns, Prudence was often tired, her sexual appetite had ceased, even making excuses for the first time in the relationship.

Prudence joked to Sky and AJ," Well, it's about time you two had more of the share in lovemaking!"

The big weekend came and as usual hundreds turned up. Sky and Edward came up from Tasmania, Mary and David, as usual, came early from Sydney. It was a magnificent family time. Prudence threw herself into the weekend. She and AJ were first up on the dance floor, never missing a dance; she clung to AJ, both swirling like young lovers around the lawns to the singing of Rose and Sky, collapsing with exhaustion in the early hours of the morning.

The Big Sky bash lasted from Friday evening until Sunday morning when everyone started straggling home either by plane, helicopter or road transport. It was a time when all the station owners, workers and others caught up with each other, every year. It had turned out to be the main event in the Kimberley calendar with many a business deal and romance started off at the annual event.

On that Saturday, the barbecues operated all day. Some visitors slept in after participating beyond their capacity in dancing, drinking and eating. Swags and tents had taken up all positions within a kilometer around the homestead. The band cranked up again in the evening at dusk, for the last night of the get together. New loves and old danced to the music under the Kimberley stars and it had been as good as ever. Snowy usually gave his address about ten at night but Prudence had requested that he allow her to speak instead this year. Smiley agreed; if Prudence had asked old Snowy 'to jump', as would any of her workers, he would have said 'how high?' such was the respect all held for her.

Prudence gave a remarkable speech thanking all for their friendship and mainly, for the loyalty and hard work all had given to make the company, to build it up to what it was today.

"Thank you from Sky and AJ also, we intend to slow down and let the youth of today take over. In ones life a time comes when enough is enough, the older generation can stifle the talent of the young if they impose old ideas onto the young. I came to the Kimberleys, thanks to Sky, thirty six years ago with a young baby on my hip. Immediately I fell in love with the land and its people, tough, loyal and hard working. It has been my life's greatest privilege to have worked, laughed and cried amongst you, sharing both good and hard times."

A thunderous applause arose from the crowd, all the young

ringers whistling and clapping, yelling for Prudence to breast the bar to have her usual drink with them; they adored her, her sense of humor and fair play, they gave her the best they could, her mere presence demanded it always and they called her the 'queen of the Kimberleys'.

Prudence said them before she left the verandah, "Just one last dance with AJ, then get ready boys, I'll be over."

She then requested Snowy and the band, which over the years had grown to nearly an orchestra, to play 'Dance with me Molly', one of her favorites.

Sky and the singers seemed to put greater effort into the song than ever, as Prudence, AJ, and dozens of revelers joined them, all trying to get close on each pass to thank Prudence for the lovely speech. They all appreciated what she had told them.

Prudence seemed exhausted after the dance, her vibrancy gone. Rachael, who had been worrying with Sky about her, walked over after the dance and suggested she retire early; Prudence insisted on having a drink with the ringers as usual, it was a highlight of their year to have the boss have a few drinks with them.

As they made their way to the bar, followed by fifty or so young males and females, Prudence faltered and collapsed. Rachael and AJ rushed to her side, the band stopped and a hush came over the gathering of hundreds. Sky placed her guitar on the chair and ran, pushing her way through the crowd. With the help of some of the guests a distraught AJ, Sky and Rachael carried Prudence inside to her bed. Rachael insisted all leave, apart from family, who were now all by their parent's side.

Rachael wiped her face with a moist towel and opened up a bag she had been carrying, shading Prudence all weekend, looking at the others she sobbed, "Well perhaps I can now tell you what I should have before, but Prudence made me swear that we tell you after this weekend, when we got back to Tasmania. You know, she had a mind of her own and as usual not wanting to spoil the weekend. Our Prudence has cervical cancer, it's inoperable and sapping the life out of her. Yet she went beyond whatever time left the doctors diagnosed, even now, she perhaps only has two or three weeks to live. Tonight she did what she did on morphine which I have been giving her regularly."

AJ and Sky lay down beside her, heart wrenching sobs coming from their grief stricken bodies, holding her hands as they often did over thirty five years of this glorious union, unable to comprehend what they had just heard, even while dying, she thought only of others before herself.

The news was given to the revelers who sat stunned after her collapse. A whisper could have been heard, where minutes before, a party had been in full swing. Tears flowed over the Kimberleys that night.

The next day, the Kimberley Echo ran headlines. *'Tears over the Kimberleys'* the front page article read: *'Well known and respected member of one of Australia's leading pastoral companies, Prudence Forsyth-Wilson, collapsed at the annual and well attended Big Sky Bash, the regions premier event. It appears she has been suffering from inoperable cancer but did not wish to spoil the event for others and had suffered in silence allowing the event to continue. Known for her unusual domestic situation, and unlimited drive and enthusiasm, Prudence came to the Kimberleys as a teenager with a young baby, and from that day, became a legend, buying up stations throughout the region in Queensland and the Northern Territory. Always in the company of her two dedicated family members, Anthony and Sky Wilson, the three have become icons in the cattle industry, well know in Northern Australia. The union has produced four children, who it is reported, will take over the running of the empire.*

'In an amazing event the family was escorted from the station to Kununurra airport by dozens of aircraft and helicopters and on arrival a commercial flight was forced to circle while the plane with escort landed. The private company jet with the ill Prudence on board, took off for Tasmania and the pilot informed us the convoy of aircraft and helicopters coming in was like watching a swarm of bees land.

'The paper wishes all members of her family and indeed hundreds of friends and employees every sympathy and thought in the coming weeks. The Kimberley region will be much the poorer for one of its most outstanding members'.

The paper phoned the station for comment and spoke to another Kimberley legend and long time employee, as well as friend, Snowy Figg.

He was too upset to comment, but did say, "She was the queen of the Kimberleys mate, absolutely and unquestionably a swan amongst bloody geese."

Chapter

28

The family had arranged for an ambulance to be waiting at the Launceston airport to take Prudence home to Forth, it had been her wish to die in Tasmania and naturally, be buried next to her grandfather.

It was a solemn homecoming for the family. Mary had resigned from work, this being the catalyst. David, as was the other family members, absolutely gutted and distraught, and all found it impossible to believe the head of the family would ever die or become ill. Her zest for life had been infectious.

Annie perhaps of all, was unable to cope; the family had been her life. Albert sent for the children as Annie became more grief stricken, unable to stop or control the emotions she felt.

Prudence sat up in bed and Sky and AJ sat either side of her, holding her hands, both dumbfounded, lost and unwilling to accept the coming death of the one who always made things right, the decision maker and light of their lives. Neither could imagine life without Prudence and the family worried for them also.

One of Annie's children, Helga, a lovely tall blond girl who had grown up with the family, became a tower of strength. Never married and now thirty, she sat for hours with her childhood playmate David, seven years older. They soon became more than friends. David had met many girls and dated but he found most of them to be false. Now, in this time of grief, the genuine respect and love Helga had for his grieving mother showed clearly, it was plain to see they had a close bond.

Prudence made him realise that he was crazy not to have done something before, as his mothers wish was for him to marry and have children. Now she would never see his grandchildren and this distressed him. Though Prudence was thrilled to hear the news her son and Helga told her, as was Annie and in all the grief, shone a light of hope.

Sky and AJ lay every night holding Prudence in between them, only leaving for a small meal occasionally; it was during one such event Prudence called all the four children in for a private talk. Aware she was slipping fast, Prudence wished to organise even her burial.

That evening, to everyone's surprise, an old caravan followed by several troop carriers drove up the driveway. It was Snowy and Rose along with twenty or so of 'Auntie Pruey's old playmates from the early station days; they had come to sing the death songs of their people to a respected old friend.

It seemed almost unreal as they refused to go to the shearer's quarters of cottages but quietly sat around a camp fire under the huge spruce in the homestead gardens.

Sky's two faithful kelpies lay buried behind the tree, having been a part of her life for fifteen years, both died within weeks of each other. Sky refused to have any other pets in her life, she reckoned, in her own way, your heart can only be given and stand so much, once it all goes then life ends.

When Prudence died, Sky would cry only enough so that the rest of her love was left for AJ. If he died, then so would she, as only then she would have used up all her love and her heart would die also.

Prudence propped herself up on the pillow, a frail vulnerable little woman near death, but she insisted on a visit from her aboriginal friends who had came so far to see her.

They had left their tribal grounds which she knew was something special.

That morning at two o'clock, with AJ and Sky holding her gently between them, Prudence Forsyth-Wilson died peacefully. A remarkable woman, her short life had ended. A wail went up from under the spruce tree as the aboriginals sang their death songs, indeed a good friend had died.

Rachael attended to matters the following day as all the family members were too upset to think or do anything. The light in their life had gone out, the she wolf leader of the pack, had died.

Prudence left a note for AJ and Sky which only added to their grief. She thanked them for the incredible years they had let her share in their lives. She had written that Sky had told her she gave her heart to AJ and that they both held the chains to her heart and at anytime may have destroyed her if they had chosen, but instead shared their unmitigated love in a lifetime of dedication and friendship. *'One year with the two of you was worth one hundred alone, so I have been lucky. Do not weep for me, I now give you two loveable people to each other. I only have one wish and that is that you are both buried either side of me so we may lay in death as we did in life. I hope you have many years of happy life together, my two most precious people in my life, you were the sunshine of my life, my reason for living. Love Prudence.*
PS. Sky, if we had lost AJ in Vietnam, we were so close we may have become lesbians. One last joke from Prudence!'

People from all over Australia attended the funeral. The aboriginals looked on in respect, an unusual sight, but then Prudence was an unusual person, everyone agreed, different from the average.

The minister gave a lovely sermon, explaining that Prudence had not wanted a church service but a simple burial. He talked about her unusual life, her fire for life and friends, her talons in protecting her family if need be.

As the casket sat covered in flowers over the grave, the Minister turned to AJ and Sky and said, "I know this is highly unusual, but then so was your late wife and friend. Her wish was to attend your wedding ceremony, it was her last instruction to your children and in fact sternly to me."

And so a simple ceremony was conducted by Prudence's casket as a stunned and grieving couple were married. Prudence's last wish. The minister also placed Prudence's wedding ring on Sky's finger with the one she already wore.

"This ring is to remember her by," said the minister, "also her wish."

The casket was gently lowered into the ground as the music of Isla Grant, her favorite singer, played softly in the background. Prudence had chosen the song, Like Leaves in the Wind; it seemed appropriate and she had chosen well.

After the funeral, Sky and AJ returned to Forth. They did not want to leave anymore, to go north, and leave Prudence behind. She had made all decisions, they had both happily followed her. They seemed lost visiting her grave with flowers weekly. Christmas was a sad affair, solemn with no one enthused about the occasion; the spark that ignited family time had been snuffed out.

Sky and AJ began to take showers, it did not seem right to lay in 'the think tank' without Prudence. They withdrew into each other for comfort, laying in the huge bed as if waiting for Prudence to walk through the door, sashaying along in her brief underwear, igniting passions and laughter. A dark cloud now seemed to hang over Forth.

Sky and Snowy refused to play ever again; it seemed their desire had gone. Snowy and Rose took months to return to the Big Sky, they just ambled along having lost all desire to return home, lost in grief.

David married Helga and they moved in with Mary. The trio

ran the Cattle Empire. Prudence, as always being fair, left her fortune equally divided amongst all four children, now worth over two hundred million in investments. William Browning retired and went to live in Queensland, shattered by the death of Prudence; he had no heart anymore for the family business.

Sky and AJ had been paid as company directors over the years, hardly ever spending any money, the joint account was worth many hundreds of thousands. It was their wish for Prudence not to complicate their remaining years with finance and they were glad to see the children of Kimberley Cottage take over the lot.

In the first year of marriage, David and Helga had a daughter and the bouncing infant was christened on the verandah of Forth, they named her in honor of her remarkable grandmother, Prudence Forsyth-Wilson.

William and Anna produced their first child, also a girl, the following year and named her Agnes Rose Wilson. It seemed a tradition had been formed to call new members of the family after their ancestors; Prudence had named Sky after her friend and husband's love, Sky, a truly admirable and benevolent gesture of a beautiful mind.

Sky at last gave birth to twins, a boy and girl, naming the boy Braidwood John and the baby girl Eileen Isabella. AJ and Sky relished nursing and playing with the grandchildren on the verandah, always under the watchful eye of the loyal and loved family members Annie and Albert. AJ and Sky often escorted the children to their grandmother's gravesite and told them wonderful stories of her life and that of the old Colonel.

The company sold off ten of the marginal stations and started investing in other ventures. AJ and Sky listened to the children telling them of their investments but in realistic terms, never held any interest in such matters, as long as they had each other, nothing was of any consequence.

The Big Sky bash never took place again. After the death of

Prudence it seemed somehow all wrong, with the main instigator of the event having gone,. No-one questioned why it had ceased; the fact Prudence would not be there seemed sufficient a reason for the legendary event to end.

Mary and David sold the little jet which was Prudence's aircraft; it had served them well when the trio and children, along with Annie, Albert, William Browning and families had criss-crossed the country, but now it was a costly exercise to maintain, so they used commercial aircraft.

Prudence became a legend as stories of her circled around the top end of Australia; she had left a legacy never to be forgotten.

Chapter

29

In the fifth year after the death of Prudence, Christmas had passed by when the muster had started in the north. They got news that William, known as Billy, and Susan were expecting their second child.

Rachael had been living at the Big Sky since the death of her best friend; Sky suggested they go north gain. AJ was surprised when she suggested they take the Holden and retrace the trip they had taken forty odd years previously. Never had he questioned either of the two women who shared his life; as always, AJ readied the old Holden for the trip, adding a tow bar and small trailer for the tent and equipment.

A worried family waved the couple off from Forth, insisting they take a mobile phone and to keep in touch, phoning at least once a week to home or to the Big Sky. Mary was especially worried, the old couple had entered a world of their own and she fretted at what would happen if either became sick or worse, the consequences were unthinkable.

There was a long line of people and cars waiting to board the ferry at Devonport. People looking at the immaculate old vehicle asked the occupants where the rally was. Onlookers chuckled when AJ informed them they were on their honeymoon.

Driving off the ferry they headed along the highway over the West Gate Bridge and swung north following the same route that three excited youngsters had followed decades before. Several times AJ got lost as highways had changed with new sections sealed and routes changed.

Reaching Mildura they camped in the local caravan park, exploring the region, but always, Sky seemed to be on a quest and anxious to continue the odyssey.

They visited the hotel car park where 'that fight' had taken place, camped overnight and swam in the river where they had first made love. Entwined in each others arms, they relived the moment so long ago, when two young people had been innocent in love, and recalled the long trail they had walked since.

Always remembering Prudence who had made their lives so perfect, AJ mused, *Perhaps we would still be working in the shearing sheds had Prudence not entered our lives.*

Several times on the journey, fellow travelers felt sorry for the older couple with the few camping items they seemed to have. Thinking they did not have much money, several times campers in caravans or motor homes cooked meals to give to the couple, which they gracefully accepted, thanking them for their generosity. Perhaps had they known the two were the founders of the well known company, Wilson Pacific, they may have not been so generous.

AJ and Sky drove along the dusty road to the shed where they first met. A caretaker now lived in the homestead but they were both shocked at the run down condition of the station. They stayed and camped for two days, catching yabbies in the waterhole, remembering they had first spoken to each other sitting on the same gnarled old tree, unbelievably still having survived the test of time.

Heading north they called into Longreach, saddened to find old Smiley had passed away a year before. Mrs Mancey made them welcome, she was lonely and missed old Smiley, she reckoned he was like Prudence, tough on the outside but a marshmallow on the inside. They stayed for a week with their old friend. Mrs Mancey cried when they left as she knew it would be the last time they would see each other, she was very fond of the couple, sad to hear about Prudence, but glad to see both still basking in each others company.

Traveling north still, they followed the highway to Mt Isa, heading west to Three Ways before north to Katherine. In many instances the highway, now all sealed, had changed. The old camp sites hard to find or gone, but on a few occasions they rejoiced in finding spots they had camped at previously, exploring the area as they did on the first trip.

AJ and Sky seemed to have a new lease on life, remembering the time they first made the trip when so young, carefree and in love, unaware of the future, living and loving for the day, soaking up the love they held and still do to this day. Back then the future hadn't even been a topic for discussion and they now laughed about how unaware they had been of where the future would take them.

Reaching Kununurra, they stayed with friends camping near their huge dam surrounded by palms and frangipani. AJ had been in the army with the husband. He and his wife ran a small tourist enterprise, that was quite popular, making a host of drinks and selling tropical fruit to the travelers.

Both men discussed the war and the effect it had on many, even years after. Michael Webb had been one of many casualties of the conflict even years after hostilities had ceased, and now it seemed they both agreed Australia once again was sending its finest young men into war with the Americans on a lie. Once because the commies were streaming down from the north about to take us over, and now weapons of mass destruction bombarding the airways and print media daily. AJ reckoned that the American ideology of 'I will bomb you until you accept my democracy' was as corrupt as the men who sent youngsters off to die. Perhaps, his friend added, if the politicians had to go or send their sons and daughters into these theatres of death, wars may end forever.

They camped for over a month with their friends, Sky helping in the shop while AJ and his old army mate had a few drinks while fishing for Barramundi in the Ord, it was a peaceful and relaxing month. Both Sky and AJ had come to realise, as had Prudence, that good times only last a short time and that you must grasp them with both arms.

AJ thought that they would leave Kununurra and drive down the Great Northern to Fitzroy Crossing, then on to the station, but Sky seemed to have other ideas. She had been a bit mysterious, making phone calls and instead drove on towards Wyndham. Driving up the overgrown track she pulled up at the long abandoned settlement where both had received such a joyous greeting on their first trip. Sitting under a tree, to AJs surprise, was two aboriginal men; he recognised them both, they had in fact been in Tasmania at Prudence's funeral. Greeting them, they untied two ponies which were tied up in the old derelict community kitchen and passing the reins to Sky, they sat down again. They would wait until the couple's return and watch the vehicle and contents.

Mounting the tough little animals, AJ questioned Sky that they had no food this time, and she quietly told him all was arranged. Setting off, memories of the first trip came flooding back to AJ.

He watched Sky as she led them to the top of the mountain range, nothing had changed, and still her long legs and angelic face enthralled him as he rode behind her. The journey seemed longer than the first time, they had to rest more often, but on dusk, they broke onto the top and traveling the short distance, he immediately recognised the outcrop. A tent had been set up in front of the crevice they had previously slept in. Dismounting and tying up the ponies, AJ was astounded to see a double bed and gas fridge set up inside, it appears Billy had made all the arrangements and had flown the gear up by helicopter.

Taking AJ by the hand, with lightening and thunder pealing the distant clouds, Sky again dropped off her dress to stand naked in the rushing cool air, the whole scene once again seemed to be magical as large spots of rain, as if on cue, soaked both and standing with glistening bodies AJ felt as if a great weight of grief lifted from his body. He felt young again, invigorated after the long ride as the stiffness and pain from the ride disappeared. Taking Sky by the hand they entered the tent and sinking into the soft bed, made love and drifted off to sleep.

For two days, Sky sat on the mountain looking north as if for some sign. Every evening she did the same ritual as if she was talking to someone or some strange event was taking place.

On the last evening she led AJ into the tent and gently laying down next to him, entwining her long legs around his as she gently told him, "I have farewelled my ancestors, now I can go home to Prudence's and your country and keep my promise to be buried next to both of you. I am ready to die whenever the spirits choose to end my life".

The End

The sequel to this novel
'The Children of Kimberley Cottage'
will be published next year by the author.

www.ingramcontent.com/pod-product-compliance
Lightning Source LLC
Chambersburg PA
CBHW072229170626
46813CB00003B/1147